FLORENCE

A SLATER AND NORMAN MYSTERY

P.F. FORD

BOOKS BY P.F. FORD

To my amazing wife, Mary – sometimes we need someone else to believe in us before we really believe in ourselves. None of this would have happened without her unfailing belief and support.

PROLOGUE

It had been a cold, frosty February night. Now, in the early morning darkness, well before dawn, parts of the little town were beginning to come to life and prepare for the coming day. On the outskirts, away from the town centre, the lights were on in the small supermarket. Nearer the centre, the mouth-watering smell of bread, fresh from the oven, wafted from the open door of the bakery. A little further along, light shone across the pavement from the open door of the newsagents as the owner grappled the bundles of today's news into the shop. An occasional car stopped outside and disgorged its occupant in search of an early morning newspaper and maybe a pack of cigarettes.

In the shadows, a small, tatty-looking old woman flitted from doorway to doorway, a grubby off-white coat tied around her waist with what appeared to be string. She seemed to be looking for something, and as she searched she muttered quietly to herself, absently running her fingers through her long silver-grey hair, much as a child might do.

As she got to the bakery, she hovered in the doorway, peering inside until a kindly woman dressed in white overalls came out carrying a large brown paper bag.

'Morning, Florence,' said the woman cheerily, her face glowing red from the heat inside the shop. 'How are you today?'

The old woman in the grubby coat smiled uncertainly.

'Have you seen Dougal?'

'Still not found him, then?' The lady from the bakery smiled kindly back at her, knowing she wouldn't get an answer, but feeling she should ask anyway.

She handed the paper bag to the old woman, who looked down at it as if it didn't belong there. Then she hugged it to her chest as if frightened it was going to be snatched away. She nodded her head in thanks and as she looked up at her benefactor, a tear slid down her grubby cheek. She was overwhelmed by this act of kindness, even though it happened every time she came into town.

'I've done you a loaf of bread, two of those pies you like, and a couple of cakes,' said the kindly woman. 'And there's a hot pasty on top. You should eat it now before it gets cold. Would you like to come in? I can make you a cup of tea to go with it.'

The old woman shook her head and backed away. She wasn't being ungrateful, she just couldn't risk going inside, no matter how kindly the lady in the shop might be. She gave another uncertain smile and then hurried off down a narrow passageway that led off in the direction of the old canal and the adjoining towpath, still clutching the bag to her chest.

The lady watched her go and let out a long sigh. The baker, a large, ruddy-faced man, emerged from the shop and slid an arm around her waist.

'Never mind, love,' he said to his wife. 'You can't make people accept your help. At least you know she won't go hungry today.'

'I know,' she said, sadly. 'I just wish I could do something more. I don't even know where she lives, and I dread to think how she survives in this cold.'

'Come on inside,' he said, giving her a hug. 'We'll just have to drink the tea ourselves.'

The kindly lady was not alone in her ignorance. Not many people in Tinton even knew of the tatty old woman's existence. Those that were aware of her called her Florence, because that's what they'd always called her. It was doubtful if anyone could remember if it was her real name. In much the same way, no one really had any idea where she came from, or how she existed.

She made this journey into town two or three times a week, and had done for years. She always came under cover of darkness because she knew if she came into town any later, she would have to cope with more traffic than she could handle, and people would see her and stare at her. Some might even feel the need to pass nasty comments and tell her how she wasn't wanted in this town. They didn't seem to understand. They never had.

She just wanted her Dougal back, and then everything would be alright.

CHAPTER ONE

The Night Caller had been targeting the larger houses of Hampshire for some weeks now. Acting with impunity, he had so far robbed over a dozen homes, netting a haul of jewellery and works of art worth several million pounds. To date, no one had the faintest idea who the culprit was, despite him leaving a 'Night Caller' business card at the scene of each robbery. Last night, it appeared he had made his latest call – this time in the Tinton area.

DS Norman Norman hated going to these great big houses out in the country. It wasn't that he had a problem with the people who inhabited them, it was more the case that they seemed to have a problem with him. He couldn't see what their problem was. Okay, so he was a little untidy sometimes, but did that matter? As long as he was good at his job (and Norman thought he was pretty damn good at his job), what did it matter what he looked like?

He had an especially bad feeling about this one. This guy was a retired chief constable and had been knighted for his services to law and order. Norman was convinced this more or less guaranteed he was going to be given a hard time, and as he turned his car off the road and onto the long driveway and got his first glimpse of the enormous house, he just knew he wasn't going to enjoy this job.

Sir Robert Maunder was an inch or two shorter than Norman and yet, when he opened the front door and stood silently looking Norman up and down, there was something about him that made him seem rather grand. But in that initial silence, Norman wondered if perhaps the only thing grand about this man was his own sense of self-importance. Perhaps it was the result of having spent much of his life looking down on people he perceived to be of lesser rank.

'I'm sorry,' said Sir Robert at last. 'But we don't allow your sort of people here. Now go away or I'll call the police.'

Norman sighed heavily and began rummaging in his pocket for his warrant card. He could see this was going to be even worse than he had expected.

'DS Norman.' He held up his warrant card and rolled his eyes slightly as Sir Robert scrutinised it for a good few seconds. 'I understand you've reported a crime. I'm here to investigate.'

'Good Lord,' said Sir Robert, looking at him suspiciously. 'I knew things were getting bad, but is this the best you could do? I'm a knight of the realm, you know.'

'I'm sorry,' said Norman. 'We understood this was a simple break-in and no one got hurt.'

'Yes, that's right,'

'Well frankly, Sir, you're lucky to get a DS and a forensics team.'

'I don't like your attitude, Sergeant,' said Sir Robert, angrily. 'You seem to forget I used to be a chief constable. I know how these things work.'

Norman didn't like Sir Robert's attitude either, but he didn't say as much. He could imagine Sir Robert in his heyday, looking after his cronies regardless of the crime that had been committed.

'With respect, Sir,' replied Norman, 'I think you'll find things have changed a bit since you were in charge. These days we rarely get to pick and choose our jobs. I just go where I'm sent and try to do my job to the best of my ability. You could put in a request for someone more important to come out if you like, but I wouldn't expect too much if I were you.'

For a moment, Norman felt as if he and Sir Robert were engaged in some sort of stare-off, and he waited for the inevitable storm to break, and for him to be sent packing.

'Don't you even have scene of crime officers?' Sir Robert said, suddenly, his voice calmer.

Norman was surprised by the sudden change of attitude.

'There's a forensics team on the way,' he said. 'They should be here in a few minutes. Perhaps you could show me the crime scene while we're waiting.'

Sir Robert backed up and Norman stepped into the hall. He took a pair of thin forensic overshoes from his pocket and slipped them over his shoes. It was unusual for him to think of such a thing, but Ian Becks, Tinton's forensic expert, had been very insistent on the phone. If this was the work of the Night Caller, Becks had warned, he didn't want Norman leaving his 'great big, heavy hoofprints' all over the scene.

Sir Robert led the way through the house and up the stairs.

'It was this Night Caller chap,' he explained to Norman. 'There's no doubt about it. He even left his calling card.'

Norman didn't comment on Sir Robert's speculation, preferring to make up his own mind based on the evidence.

'Is there much missing?' he asked.

'Most of my wife's jewellery. I'm afraid she left her jewellery box out where it was easy to find.'

'Don't you have an alarm?' asked Norman.

'Damned thing didn't work.' Sir Robert sighed, exasperated.

They reached the bedroom where the theft had taken place.

'In here,' said Sir Robert, as he pushed the door open.

The room was palatial in size and design with a huge four-poster bed at one end, tapestries on the walls and what appeared to be expensive Persian rugs on the floor. Norman thought it was way over the top, but then he supposed you have to fill a room this size with something, and modern furniture would definitely have looked out of place.

A large jewellery box sat on a dressing table. The lid had been thrown back, and several small drawers in the front were open. Norman peered inside to see what could best be described as a few scraps of jewellery in the bottom. Inside the open lid, a brilliant white card, about the size of a standard business card, stated clearly and simply 'You're a victim of The Night Caller'. The words 'Night Caller' were inscribed in a large fancy font.

'Do you have a list of what's missing?' asked Norman, staring at the card.

'Downstairs, on my PC,' said Sir Robert. 'I'll print a copy for you.'

'Where were you and your wife when he was emptying the jewellery box?'

'Err, yes. That's a bit embarrassing.' Norman was surprised to see that the Knight of the Realm was actually reddening slightly. 'I was actually hoping you wouldn't ask.'

'I'm a police officer, Sir Robert,' Norman said, sighing. 'It's my job to ask questions, remember?'

'Yes, of course.' Sir Robert pointed to the massive four-poster bed. 'We were both sound asleep in there.'

'In the same room?' said Norman, not bothering to hide his surprise now. 'So, the alarm didn't work, your wife left her jewellery box out in the open and you both slept while someone broke in and helped himself to its contents. Is that right?'

'Yes. It sounds very careless of us, when you put it like that,' mumbled Sir Robert sheepishly.

'I would say careless is quite a good word,' said Norman pointedly, but before he could say any more there was the sound of a doorbell ringing downstairs.

'I must get that,' said Sir Robert, looking as if if he had been saved by the bell. 'My wife's resting. She's very upset.'

'That'll be the forensic team,' said Norman, following the older man back down the stairs.

CHAPTER TWO

Detective Sergeant Dave Slater breathed a sigh of relief.

'It wasn't that bad was it?' PC Jane Jolly asked, laughing. 'Anyone would think you don't like children.'

'It's not that I don't like them,' said Slater. 'I used to be one. It's just that I feel so awkward around them and I'm never quite sure how to speak to them.'

'You worry too much,' said Jolly. 'You were fine once you relaxed.'

'I was?' he asked, doubtfully.

'Yes, you were. Didn't you notice? Once you started talking about your job, they were hanging onto your every word.'

'Yeah,' he said. 'But that's the easy bit. It's when I have to engage with them informally. That's when I feel awkward. And then I look across at you, and you find it so easy. It makes me feel totally inadequate.'

'I have three kids of my own,' explained Jolly. 'I find it easy because I do it all the time. I suspect you don't have much contact with kids. Are there no nephews or nieces? No friends with small children?'

'No. You're right. I don't get any practice. But I can hardly go around accosting small children and engaging them in conversation, can I? I'd get arrested.'

'Never mind,' Jolly said, smiling at him. 'If this is going to be a regular gig you'll be getting plenty of practice.'

'Norman's the same rank as me. He can do the next one,' said Slater, as he gathered up their stuff. 'Come on, Jane. Let's get out of here.'

The source of Slater's discomfort was the latest idea to come down from the chief constable's think tank. The Children's Community Initiative was intended to demonstrate to children that the police weren't the enemy that many of them seemed to think they were, by sending out 'appropriate' officers to prove otherwise.

To this end, Slater and Jolly had just spent the best part of two hours talking about their work and fielding questions. It had seemed to Slater that most of the questions seemed to be about how to avoid getting caught. Not for the first time, he thought their time would be better spent re-educating the parents who taught their children to think that way.

'Was it me,' he asked, as they walked towards their car, 'or were most of the questions about how to get away with crime?'

'I think you must have your cynical head on this morning,' said Jolly, laughing. 'It wasn't that bad.'

'Are you sure? It's left me thinking the baddies are beginning to outnumber the goodies.'

'I was wrong,' Jolly said, shaking her head at him. 'It's not just the cynical head today, but the full Mr Negative head. Did you find something nasty in your breakfast this morning?'

'Am I that bad? I just get frustrated when there's so much petty crime going on. I mean, what's wrong with people?'

They had reached their car now and they climbed in.

'I'm just a lowly PC and you're a DS, so it's not really my place, but shall I tell you what I think?' said Jolly.

'I think we've known each other long enough to forget about rank in these situations,' said Slater. 'I also think we've been friends long enough for you to know I value your opinion, so go ahead, Jane. Fire away.'

'I think you're getting bored. You like the big cases. They're a challenge and you have to think. The small stuff, which is just about all we get here in Tinton, doesn't challenge you at all. Maybe it's time you moved on to somewhere bigger. Perhaps you should try to get into a murder squad somewhere.'

'Move on?' said Slater, in surprise. 'Do you really think so?'

He thought she was probably right about him being bored with the jobs he got to do, but moving on wasn't something he'd really thought about. It was a bit drastic, wasn't it? For the first time in a long time, he was in a serious relationship and he certainly didn't want to walk away from that. But then if his job was making him unhappy he wasn't going to be much fun to be around, was he? Perhaps she had a point.

U nfortunately, the dull, grey morning they had left outside earlier showed little sign of improvement now they were back in the car. The only good thing was that it had finally stopped raining, but black clouds still lingered overhead. It was a typical Tuesday in late February.

As Jolly started the car, she called in to let control know she was available.

'Thank you one-seven,' the radio crackled back at her. 'I know you've got DS Slater with you, but could you look in at 17 Canal Street? It's probably nothing, but the milkman's called in to report his concern. Apparently it's the home of an elderly person and the milk hasn't been taken in for a couple of days. I've got no one else free at the moment so if you could take a look on your way back, it would help.'

Jolly turned to Slater.

'Is that alright with you?'

Canal Street was only a short detour on the way back to the station. They would be there in about five minutes.

'Sounds like another one of these big cases you were talking about,' he said, smiling at her. 'Yeah, let's do it. I've got nothing to rush back for.'

As they emerged from the school car park, a fine drizzle began to fall, and by the time they reached Canal Street it had turned into steady rain once again.

As its name suggested, Canal Street ran parallel to the old canal, with the back gardens of the houses only separated from the water by the old towpath. Many years ago, this waterway had been a hive of activity and then, like so many other canals, it fell into disuse and disrepair after the Second World War. More recently, it had been recognised as one Tinton eyesore that could be cleaned up and now, rubbish removed, banks rebuilt, and towpaths gradually being restored, it was becoming a popular place of retreat for many locals.

The house was easy enough to find, the milk delivery van parked outside taking the guesswork out of the task. As they pulled up behind it, the driver's door swung open and a soggy, bedraggled milkman emerged. Jolly felt a certain empathy for the milkman's plight – she had spent countless hours standing on cordons while the rain lashed down around her, and she knew from experience that it didn't really matter how good your waterproofs were, in this kind of weather, the rain still managed to get inside and soak you if you were out there long enough.

'Are you coming in?' Jolly asked Slater as she climbed from the car.

He looked out at the increasingly grey day.

'I think this is one of those situations where rank does count,' he said, grinning at her. 'I'll wait here.'

'I thought you might.' Jolly sighed, closing the car door. She couldn't really blame him – she would have much rather stayed in the comfort of the car too.

'Are you the guy who called in?' she asked the milkman as she walked over to him.

'Yeah. I'm worried about Mr Winter, the old guy who lives here. This is one of the days I call in and see if he's okay when I've finished my round. He usually makes me a cup of tea and I sit with him for a while and have a chat. But there's no answer today.'

'Maybe he's gone out,' said Jolly. 'Perhaps he's gone shopping.'

'He has his shopping delivered,' said the milkman. 'If he needs anything else I get it for him. And he always tells me if he's not going to be here.'

Jolly could see the man was genuinely worried.

'Have you looked round the back?' she asked.

'Yeah, of course,' he said. 'There's no sign of life, and yesterday's milk is still on the step. It's been there since six yesterday morning. That's just not right. He wouldn't do that. And the dog's not barking.'

'Perhaps he's taken the dog for a walk?'

'He'd be back by now,' said the milkman.

Jolly banged on the front door of the house and rang the bell.

'I've done all that,' said the milkman. 'I told you. There's no answer.'

'I'm sure you have,' said Jolly. 'I'm not doubting you, it's just procedure I have to follow. I can't go busting in without good reason.'

She looked up at the house.

'Right, she said. 'Elderly person not answering the door. That's a good enough reason for me. Let's take a look around the back.'

River Lane was tightly packed with small Victorian semi-detached houses. Narrow passageways ran down between each pair of houses, leading to the back gates. Jolly led the way down the passageway to the left of the house and through the open gate that led into the back garden. A paved area led across the width of the narrow garden to the back door, and an adjoining window looked out onto the garden. Jolly peered through it into a kitchen that looked badly in need of updating, but for all that she could see, it was kept neat and tidy by the owner.

She noticed the light was on and wondered if that meant it had been on all night. At the same time, she acknowledged just how gloomy it was at the back of these houses. You'd need a light in there on a day like this.

'I can't see anyone,' she murmured. 'It all looks neat and tidy enough.'

'Suppose something happened to him upstairs,' the milkman said over her shoulder.

'I'm not supposed to break in unless I know for sure'.

'There's a key,' said the milkman. 'It's so I can let myself in, but I've never felt the need to.'

'Now might be a "need to" time, don't you think?' Jolly wondered why on earth he hadn't done this already. Some people seemed to lack common sense.

The milkman turned back the corner of the doormat. Then he pulled it back a bit further, until finally he'd lifted the whole thing.

There was no key to be seen, but they could both clearly see the imprint of a key in the dust that had collected under the mat.

'He kept it under the doormat?' asked Jolly in dismay. 'And you knew?'

'I told him, but he wouldn't listen to me,' said the milkman. 'I told him it was the first place anyone would look.'

Now Jolly was worried. Of course, it was possible the key had been removed by the old man himself, but her instincts were telling her something very different.

'Right,' she said. 'I'm going to let myself in. I want you to stay out here.'

'But what if someone's already let themselves in and-'

'That's precisely why you need to stay out here,' interrupted Jolly. 'If someone has been in there, this could well be a crime scene. If it is, we don't need you contaminating it.'

'Let me do something to help,' pleaded the milkman. 'Maybe I could knock the door down for you?'

'You've been watching too many TV shows,' said Jolly. 'It's not as easy as it looks. And anyway, that won't be necessary. There's a much easier way that makes much less mess and doesn't take so much effort. Just turn around and look the other way.'

'What?'

'Just humour me,' she said, pulling on a pair of latex gloves. 'It'll be better if you don't see what I'm doing. And the sooner I get in there, the sooner we'll know what's happened.'

Reluctantly, the milkman turned his back. As he did, Jolly fished a set of picks from her pocket and knelt before the lock. It was unofficial, of course. She knew very well that a police officer picking locks could never be condoned, but sometimes these things just had to be done. And it just so happened she was rather good at it.

After less than a minute, she felt the tumblers fall into place.

'Just in case he's standing guard, what's the dog's name?' she asked over her shoulder as she stood up.

'Dougie,' said the milkman. 'He's only little but like I said earlier, if he was in there he'd be barking his head off by now.'

'Right. You wait here,' she said quietly, as she gently turned the handle and eased the door open.

Inside, the house was still and silent but for a loud, regular tick, tock, tick, tock, that seemed to be coming from the hall.

'Hello?' she called out, as she walked across the kitchen. 'Is there anyone home?'

She stopped to listen, but there was nothing above the noise of the clock. She continued slowly into a tiny hall. Sure enough, a huge grandfather clock dominated the narrow space, the tick-tocking becoming even louder now she was right next to it. An open door led off to the right. She peered through it into a tiny living room with two shabby armchairs and an ancient television set. A huge, ornately framed landscape dominated the biggest wall in the room. It was obviously a print of something, maybe a Constable, Jolly guessed. Again everything appeared neat, and tidy, and in order.

She began to ease her way carefully up the narrow staircase, careful to tread as far from the centre as possible, but even so, the ancient staircase creaked loudly about halfway up. She paused to listen once again but there was nothing to hear except the noisy clock below her.

There were three doors off the landing. To the left, an open door led into a bedroom. The quilt had been folded back from the single bed and a bedside lamp was on, but the room was empty. Behind the middle door was the tiny bathroom. This, too, was empty.

She found Mr Winter behind the only closed door in the house. It hid the smaller of the two bedrooms, which was obviously being used as an office. He was in his pyjamas, lying on his back on the floor in a corner. She checked his pulse but this only confirmed what she could see easily enough with her own eyes. Mr Winter was dead, and she thought he'd probably been there for at least 24 hours, and maybe even longer. She stood up, sighing heavily. You got used to death in this job, but she still always felt affected when confronted with a dead body. Edging out of the room, careful not to disturb anything, she headed back downstairs and out to the car.

'T he doctor's on his way,' Jolly told Slater, after she had called her find in to the station.

'Waste of bloody time,' muttered Slater. 'The poor old guy's obviously dead.'

While she had radioed back to the station, Slater had gone for a nose around the house and after a few minutes, Jolly had forced herself to join him.

She had been deeply affected at finding the little old man lying on the floor all alone, and two things were niggling away at her. First, there was the missing key. Although it didn't seem to have any obvious relevance to what had happened, she would have been much happier if they knew where it was. And then, perhaps most worrying, the milkman had assured her Mr Winter and his little dog were inseparable. If that was the case, it would be reasonable to expect to find the dog close to his master, but there was no sign of him. It's not as if he could have let himself out, so where was he?

She took a last look around the tiny office where the body had been found. An old table had been put to use as a desk, while a rather uncomfortable-looking chair sat before it. A relatively new keyboard, mouse and screen sat on the table with a small printer off to one side. The cables ran tidily down the back of the table, where they were plugged into the back of a home computer. A small filing cabinet sat alongside the desk. She slid out the single drawer and peered inside. There was just the one file inside, which seemed to be crammed with household bills, statements, etc. Everything seemed to be in order. Whatever Mr Winter used this office for, he was obviously a neat and tidy worker.

She closed the office door and then, carefully and deliberately, closed all the other doors as she made her way slowly back downstairs to the kitchen. As she closed the kitchen door, she leaned back against it and surveyed the tiny room. Slater had his back to her looking through the window and down the garden.

'Are you going to call SOCOs out?' she asked.

'I don't think so,' he said. 'It's a bit worrying about the missing key, and the missing dog, but really there's nothing here that makes me think a crime's been committed. We just need to notify the next of kin.'

An ancient refrigerator whirred away in the corner of the room. Three business cards were held to the fridge door with magnets. There was one for a plumber and another for a painter and decorator, but it was the third one that interested Jolly. She'd noticed earlier that this card was a solicitor's business card. From its tatty appearance, she guessed Mr Winter had had the card for quite some time, so hopefully John Hunter, the solicitor in question, would be aware of who to contact. She made a note of the name and phone number in her notebook.

'According to the milkman there are no next of kin,' she said, sighing sadly. 'And I haven't found anything to suggest he's wrong. It looks like the poor old guy was all alone. Perhaps this solicitor will know a bit more about him.'

Finally, they slipped out through the back door and locked up, using the house keys Jolly had found in a kitchen drawer earlier. She was careful to leave the gate slightly ajar – at least if the missing dog came home he would be able to get into the garden. As if the weather felt the need to match their mood, the rain was now falling even harder, and the sky seemed to have become even more grey and gloomy than before.

She thought it was a fitting tribute to the demise of another lonely old person, and she let out a long, sad sigh as she sank into her car seat. Slater was silent, and Jolly thought he had been affected by the whole thing too. After a few minutes, she decided to pull herself together. She was a tough cookie, after all, and had seen it all before. She put the car into gear and Slater looked across at her, surprise on his face.

'Right,' she said. 'There's not much we can do about what's happened, but perhaps I can make sure he gets laid to rest in the right way. I think the world owes him that much, at least.'

CHAPTER THREE

Up in the canteen at Tinton police station, Norman surveyed the room from a corner table. He had become something of a legend within the small community of Tinton police station. He had arrived with a reputation for being a lazy loner but had quickly disproved the reputation and was now held in both high esteem and great affection by all his colleagues. His positive attitude could always be relied upon to lift spirits and raise a smile if needed, and with his unruly hair and creased clothes (Norman didn't do ironing, and appeared not to even own an iron), he had a unique style all of his own. Some might call it casual, although his friend and colleague Dave Slater was always quick to remind him, rather fondly, that 'dragged through a hedge backwards' would be more appropriate.

Although equal in rank to Slater, Norman was older and not interested in climbing any greasy promotion pole. When they worked together, he was happy to defer to his younger partner as he knew that in return, Slater was more than happy to accept Norman as a valuable source of experience and ability. After working together for a few months, they had developed a healthy respect for each other, and a friendship that seemed to grow ever stronger. Combining this respect for each other with their complementary abilities had enabled them to create a formidable partnership.

Right now, though, Norman's attitude was anything but positive, having just received what he considered to be a totally undeserved bollocking from his boss, Detective Chief Inspector Bob Murray. He bore no real malice towards his boss, whom he knew was simply passing on the dressing down he had no doubt been given from above earlier that day. What irked Norman was the injustice of it all.

Norman had known the old fart, Sir Robert Maunder, was going to cause trouble the moment he had arrived at his house. The man had been a complete arsehole, not just filled with his own self-importance, but positively over-flowing with it. A clash of personalities had been inevitable, but Norman hadn't expected to be on the receiving end of the backlash quite so quickly. Now it seemed it was Norman's fault Maunder and his wife had slept while the thief broke in. It appeared it was also Norman's fault the burglar alarm hadn't worked. And who left all that jewellery out in the open? Apparently that was Norman's fault too. According to the retired chief constable, everyone at Tinton was totally incompetent and he had convinced the current chief constable to agree with him.

Norman wasn't one to dwell on negatives, however, and he knew there were two things that would quickly restore his good humour. The first was the huge, bacon-filled, torpedo roll he was about to devour. The second was the eagerly anticipated, imminent arrival of Dave Slater. Slater had been complaining about having to speak in front of all those kids from the moment Murray had bestowed the honour upon him and Norman couldn't wait for him to get back. Winding up Slater was almost like a hobby for Norman. While he waited and chewed on his bacon roll, he thought about what he would say to Slater.

When the doors swung open and Slater and Jane Jolly pushed their way through, it only took Norman a quick glance at their faces to see they'd had a bad morning. As Norman watched them queue for their food and then walk slowly across to join him, he decided maybe it would be better to test the water before he started taking the piss.

Everyone at Tinton had a big soft spot for PC Jane Jolly, and

Norman was no exception. She was one of the station stalwarts, always there, and always with a kind word and a smile. She wasn't known as Jolly Jane for nothing. Norman had been particularly impressed with her efforts when they had worked together in the past and, despite the difference in rank, he regarded her very much as part of their 'team', and he knew Slater did too. Norman thought he probably had a larger soft spot for her than most because she reminded him of his wife, although he'd never told her as much.

He looked at her as she approached. The smile was there on her face, but it was half-hearted, lacking its usual vibrancy.

'You two had a shite morning too, huh?' asked Norman.

'It started off okay,' Slater said, sitting down opposite him. 'We got through talking to the kids alright, but then we got the call to deal with an old man who wasn't answering his door.'

'Poor old bloke was dead when I found him,' Jolly said, sighing. 'He had died all on his own and he'd been lying there for at least a day.'

'Ah. A really shite morning, then,' Norman said, sympathetically. 'That's never a nice thing to have to deal with. So how come you got to find him?'

'The milkman cared enough to look in on him three or four times a week,' she said. 'He knew as soon as he got there this morning that something was wrong, so he called us.'

'This seems to be becoming more and more common as more and more people live on their own,' said Norman, gloomily. 'There used to be a time when everyone knew their neighbours and those neighbours looked out for each other, but this is fast becoming a land of strangers.'

'Looks like he died of natural causes,' Slater said. 'There's no sign of a break in and I couldn't see any sign of a struggle or anything like that.'

'It's a bit odd his dog is missing though.' Jolly looked slightly puzzled and Norman raised a quizzical eyebrow.

'According to the milkman, they were inseparable,' she explained. 'So why wasn't the dog there? I thought it seemed a bit strange that's all.'

'Maybe he'd run away,' Norman ventured.

'Maybe,' agreed Jolly, but she sounded doubtful. 'But I'm going to look in every time I go past in case he turns up.'

'Isn't that something for the family to sort out, or the RSPCA?' asked Slater.

'But it looks like there is no family, remember?' said Jolly. 'I suppose that's why the poor old bloke was living on his own. All I've got is the name and phone number of his solicitor.'

'Well, give him a call,' said Norman. 'Let him sort things out and earn his keep.'

'Yeah. I suppose I should.' Jolly looked unhappy, though, and Norman knew she would want to do everything herself.

'So, why was your morning shitty?' asked Slater.

'Oh, it's been great,' said Norman, sarcastically. 'Remember that Maunder guy I told you about?'

'The one who got a knighthood because he was a chief constable?'

'Huh. He could easily have got his knighthood for being a complete arsehole,' said Norman. 'He's certainly damned good at it. Anyway, it turns out he knows the current chief constable and he's complained about me.

'Apparently it's my fault his alarm didn't work, and that his wife left all her jewellery out. It's even my fault him and his wife slept through it all.'

'Great mornings all round then,' Jolly said, smiling sadly.

When she called on him later that day, Jane Jolly thought solicitor John Hunter was a kindly looking man. In his sixties, he obviously looked after himself, but didn't seem vain enough to worry about the fact that his hair was grey or anything like that. Jolly approved of that. As he came from behind his desk and extended his hand to greet her, he scored more points for his engaging smile and easy manner. A waft of aftershave came her way. She didn't know what it was, but it was rather pleasant, and she added a few more points to his score.

'Good morning, Mr Hunter. I'm PC Jane Jolly from Tinton police,' she said, shaking his hand.

'My secretary tells me you think one of my clients has met with a fatal accident,' said Hunter, looking concerned. 'What terrible news. Of course I'll help in any way I can.'

'Thank you,' said Jolly.

'Please sit down.' He indicated a chair and she sat down. He sat down opposite her.

'So what happened?' he asked.

She gave him a brief rundown on what had happened to Mr Winter.

'So he fell and hit his head?'

'That's how it looks,' said Jolly. 'The thing is, we could find no evidence of any next of kin. I was hoping, as his solicitor, you might be able to help us out there.'

'I'm afraid I didn't know him very well,' said Hunter. 'He only came to me a few weeks ago to make his will.'

'Ah.' Jolly pulled out her notebook. 'So he'll have told you about his family.'

'I'm afraid what he told me isn't going to be much help,' Hunter said. 'According to Mr Winter, his only living relative is a sister, Julia, but he had no idea where she is now.'

'Oh.' Jolly was crestfallen

'I'm sorry,' he said. 'I've been trying to find her but with no success so far. I'm going to have to redouble my efforts now – he's left everything to her in his will.'

'We were hoping there would be someone who could identify the body, and maybe arrange the funeral.'

'Oh. I see. Why don't I do it?'

'Are you sure?' asked Jolly.

'Identification's just a question of looking at his face, isn't it?' asked Hunter.

'It'll only take a minute,' Jolly said. 'It's just a formality.'

'It's the least I can do. And I'll get my secretary to arrange the funeral. It won't be anything fancy, but at least he can be sent off with a bit of dignity.'

'That's so very kind of you,' said Jolly. 'Could you let me know when the funeral is arranged? I found him you see and it seems a bit sad dying all alone like that. I'd like to be there.'

'How very thoughtful,' said Hunter. 'You're a credit to the police, Miss Jolly. Leave me your number and I'll make sure to let you know.'

John Hunter scored a few more ranking points for calling her 'Miss' Jolly. She knew she looked like a typical, harassed mother-of-three, and couldn't remember the last time anyone had called her 'miss'.

N orman snatched the phone from his desk and answered it with his usual professional manner.

'Yo. Norman here.'

'Hi Norm, it's Ian Becks,' replied the voice in Norman's ear.

'What can I do for you, Becksy?'

'Are you ok?' asked Becks. 'That self-important twat was giving you a hard time this morning.'

'I have broad shoulders,' Norman said, sighing. 'I've come across guys like him before. He can't help it. He thinks that title makes him better than everyone else. He's also missed the fact that time has moved on and he's no longer in charge. And, of course, he was probably embarrassed at having to admit his alarm didn't work and he slept through the robbery.'

'Yeah, well that's what I was calling to tell you. This might cheer you up. The alarm didn't fail – the old duffer didn't even switch it on.'

'Are you sure?'

'Absolutely. I've checked and double checked. It wasn't switched on last night.'

'Does that happen often?' asked Norman, feeling slightly suspicious.

'Can't say for sure without a lot more testing,' said Becks, 'but I'd bet on it being an isolated incident.'

'Are you suggesting what I think you're suggesting, Ian?'

'Hey. It's not my place to speculate, Norm, it's my job to supply you with evidence and facts. And that's just a fact.'

'What else have you got?'

'Not much if I'm honest,' said Becks, grimly. 'There's no sign of forced entry, no unexplained fingerprints, and bugger all else, apart from that calling card.'

'Anything on that?'

'Nothing to get excited about. I have to send it off to Winchester so they can compare it to the cards they've got so far. Apparently, a lot of people are doing break-ins and leaving these calling cards, but when you put them next to each other the fakes are easy to spot. They tell me the real Night Caller uses very special ink and card. By comparing them, they can tell us if we're dealing with the real Night Caller or not.'

'Let's hope it is,' said Norman. 'Then they can take over the case and I don't have to deal with that pompous arse again.'

'I'll keep my fingers crossed for you,' Becks said, laughing.

'Thanks for letting me know, Ian.'

As Norman put the phone down, he wondered about Sir Robert Maunder. It was a bit of a coincidence, wasn't it? Forgot the alarm, left out the jewellery box, and then slept while the guy was there in the same room helping himself. And there was no sign of a forced entry. Someone could easily be forgiven for thinking there was some sort of insurance swindle going on.

But then, that someone would need to get their hands on the old guy's financial information to take that suspicion any further. Norman thought he would stand more chance of finding a snowman on the equator.

CHAPTER FOUR

Dave Slater hated funerals. He subscribed to the idea that a funeral should be a celebration of a life gone by, but in his experience, that just didn't happen. To be fair, he had only ever attended three in his life so far, but he had found each of them to be a very morbid affair. He knew it was probably down to the fact that all those funerals had been those of his grandparents, and each one had been very old fashioned. Whichever way he looked at it, though, and no matter how much allowance he made, he couldn't deny he had found each one deeply depressing.

On this drab, grey Monday morning, he could see no reason to think Mr Winter's funeral was going to be any less depressing. In fact, he was sure it would be even worse because, as far as he could make out, there were going to be very few people attending this particular interment. He'd shared his misgivings with his girlfriend, Cindy, and, bless her, she'd offered to come with him. But this was no place for her; he was only here himself because Jane Jolly had spent the past few days making him feel guilty about Mr Winter's death. It wasn't his fault the poor old guy had no friends or relatives, was it? Nor was it his fault the guy's death had been an accident and he hadn't been murdered.

Even so, in the end he had agreed to come as long as Norman came too so here they were, like three stooges who'd come along to make up the numbers – which was *exactly* what they were.

Now he was looking round the inside of the crematorium, Slater thought he had been correct in his assessment of the numbers attending, and apart from himself, Jolly, and Norman, the only people inside the church were John Hunter and his wife, a small, grey-looking man whom he vaguely recognised from around town, the small team from the undertaker's, and the vicar who was conducting the service. He thought it very sad there were so few people here to pay their respects, then he felt worse still when he realised he and Norman wouldn't have been here but for Jane Jolly cajoling them along.

The three police officers had at first chosen to sit several rows back, but they soon realised they had only succeeded in drawing attention to their presence. This made Slater feel even more uncomfortable, but Norman didn't seem to notice. Enviously, Slater wondered how his colleague always managed to look at ease whatever their situation. The vicar was obviously doing his best to sound upbeat and interesting but, with such a small audience, it was hard going. Aware that he could easily fall asleep if it became any more boring, Slater tuned him out and allowed his mind to wander.

His thoughts were interrupted when Norman nudged him and then nodded towards the rear of the crematorium. Looking over his shoulder, Slater could see a figure hovering by the door. He turned slightly to get a better look at a small, grey-haired old woman who stood there in a shabby off-white coat. She looked rather fragile and fidgeted nervously as though she felt she shouldn't really be there. There was an air of distraction about her which made her look lost and confused. He thought, rather poetically, that she reminded him of a butterfly, fluttering haphazardly on damaged wings.

He had been observing her for at least half a minute or so before she noticed, with a start, that he was staring at her. Not wishing to frighten her, he turned to face the front for a few seconds before sneaking another glance in her direction, but she was gone. He turned right round to have a better look, but she was nowhere to be seen. As he turned back, he was sure he caught a glimpse of someone else, a man, he thought, stepping back into the shadows at the back of the room. He wondered why someone would be creeping about like that. Or was he just being suspicious?

A t long last, the curtains drew back and Mr Winter's coffin began its slow journey out of sight. In a few minutes, it would be reduced to ashes and gone forever. As the coffin disappeared from view behind the closing curtains, Slater took another look around. There by the doorway he noticed her again: the small, grey-haired old woman in her shabby coat. She was holding her right hand to her mouth, in a gesture of dismay, perhaps, or maybe to stifle a sob. From this distance, he couldn't tell for sure, but the gesture made him feel she must have known Mr Winter. Then, as before, she realised he was watching her and, taking a couple of steps back, she disappeared from view.

As they filed from the building, Slater pulled on Norman's arm.

'There was something weird going on at the back of the room,' Slater said, when Norman looked at him quizzically.

'You saw that too?' Norman asked, looking around. 'I thought I saw someone hanging around in the shadows back there.'

'I'm going to slip off and see if I can see anything,' Slater said, and Norman nodded.

'I'll see if I can find anything.'

S later thought he had caught a glimpse of her as he left the building and he hurried across to a nearby clump of trees where he thought she'd been, but his elusive butterfly seemed to have flown. He searched around for few minutes, following a footpath that led through a small gate to the road outside, but she was nowhere to be seen.

As he came back through the gate, he could see Norman had returned and was now talking to Jolly and the Hunters and the small, grey-looking man Slater thought he should know. He briefly searched in and around the trees again, wondering how the woman could have just vanished without him seeing her go. It made no sense, but she was nowhere to be seen.

Cursing quietly, he made his way back. The tiny gathering had dispersed now, leaving just the solitary figure of Norman waiting for him. As he approached, Norman's mobile phone started to ring. He watched him take the phone from his pocket and look at the screen before he turned his back and answered it. Slater assumed it must be a personal call, so he kept a discreet distance until Norman had finished. As he turned back to face Slater, it was obvious Norman was none too happy.

'You okay?' asked Slater.

'Yeah, yeah,' said Norman. He looked a bit pale, and he was turning the phone over and over in his hands. 'These sales people just don't know when to stop, do they?'

He thought Norman's reaction was a bit over the top for a telesales call, but then Slater remembered how annoying he found them, and thought perhaps it wasn't an overreaction after all.

'What a waste of bloody time that was, Norm,' he said as they headed back towards their car. 'Maybe I'm losing my touch. I can't even remember who that bloke was in church doing all the singing.'

'Fred Green,' said Norman. 'He owns the greengrocer's in town. He used to deliver to Mr Winter every week, had done for years.'

'Ah, that's it! I knew his face but I just couldn't think who he was or where I knew him from.'

'And it definitely wasn't a waste of time,' said Norman, smugly.

'It was for me,' Slater said, sighing. 'She looked like some old bag lady or something, but I got the feeling she knew Mr Winter. Then when I went to talk to her, she just seemed to vanish into thin air. Did you manage to catch up with the guy who was hiding in the shadows?'

Norman shook his head.

'He was way too quick for me,' he said.

'Bugger!' said Slater, vehemently. 'What a bloody useless pair we are. But then I suppose it doesn't really matter. It's not as if it's an ongoing investigation.'

'Speak for yourself.' Norman waved his mobile phone at Slater. 'I got a good photograph, and I got his car registration too!'

'Well done, Sherlock,' Slater said, smiling at the smug look on Norman's face. 'But you really ought to delete them. This is not a case we're working on.'

'Yeah, I know.' Norman shrugged, chuckling. 'It doesn't hurt to practise though, right?'

CHAPTER FIVE

I t was late on Wednesday morning, two days since Mr Winter's funeral. Jolly was supposed to be heading back to the station, but she had chosen to take a diversion which took her down Canal Street. Despite her best efforts, and making the RSPCA aware of the lost dog, there had been no sign of him anywhere. She was reluctant to give up on the dog and still felt it was somehow her responsibility to find him. Deep inside, though, she knew there wasn't much chance of finding him now.

She pulled up outside the little house and stared up at the windows. Quite why she felt so sad about, and responsible for, this particular little old man dying, she couldn't say. He wasn't the first old person she had found dead in their home, and she very much doubted he would be the last.

As she closed the car door and turned to walk down the side path, she noticed the gate was wide open. She had left it propped ajar in case the dog came home, but now it was completely open. It was one of those gates that dragged on the ground, so it had to have been pushed. She quickened her pace, hoping the little dog was going to be waiting at the back door and pleased to see someone at last. To her disappointment, there was no dog waiting to greet her. She stopped to look in through the kitchen window, just in case it had somehow got inside. As she peered in the window, her heart leapt as a movement behind her own reflection made her jump.

She spun round to see a gate at the bottom of the garden – some hundred feet away – slamming shut. She sprinted down the garden, cursing herself for those wasted few seconds squinting into the dark kitchen.

She threw the gate open and ran out onto the towpath, but she had no idea which way the culprit had gone. She stared around wildly but there was no sign of anyone in either direction. She thought about starting a search, but she wasn't even supposed to be here, so she couldn't really justify wasting time on what was likely to be a fruitless exercise. Annoyed with herself, she made her way back into the garden, making sure to close the gate and put the bolt across. It wasn't going to stop anyone who was determined to get in but it was the best she could do for now.

She hadn't been down this end of the garden before, and for the first time she became aware of a tiny shed hidden away behind a small, weather-worn greenhouse. She wondered why she hadn't noticed it before, then realised it would be hidden from view to anyone looking from the house. There was a small padlock on the shed door, but it was broken, and on closer inspection, Jolly thought it had been broken very recently.

As she pulled the door open, she could see there was hardly anything in the shed, and she wondered why anyone would have wanted to break in. She thought this was probably the work of some junkie looking to pinch a lawnmower or something similar – they'd do anything to make a few quid to help feed a drug habit these days. With a sigh, she made her way back up the garden to the house.

Again, she glanced through the kitchen window. She could see through the kitchen door and on into the hall. Everything looked neat and tidy, just as she'd left it. She had already turned away and taken a couple of steps towards the gate before the realisation struck her – she had closed all the doors inside the house, including the kitchen door. Someone had been inside the house after she had locked up.

S later turned into Canal Street and made his way slowly towards the two patrol cars and the SOCO's transit van that were parked outside the crime scene, making it impossible for him to park anywhere close by. Grumbling quietly to himself, he found a space a few houses down and walked the last few yards.

He stopped in the street and looked the house up and down. The houses the Night Caller had robbed so far were all pretty big and expensive. This was a tiny two up, two down. He thought they could probably rule him out as a suspect before they even started.

'Hi, Jane,' he said to the waiting PC Jolly as he approached the front door. 'I didn't think I'd be coming back to this house any time soon.'

'It's a bit of a coincidence, isn't it?' she said, with a grim smile. 'But I think we can rule out the Night Caller for this one.'

'It's certainly not his preferred size of house, that's for sure.'

'I said there was something funny about his death,' Jolly said, smugly.

'Now let's not jump to any conclusions,' he said. 'It's probably just kids taking advantage of an empty house. What does it look like?'

'Imagine a bomb going off in a house this small, but without the fire, and you'll have a pretty good idea. Come round this way and I'll show you.'

She led him down the side of the house and around to the back, stopping to indicate the kitchen window. Slater peered through the kitchen and on into the hall.

'The kitchen's still neat and tidy,' said Jolly. 'The mess is in all the other rooms.'

As Slater looked through the window, a blue figure walked from left to right beyond the doorway.

'Bloody hell,' he said. 'Is that a smurf in there?'

'You'd think so, wouldn't you?' Jolly said, laughing. 'It's the SOCOs in their new paper overalls. Apparently white's no longer the in colour. It seems this season it's all about blue.'

'I think pink would have been far more fetching,' Slater said. 'I hope that's not going to affect their performance.'

'To be fair,' said Jolly, 'they're all over it, but so far they've found nothing obviously useful. They're hopeful there might be some good fingerprints.'

'Let's keep our fingers crossed.' Slater scanned his surroundings. 'Any sign of a break-in?'

'No,' she said, pointedly. 'But then, if whoever did this has got the spare key that was under the doormat they wouldn't have needed to break in, would they?'

Slater accepted the implied criticism without response. This was no time to get into an argument about interpretation of facts and the value of hindsight. He still thought he had made the right call based on the available evidence at the time they had found Mr Winter's body.

'Have you any idea what's missing?' he asked.

'As I recall, there wasn't anything worth stealing, but I haven't had a chance to look around yet. I thought it would be better to let this lot do their thing first, but they did tell me there's a mark on the wall in the living room where something used to hang. I seem to recall that was a print of some old landscape painting. It won't have been worth much, although the frame might have been worth a few quid.'

'This doesn't make sense at all,' said Slater. 'It has to be kids.'

'There's something else. When I got here earlier I just missed someone leaving by the back gate.'

'Did you see who it was?'

'No, sorry,' Jolly said, sighing. 'Whoever it was had a head start. By the time I got to the gate they'd had plenty of time to get away.'

'Never mind, Jane,' said Slater, with an ironic smile. 'Welcome to the world of sod's law.'

'But it's not all bad news,' said Jolly, perking up. 'There was a nice, fresh footprint just inside the gate. They've made a cast of it, so at least we've got something. And I thought it might be a good idea to make a list of all the car registration numbers that were out in the street at the time. It's a long shot, but I'll do a check when I get back. Maybe I'll get lucky and find one that doesn't belong to a resident.'

'Now that's smart thinking,' said Slater, approvingly.

CHAPTER SIX

S later was busy staring into space when the phone extension on his desk began to ring.

'Chief Smurf here,' said a familiar voice in his ear. It was Ian Becks, Tinton's forensic wizard.

'Ha! So even you admit those new suits make you look like smurfs,' Slater said, laughing down the phone.

'I'll have you know they're the very latest thing,' replied Becks. 'Very high-tech, no fibre shed-'

'Yes,' interrupted Slater, 'and extremely smurf-like. You've just admitted it.'

'Only because I know you lot aren't going to stop taking the piss. It doesn't mean I agree with you. Anyway, I didn't call to ask your opinion about the new suits. I have some news for you about the break-in at Canal Street.'

'Ah! Right,' said Slater. 'I'm all ears.'

'Okay,' said Becks. 'First of all, the footprint we found out in the garden is from a man's size ten trainer.'

'So it could be teenagers?'

'Well, it's possible there were kids in the garden and Jolly disturbed them. But I'm pretty sure it wasn't kids who broke in just to trash the place. It might be someone trying to make us think it was kids, but this person was too careful for that, but then in another way they weren't careful enough.'

'Don't tell me you've actually got some evidence this time,' said Slater.

'Oh, yes indeed. We have fingerprints.' Becks sounded proud.

'Have you managed to match them to any of our regular house breaking guys?' asked Slater, optimistically.

'It's definitely not one of our regulars.'

'Why not?'

'I won't bore you with the science,' said Becks. 'But going by the ridge density, the prints we have are those of a woman, and none of our regulars are women.'

'A woman?' repeated Slater, in surprise. 'They're not Jane Jolly's, are they?'

'Wow!' said Becks, his voice heavy with sarcasm. 'We're so thick down here we didn't think to check.'

'Err, I'm sorry.' Slater knew the way he questioned every finding irritated Becks but he couldn't help himself. He just liked to be thorough. 'Of course you would have checked. I was just thinking out loud.'

'Apology accepted. We've only found three sets of prints in the whole house. Of course, Mr Winter's prints are everywhere, and we've found the milkman's in the kitchen, but that's consistent with him calling in two or three times a week for a cup of tea. But then there's this third set we can't account for. They're in the kitchen and the living room and, weirdly, the face of that grandfather clock is covered in them.'

'So, do you think it was a woman who broke in and stole the picture from the living room?' asked Slater.

'Speculation is your job, mate,' said Becks. 'We smurfs just do the clever science stuff. It's up to you to work out if it's relevant to your enquiries.'

'Yeah, right. Thanks, Becksy.'

'However,' continued Becks, 'I will offer a couple of pointers. For a start, you need to remember there hasn't actually been a break-in. Whoever was in that house had a key to get in.'

'You can be so pedantic at times,' said Slater.

'That's the scientist in me.'

'You said a couple of pointers,' Slater reminded him.

'Oh yeah. If I was a gambling man, I might put my money on some-thing odd going on in that house.'

'What's that supposed to mean?'

'We found some tiny paint flecks and dust particles on the old guy's desk. The paint is from the PC in the room and the dust is the sort that collects inside a PC.'

'Is there a point to this?' asked Slater, his patience wearing thin. Becks liked to go all round the houses rather than coming straight to the point.

'Well, the thing is, the PC lives on the floor so for the paint and dust to get on the desk it would have to be lifted up there and opened up.'

'So, you've done that, and?'

'We found there was no hard drive in the PC, and the insides have been effectively destroyed.'

'What's the use of a PC with no hard disk?' asked Slater. 'And why would you keep a PC that didn't work?'

'It's been removed and destroyed very recently,' said Becks. 'I'd guess within the last week or two.'

'Could it have been an accident?' asked Slater, immediately wishing he hadn't asked such a stupid question.

'You can't accidentally remove a hard disk,' said Becks, slowly and patiently, as if he were explaining something really complicated to an idiot.

'But why would anyone do that?' said Slater, thinking aloud.

'I can only think of two reasons. First off, you might take it out for repairs or replacement, but then why would you smash up the rest of the computer? However, if there was some information on that computer that you wanted suppressed...'

He left the sentence unfinished and there was a silence as Slater considered the implications of this latest find.

'But this was just a little old man,' he said eventually.

'I'm just putting forward a couple of ideas,' said Becks. 'I have no idea if they're right or wrong, that's your job.'

'And it was all put back together?' asked Slater.

'Oh yes. You couldn't tell from just looking at it. If we hadn't been called in I don't suppose anyone would have realised unless they'd tried to use it.'

'Do you think an old guy could do that?'

'If he knew what he was doing, yes,' said Becks. 'But why would he want to? And if he really wanted to destroy his PC, why would he keep it there? Why not just get rid of it?'

Slater's mind was racing away with him now, and he was wondering what on earth was going on. What at first had seemed to be a sad case of accidental death had suddenly opened up a can of worms.

'Are you still there?' asked Becks.

'Err, yes. Sorry,' said Slater. 'My brain's gone into overdrive.'

'So you think it's important, then?' asked Becks, satisfied with himself.

'I don't know,' mused Slater. 'I thought we had a simple accidental death followed by the trashing of an empty house. Now I'm not sure what to think. Why is it you manage to complicate things so often?'

'Smurfy's law?' Becks laughed uproariously at his own joke. 'You'd get bored if it was all straightforward. I'm here to ensure a regular supply of spanners get thrown into the works. It keeps you lot on your toes and stops your brains from rotting.'

'Right, yes. Thanks for that,' said Slater, his mind racing off again. 'Can you be more exact about when it happened?'

'Sorry mate, you've already had my best guess. What's your point?'

'Whoever trashed that house last night didn't care how much mess they made. Does it seem likely that same person would take the trouble to destroy the PC and then put it back together?'

'It does seem unlikely, doesn't it? Why not just smash it up like so much of the other stuff was?'

'Exactly,' agreed Slater. 'When do I get the full report, Ian?'

'I'll send it through before the end of the day. I'll bring it up the three flights of stairs myself. I could do with the exercise.'

Slater put the phone in its cradle, but kept his hand on it. He was getting a bad feeling about this. What if Jolly had been right and he'd been too quick to put Mr Winter's death down to an accident? He raised the phone back to his ear and began tapping in another number.

'I must admit I was a bit surprised by your call,' said Dr Eamon Murphy, the resident pathologist at Tinton hospital, as he led Slater into the morgue. 'When I did the post-mortem I was under the impression there was nothing suspicious and it was an unfortunate accident. Under those circumstances there was no reason to send you a copy of the report.'

'You're quite right. We all thought it was an accident,' said Slater. 'And that may well be the case still, but there are one or two things that have happened since that make me think we should maybe look again just to be sure.'

Dr Murphy looked doubtful.

'You do realise this man's been cremated, don't you?' he said, his voice clipped. 'So if you're not happy with my results, you can't have another PM to prove me wrong.'

'Honestly,' Slater said, trying to pacify the doctor, 'I haven't even seen the PM results, and I'm not here to challenge you. I trust your findings, I just want to see if it's possible to put another interpretation on them. I mean, you were looking for evidence of a fall, right?'

Murphy still looked a little doubtful but he led Slater over to a desk where a stack of folders leaned precariously towards the edge.

'There it is on top.' Murphy pointed to the folders. 'Help yourself.'

'Can you talk me through it?' asked Slater.

'I suppose that might be quicker.'

Murphy picked up a report, turned to face Slater, and began to read.

'There's not much to it really,' he said, scanning the pages. 'There was a contusion to the back of his head, which was consistent with hitting his head when he fell backwards. He had a broken rib that could also have been consistent with a fall. When I went inside, I found he'd had a heart attack which was brought on by the fall.'

'Is that it?' asked Slater.

'That's enough to confirm his accidental death,' said Murphy, curtly. 'And that's what I was asked to do.'

'How bad was this contusion?'

'Bad enough to cause a blood clot at the back of his head.'

'Would that have killed him?'

'Untreated it probably would have, eventually,' said Murphy.

'Wouldn't it take more than a fall to cause that?' asked Slater.

'What exactly are you getting at?'

'Were there any other bruises?'

'Well yes,' said Murphy. 'Of course there were, but this was an old man. Old people often bruise very easily.'

'Where were these bruises?' Slater felt like he was wading through treacle.

Murphy sighed heavily and thumbed through the report.

'There were bruises to the forearms and shoulders and, of course, there was a huge bruise where the rib was broken,' he said, closing the report.

'Were these old bruises?' asked Slater.

This time, Murphy tutted loudly as he reopened the report.

'No,' he said. 'They were very recent and hardly showed on the skin surface. I assumed they would have been caused by the fall.'

Slater felt a familiar tingle.

'Suppose I was an old man, and I discovered someone had broken into my house, and then this someone turned on me and tried to punch me in the face. So I put my hands up to protect myself.' He raised his arms as if to defend himself. 'Would those punches bruise my forearms?'

'Err, yes. I suppose they would,' Murphy said, looking uneasy.

'What if my attacker then punched me, or maybe even kicked me, in the ribs? I'm old and slow so my arms are still up to protect my head. Could that kick break one of my ribs?'

'Easily,' said Murphy. 'Old bones are brittle bones.'

'And then, while I'm gasping with pain from my broken rib, my attacker grabs my shoulders and shoves me back out of his way. Would I hit my head hard enough to cause a blood clot?'

'But I was told it was accidental death from a fall,' Murphy said, defensively. 'I've been rushed off my feet here. And anyway, I'm not a forensic pathologist.'

'Whoa, slow down, doc,' said Slater. 'I'm not blaming you. You found what you were asked to find. I'm just offering an alternative means by which those injuries could have occurred. And I might be wrong.'

'But I should have seen that possibility too. I should have been pointing it out to you, not the other way round.'

Slater thought the pathologist was right, but he didn't feel rubbing it in was going to achieve anything, so he said nothing. Murphy turned back to his desk and Slater thought their discussion was over, when the doctor turned round again, holding something in his hands.

'In view of what you've just said, you'd better have this.' He handed a clear plastic bag to Slater.

'What's this?' Slater asked, holding up the bag and peering at it. Inside was a scrap of paper with some numbers written in biro.

'I didn't report it to anyone, because it didn't seem important,' said Murphy. 'When he was brought in, his right hand was clenched into a fist. When I opened his hand, this dropped out. Is it important?'

'Your guess is as good as mine.' Slater sighed and studied the piece of paper for a moment.

'Any suggestions?' he asked, turning to Murphy and indicating the bag.

'Well, you're the detective.'

'Yeah,' agreed Slater, 'but that doesn't mean you're not allowed an opinion.'

'But I'm not qualified–' began Murphy.

'I'm not asking you to solve the case,' interrupted Slater. 'And you won't get fired if you're wrong.'

He placed the bag down flat on the desk in front of them.

'Come on, Eamon,' he said, encouragingly. 'You must have an opinion, right?'

'Well,' said the pathologist, reluctantly, 'now we've decided there was a struggle it changes everything doesn't it? So how about during that struggle, our victim was holding a sheet of paper in his hand. His attacker pushed him away and snatched the sheet of paper, but didn't get all of it.'

He pointed to the edges of the paper.

'If you look here, you can see it's been torn.'

'That adds up,' agreed Slater. 'I wonder what the numbers mean,' he added, thinking aloud.

'It's not the complete sequence,' said Murphy. 'If you look to the left side you can see there's half a digit missing. It could be a three, or maybe an eight. And it's quite possible there are more digits missing from the right side. There's no way to tell.'

'So it could be a phone number or a bank account number,' Slater mused.

'Not my field I'm afraid,' said Murphy, with a wry smile.

'It's not mine either,' said Slater, 'but it could prove to be a key piece of evidence. Well done for holding onto it, Eamon.'

'You need to get this to the Chief Smurf,' said Murphy. 'This is more his field. He'll figure it out for you.'

'Ha!' Slater smiled broadly. 'So you've seen the new suits, too.'

CHAPTER SEVEN

S later thought his boss, DCI Bob Murray, seemed to have aged noticeably over the last couple of months, and he looked particularly tired today. Murray had never been one to complain, but Slater knew he was getting sick and tired of having to spend all his time playing politics and balancing budgets. It went with the job, of course, and anyone achieving such a rank these days knew what they were letting themselves in for, but it wasn't like that when Murray had made his way up through the ranks. Slater knew he found it frustrating spending almost all his time filling forms – he would have been frustrated, too.

There had been a whisper that Murray had expressed an interest in the latest round of voluntary redundancies, but Slater didn't know if it was true. He found it hard to imagine Murray anywhere else but behind his desk.

'So,' growled Murray. 'What the bloody hell's going on at Canal Street?'

'It's beginning to look as if Mr Winter may have been murdered for something on his computer,' said Slater.

'Do we have any idea what it's all about?'

'No, Guv. I'm afraid not,' said Slater. 'Whatever it was must have been on the hard disk.'

'So why come back and trash the place?'

'I don't think it was the same person,' said Slater. 'I think the night he was killed he disturbed someone, probably a man, who then took the hard disk from the PC. This time we've got some fingerprints, and Becks is sure they're a woman's. We've also got a size ten footprint, and we might get lucky identifying his car.'

'How many women do you know with size ten feet?' snorted Murray.

'Yeah,' said Slater. 'I know. It doesn't add up really, does it? Maybe there's a man and a woman working together.'

Murray swore quietly.

'This is just what we don't need right now,' he said bitterly. 'We haven't exactly been covering ourselves in glory recently, and now you tell me we might have a murder on our hands. And if we have, we've given the murderer two weeks' start. Oh, and we've also allowed the victim to be cremated. Wonderful.'

Slater bridled at the criticism, but he chose not to respond to it. He could only guess at the kind of pressure the old man was under. If Murray was in this sort of mood, it would be better to ride the storm carefully, not go into battle.

'Maybe we need to focus a few more resources on the problem,' he suggested quietly. 'At the moment it's just me.'

'I know, David, I know,' Murray said, heaving a sigh. 'But you'll only have a small team, and you'll have to keep on top of anything else you're working on. I'll speak to DS Norman and he can join you on the same condition. I'll assign Jolly to work with you, and that's it. It's all I can spare right now.'

Slater considered it was hardly enough people to call a team, but again he thought better of complaining.

'Of course,' continued Murray, 'if Biddeford was still here you could have had him too.'

The implication wasn't lost on Slater, but again he resisted the urge to answer back. What had happened hadn't been his fault, and he resented Murray suggesting it was. He had just been doing his job, after all.

DC Steve Biddeford was the best young detective they had at Tinton, but after an unfortunate misunderstanding in a case they were working on a few months ago, he had first accused Slater of being a sex pest, and then requested a transfer. Murray didn't approve of people who rushed in without thinking, nor did he like people who disrupted the harmony among his staff, and so, despite Biddeford's attempts to apologise and rescind his request, he had found himself shipped out of Tinton.

Even Slater had appealed to Murray, but the boss had been adamant – Biddeford had to learn his lesson. He had, however, drawn the line at a full-blown transfer, and instead arranged for Biddeford to be seconded to a bigger station. He would, hopefully, return to them as a much more rounded individual with additional experience and training that he couldn't get here at Tinton.

'That's okay, Boss,' said Slater. 'A small team will do just fine.'

'They're all yours from first thing tomorrow,' said Murray, turning back to his paperwork. 'Just keep me informed, please.'

As Murray bent his head down to study yet another report, Slater realised the meeting was over.

'Yes, Boss,' he said, heading for the door.

'Oh by the way,' said Murray, just as Slater reached the door. 'Have you ever considered promotion?'

'What, me?' asked a surprised Slater.

'Why not? It's a natural progression from DS to DI.'

'To be honest, I've not given it much thought,' said Slater, turning back to face his boss.

'Well, perhaps you should,' said Murray. 'I'm not going to be here forever, and when I do go it's quite possible they'll take the opportunity to change the structure here, and that means there will almost certainly be vacancies created.'

Slater didn't know what to say to that so he just stared at Murray.

'Give it some thought,' said Murray, returning to his paperwork once more.

'Right,' said Slater. 'I will.'

CHAPTER EIGHT

Next morning, the two man, and one woman, team had assembled in the canteen for a breakfast briefing. It had been Norman's idea, of course, to eat breakfast while Slater brought him up to speed with the case.

'Right then, this is what we've got so far,' said Slater. 'On Tuesday the fifth, eleven days ago, Jane was called to investigate when an elderly man, Mr Dylan Winter, wasn't answering his door. When she gained access to the house, Jane eventually found Mr Winter lying dead on a bedroom floor. There was no sign of any forced entry or any sort of struggle, and nothing appeared to be missing apart from a spare back door key and his dog.

'There was no sign of any struggle or anything missing so I thought it was just a case of another sad, lonely, old person dying alone. And that was it, until yesterday. Jane looked in to see if the dog had turned up, narrowly missing someone who fled through the back gate. She noticed the shed had been broken into, and returning to the house, she then found it had also been entered, and it appears a print in a frame was stolen.

'Then, yesterday afternoon, Forensics told me a couple of things that make me feel we may need to ask some serious questions about

Mr Winter's death. First they found a set of fingerprints they can't account for, and second, there was no hard disk in Mr Winter's computer.'

He stopped for a couple of moments to take a mouthful of coffee and let Norman absorb this information.

'Murder?' said Norman. 'Just because his PC got broken, it's murder?'

'Forensics say there are traces of paint, dust etc. that suggest the PC was taken apart very recently on the table in Mr Winter's office. The hard disk was taken out, the insides smashed up, and then it was put back together and placed back on the floor. From the outside you'd never know it had been damaged,' explained Slater. 'Taken in isolation that's not such a big deal, but now we've had another look at the PM, the pathologist thinks his findings could be interpreted in another way.'

'So how do we think he died now?'

'This is just a guess, but I think he may have disturbed an intruder and then been attacked and pushed out of the way. His injuries are consistent with possibly being punched and kicked in the ribs, then being pushed backwards, banging his head against the wall,' Slater said. 'The pathologist agrees with me.'

'So not the work of your average local house-breaker, then.' Norman looked thoughtful.

'There is a possible clue in a small scrap of paper the pathologist found in Mr Winter's hand. It could be part of a phone number, but without the rest of it to match up it's not much help.'

'Maybe it was someone who isn't from around here,' Jolly said, tentatively. 'Perhaps he was working for someone else.'

'A contract killer sent to kill a little old man? That's a bit of a stretch, isn't it?' asked Norman.

'You're assuming he came to kill Mr Winter,' said Jolly. 'What if he was just supposed to steal the hard disk? What if his death was an accident? Suppose Mr Winter surprised him and he just lashed out with no intent to kill him?'

'Now, that's an interesting theory,' Norman said, smiling.

'It makes sense,' agreed Slater. 'If it was just some regular local burglar the house would probably have been thoroughly turned over, but this was a very specific, neat, tidy job. There was plenty of stuff that would have been worth pinching if the intruder was just looking to make a few quid, but it looks as though none of it was touched.'

'But I thought in the second break-in the house was thoroughly turned over?' said Norman.

'Yeah, it was,' agreed Slater. 'But Mr Winter was killed during the first break-in and that time the house was left damned near spotless. All that seems to have been taken was the hard disk from the PC.

'Do we know what he was looking for?' asked Norman.

'No,' said Slater. 'Not a clue, but it must have been on that hard disk.'

'So we need to figure out what Mr Winter had found out that someone else might kill him for. But if they already had the hard disk, where does this second break-in come into it?'

'That's a good question.' Slater rubbed his chin thoughtfully. 'But I don't know the answer I'm afraid.'

'Maybe what they were looking for wasn't on the disk?' suggested Jolly.

'What about the person you nearly caught?'

'I was nowhere near catching him, to be honest,' said Jolly. 'If he hadn't slammed the gate shut I wouldn't even have known he was there.'

'We don't know for sure if the second intruder has anything to do with the original crime', said Slater. 'But for now I think we have to assume it's all related. And now at least we've got some fingerprints and a footprint, from a size ten trainer. It's a start.'

'Probably not a woman then.' Norman smiled.

'But the fingerprints they found are a woman's,' said Slater.

'Two people?' suggested Norman.

'Luckily for us, Jane had the bright idea of making a note of all the car registrations in the street,' continued Slater, looking in her direction. 'She's going to focus on that today. We might just get lucky and find our intruder that way.'

Jolly nodded her head in agreement.

'Where are we gonna start?' asked Norman.

'We need to learn about Mr Winter, so we're going to see his solicitor, John Hunter,' said Slater. 'He seems to be the only person who might know something about him.' He looked at his watch. 'But first I'll let you eat your breakfast.'

'Good idea. My stomach is starting to think my throat's been cut,' Norman said, digging in to the mound of food in front of him.

S later had figured the solicitor wouldn't start work before 9am, so he and Norman enjoyed a leisurely breakfast in the canteen. They were just finishing up and Slater was thinking about leaving when the door swung open and a young PC entered. He stood in the doorway frowning as he looked around. He was obviously searching for someone and as Slater made eye contact with him, the frown vanished to be replaced by a look of recognition.

'I knew we should have left five minutes ago,' muttered Slater to Norman, as the newcomer made his way across the canteen.

'I'm innocent,' said Norman. 'So whatever it is, it must be your fault.'

'Err, excuse me, sir,' said the PC to Slater. 'The duty sergeant asked me to give you this.'

He handed over a sheet of paper. As Slater read the notes, Norman's phone broke into a tinny rendition of Blondie's 'Call Me'. Slater and the younger man exchanged glances.

'What the hell's that?' the young PC asked, wincing.

'A crappy phone making a mess of a ringtone,' Slater said, grimacing at the racket.

'Thanks for this,' he added, indicating the paper, then nodded towards Norman and his squawking phone. 'I should escape now if I were you, before it gets even worse.'

'I'll do that,' the young PC said, grinning. 'Thank you, sir.'

He turned on his heel and headed off. A moment later, Norman placed his phone back in his pocket.

'Important?' asked Slater.

'Nah,' said Norman. 'Just some idiot salesman. What have you got there?'

'It seems we're going to kill two birds with one stone this morning. John Hunter's secretary arrived this morning to find someone had been in their offices last night.'

'What? No alarm?' asked Norman.

'On the contrary – they have a very sophisticated system, but it was disabled,' said Slater.

'That's a bit clever for anyone local, so don't hold your breath for any obvious evidence.'

'You're probably right,' Slater said, sighing. 'I suppose we'd better go take a look.'

A man was on his knees peering at the lock of the door emblazoned with the legend 'John Hunter, Solicitor'. The man was dressed in one of the forensic team's new blue paper romper suits, and he rustled quietly as he turned towards them. Once again, Slater pictured a smurf at work. He just couldn't help it. The only thing that spoilt the image was the shape of the hood. He thought perhaps he should suggest a redesign. If they were going to look like smurfs, they might as well get it right.

'Aha! The cavalry, at last,' said the smurf. 'Better late than never, I suppose.'

Slater realised it was Ian Becks, Tinton's forensic wizard. Everyone in CID knew they were lucky to have him on their side, but just to make sure they never forgot, Becks thought it his duty to give them a hard time whenever the opportunity arose. The resulting banter kept everyone on their toes, and went a good way towards maintaining good morale between the two departments.

'Morning, Becksy,' Slater said, smiling broadly at him. 'I take it this means you've found enough clues to solve the case all on your own and we're not needed.'

'I'm afraid there's nothing to find, mate,' said Becks.

'What?' said Norman. 'You mean there was no break-in?'

'Oh, someone's been in here, alright.' Becks gestured to the office within. 'But whoever it was knew what they were doing. I'm pretty sure the alarm was switched off, or temporarily disabled using some sort of wireless jamming device, and if they didn't use a key to get in, it was picked by an expert. They were almost certainly wearing latex gloves too, so I'm sure we won't find a single worthwhile fingerprint.'

'No prints at all?' asked Norman.

'Oh there are plenty of prints,' said Becks. 'But I'll bet a month's wages any possibles will belong to the people who work here.'

'So it's going to be brains and not science that solves this one then,' said Slater.

'Well, if you two are the brains in question, you might as well put it straight into the "unsolved" folder.' Becks grinned at them.

'I'll have you know we've not had a single "unsolved" since we became a team,' said Norman, proudly.

'That's because my team have been there with the science each time,' said Becks, with an evil grin. 'And you know it!'

'I'd love to continue this discussion,' said Norman, heavily, 'but, maybe some other time. Now perhaps if you could step aside and let the professionals do their jobs...'

'You carry on.' Becks laughed as he stepped away from the door. 'I think we're about done here anyway.'

As if to confirm his statement, the door suddenly opened to reveal two more blue-suited forensic guys, carrying their cases of equipment.

'All done in here, Boss,' said the first. 'Sorry, but we haven't found anything promising.'

'No worries,' said Becks, and then in a voice loaded with sarcasm added, 'The Dynamic Duo have arrived now so we might as well head off.'

'You're done then, right?' asked Slater, ignoring the bait.

'Yeah,' agreed Becks. 'Like I said before, this guy knew what he was doing. I'll do a full report, but you've already got the gist.'

'Okay, thanks guys,' said Slater.

He stepped aside to let the forensics guys out, and then followed Norman through the open door.

'And you're quite sure there's nothing missing?' Norman asked.

'No, nothing. Not as far as I can see.' Sheila Bettsan, John

Hunter's secretary, looked a bit shaken. 'But someone has logged on to our computer system.'

'There must be some sensitive information on there,' said Slater.

'Not really,' she said. 'Mr Hunter has always been very aware of his responsibilities re: confidentiality. The last thing we do every day is back up everything onto a portable hard disk and then clean the system to remove everything from that day. The portable hard disk is taken home overnight.'

'That's quite impressive,' Norman said. 'A lot of people wouldn't go to all that trouble.'

'It is a lot of fiddling around,' she agreed, 'but Mr Hunter's a bit of a computer buff. He likes to dabble with designing software in his spare time and he's created a programme that creates the backup and cleans up behind it. All I have to do is click a mouse, wait ten minutes, and it's done. It means whoever was searching last night wouldn't have found anything worthwhile.'

'Do you actually have any information that someone would go to all this trouble to find?' asked Slater.

'You'll have to ask Mr Hunter that question. But, as far as the stuff I deal with is concerned, it's mostly small stuff like wills and property conveyancing, so I wouldn't have thought so.'

'Right. Thank you, Mrs Bettsan, you've been very helpful. We'll let you get on now and we'll talk to Mr Hunter.'

Slater's first impression of John Hunter was of a kindly looking man, and he remembered that Jane Jolly had reported similar. Slater thought Mr Hunter looked the sort who wouldn't get easily ruffled.

'Mrs Bettsan is right,' he said. 'I can't imagine there's a single thing in our files that would be of that much interest to anyone, and certainly nothing worth breaking in for.'

'It does seem strange,' said Slater. 'But thanks to your back-up system, whoever broke in has wasted their time anyway.'

'Yes.' Hunter smiled, ruefully. 'We've been doing it for years, but I always thought I would reach my retirement without ever knowing if it had been worth the effort. Well, I know now, don't I? But I'm going to have to do something about the alarm. Your man said he thought it had been disabled with some sort of jamming signal.'

'Yes, that's right,' said Slater. 'I'm afraid I don't know much about that stuff, but Ian's quite clued up. If he says that's what happened, he's usually right. At the very least you need to change your codes.'

'So much for sophistication,' said Hunter, disappointed. 'That's supposed to be the latest, state-of-the-art system.'

'The problem with these things,' said Norman, 'is that for every genius coming up with new technology, there's another ten geniuses dreaming up ways of breaking it.'

'Yes,' agreed Hunter, gloomily. 'It's a pretty grim outlook, isn't it? I wonder if anything is ever really secure. But then I suppose it's up to us to try to stay one step ahead.' He brightened. 'Don't let them grind you down, eh?'

'It's about all we can do,' agreed Slater.

'Anyway,' said Hunter, 'weren't you coming to speak to me today anyway?'

'Yes, that's right,' said Slater. 'It's about a Mr Dylan Winter from 17 Canal Street.'

'Ah, yes. I spoke to your PC Jolly. I had to arrange the funeral. It's a bit sad when there's no family or friends to contact and your solicitor is the only person left.'

'So there's definitely no family at all?'

'Well, he's left everything to his sister, Julia, but I have no idea where she is. He was adamant she was still alive when he came in to make his will a few weeks ago. I have to find her so she can have every-thing, but it seems she vanished years ago and I have no idea where she is. I've tried all the usual things, like adverts in all the newspapers, and even online searches. But so far I've drawn a blank.'

'So he's only just made the will?' asked Slater.

'Oh yes. I didn't even know he existed until then.'

'Did he say why he suddenly needed to make a will?'

'He just said it was something he'd been meaning to do for years but he'd never got around to it. There didn't seem to be any special reason at the time,' said Hunter. 'Although now it does seem rather prophetic, don't you think?'

Slater agreed with Hunter, but chose not to say anything.

'We can take look into this as part of our inquiry,' said Slater. 'I can't guarantee we'll find her, but we've probably got more data at our disposal.'

'That would be very helpful, thank you, Sergeant.'

'Did he have much to leave?' asked Slater.

'There's his house in Canal Street,' said Hunter. 'That's about it. There are no other assets, and no cash to speak of.' He paused for a moment. 'Can I ask a question?'

'Sure,' said Slater.

'Do you usually send two detectives to investigate these things? Is there some problem with Mr Winter's death? '

'We have reason to believe Mr Winter's death may not have been an accident,' said Slater.

'Good Lord. Really? But he was just a harmless little old man.'

'Doesn't make a lot of sense, does it?' Norman pitched in. 'That's why we need to ask questions. What else can you tell us about him?'

'Not much really,' said Hunter. 'As I told PC Jolly, he came to me to make his will, but he was a very private person so he didn't really reveal anything about himself. I know he owned his house and he lived on his own with his dog. That's about it.'

'So you can't tell us where he was born, or about his childhood, or anything like that?' asked Norman.

'I don't have to know any of that to help someone make a will, Sergeant, and if he doesn't want to share that sort of stuff with me...'

'I'm sorry,' said Norman. 'I didn't mean to imply you're not doing your job properly, we were just hoping you might know a bit more about him than we do.'

'I'm sorry, but I can't help you,' said Hunter. 'I wish I could.'

'That's okay, Mr Hunter,' said Slater. 'Thank you for your time and your help.'

'Sounds to me like old Mr Winter knew he was going to die,' said Norman a few minutes later, as they reached their car. 'In view of what's happened so far it has to mean he was threatened, doesn't it?'

'I don't think there's much doubt about that,' agreed Slater. 'All we've got to do now is figure out who... and why.'

'Do you think we should have told Hunter about the break-ins at Winter's house?'

'Right now, we suspect they might be linked but we have no clear evidence to suggest they are, do we?'

'We don't?' Norman stared at him.

'Not unless you know something I don't,' said Slater, opening the passenger door.

Norman shrugged his shoulders and climbed into the driver's side.

'Okay. Whatever.'

He sat in silence for a few seconds, but Slater could tell something was weighing on his mind, and it was only a few minutes later before he spoke up again.

'So anyway,' he asked. 'How did Jolly Jane know Hunter was Mr Winter's solicitor?'

'She said one of his cards was pinned up in his kitchen. She took his phone number from there, I think.'

'And she left the card where it was?'

'As far as I know,' said Slater.

'So the guy who trashed Winter's house could have seen the card and put two and two together just like Jane did, right?' asked Norman.

Slater's felt like a fool. Why hadn't he thought of that?

'Okay, but it's not clear evidence, is it?' he said, even though he knew it had been a good spot. 'And why didn't I think of that?'

'I'm sure you would have thought of it, too,' Norman said, smiling. 'Of course, it's possible I might be way off course and talking through my backside.'

'No,' said Slater, 'I don't think you are. Maybe our burglar thinks Mr Winter passed whatever he was looking for on to Hunter for safe keeping.'

'It fits, doesn't it?' Norman's smile broadened. 'And who better to leave it with than your own solicitor?'

'We'll have to go back and ask him,' said Slater.

'Go on. 'I'll wait here.'

'He says Mr Winter definitely did not leave him anything to look after,' said Slater, five minutes later, as he climbed back into the car.

'Rats!' said Norman. 'So much for that brilliant idea. I told you I might be talking through my arse.'

'It was good thinking,' Slater said, encouragingly. 'And I think our burglar thought so, too. And at least now we know for sure that Mr Winter hadn't given anything to John Hunter.'

'Yeah, that's true enough,' agreed Norman. 'But if we assume all this theory is correct, it means we still have no idea what we're looking for, and even worse, we haven't a clue where it might be hidden.'

'But this guy seems to be desperate. If you thought Hunter had the thing you were looking for, where would you look next?'

'You mean his house?' Norman let out a whistle. 'We could always stake it out. Maybe we'd get lucky.'

'I doubt Bob Murray would agree with you, but I guess it wouldn't hurt to ask,' said Slater, not looking forward to that particular conversation.

CHAPTER NINE

As they were just a very small three-person team, they didn't have use of the main incident room. Instead, they were crammed into a much smaller room with barely enough room to swing a cat. The single window hadn't been cleaned in years and permitted just a small amount of light to penetrate the layers of grime.

'So,' Slater had asked Norman, mischievously, 'how are you going to apply your positive spin to *this* particular situation?'

'It's sort of like an old telephone box, but with barely any windows,' Norman had said, glumly. But then, he brightened and with a beaming smile, added, 'On the bright side, it'll give us a good incentive to get out there and do some real investigating.'

Slater rolled his eyes, and Norman laughed.

It was almost eleven when they got back to the tiny office, which had undergone something of a transformation at the hands of the ever-efficient Jane Jolly. When they had looked in earlier, it had resembled a store room with desks and chairs all pushed to one side. Now it looked like a reasonably orderly workspace for three people.

On the basis that she had done all the work sorting out the room,

Jolly had chosen to place her own desk under the window, where she now sat pecking away at the keyboard of her computer.

'Wow!' said Norman, as they walked in. 'You know you should be on TV, Jane. Magicians are really popular right now.'

'I don't know how you do it,' Slater said, gazing around the room.

'Application,' said Jolly. 'That and an acceptance that no one else was likely to do it.'

'Any calls, Jane?' asked Slater, ignoring the implied slur.

'No, sorry. Deathly quiet,' she said.

'Don't apologise,' said Norman. 'Deathly quiet is okay. How's your search coming on?'

The two detectives huddled behind her desk so they could look over her shoulder.

'I've got a result,' she said. 'I've been through every car registration number on my list, and there are just two that belong to people who don't live in Canal Street. Then I called in a favour with the traffic division and got them to run the two registration numbers through their search programme on the date in question. One of those cars was picked up on CCTV heading towards Canal Street and then away again a bit later. The recorded times are a good fit for this car to be the one our intruder was driving.'

'Have you got a name and address?' asked Slater.

'I certainly have.' With a broad grin, she waved a sheet of paper in the air.

'Look out, Tinton,' said Norman appreciatively, patting her on the shoulder. 'Jolly Jane strikes again!'

He took the sheet of paper she offered and looked at the address.

'Do you know where this is?' he asked her.

'Uh-huh.' She nodded.

'Want to come with me and ask our new friend some awkward questions?'

'I'll just finish my tea,' she said, beaming. 'And I'll be with you!'

'And I suppose that while you're gone, I'd better go tell the boss we want to mess up his overtime budget,' said Slater, gloomily.

W hile Slater set about trying to convince Bob Murray that it would be a good idea to blow his overtime budget, Norman hoped he and Jolly would make some progress in their enquiries via a nice quiet chat with Danny Trent, the owner of the vehicle in question.

'What if he does a runner out the back?' asked Jolly, as they drove down the road towards his house.

'I thought of that,' said Norman, from the passenger seat. 'There are two uniforms waiting out the back just in case.'

'Thinking ahead,' said Jolly, approvingly. 'I like it. At least now I know I'm not going to have to do all the chasing if he does make a break for it.'

Norman smiled broadly, and tilted his head to acknowledge the truth in that statement. He didn't do running.

'Just looking after my partner,' he said, as she eased the unmarked car into a handy space right outside Trent's house.

'Thank goodness,' she said. 'He's only nineteen and I'm old enough to be his mother. I'd never be able to catch him.'

In the event, they didn't need to worry about their suspect doing a runner.

'I'm Detective Sergeant Norman and this is PC Jolly,' Norman announced, showing his warrant card when the door opened. 'We'd like to speak to Danny Trent.'

The young man who had answered the door looked shocked initially, but he quickly recovered his composure and the shocked expression was replaced with a smug grin. Youthful arrogance, Norman thought.

'He's not here. Why do you want to speak to him?' he asked.

'Who are you?' asked Norman, noting the attitude. He liked a challenge.

'Err, I'm John, his brother.'

'Are you twins?' asked Norman, looking him up and down.

'What?' he said, uncertainly. 'Erm, no, of course not.'

'Wrong answer, sunshine,' said Norman.

Then, turning to Jolly, he said, 'Got your cuffs handy?'

She nodded.

Norman turned back to face the now not-quite-so-smug looking young man.

'Then arrest this man, Constable.'

Jolly took a step forward.

'Now hold on a minute. You can't just arrest me like this. You might think you can go around bullying people, but you're not going to get away with it here. I'm a newspaper reporter.'

'Really?' said Norman, in mock wonder. 'Oh wow. Who do you write for? The Times? Or maybe you're a Telegraph man.'

'The local newspaper,' said the mystery man, looking as if he wanted a hole to open up in the ground and swallow him.

'We'll check that,' said Norman.

'And anyway, I haven't even done anything wrong,' bleated Trent.

'Well now, let's make a list, shall we?' said Norman with an evil grin. 'For a start you've just given a false name to a police officer. By doing that you're obstructing a police inquiry, and you should understand we're not talking some piffling little case. This is a murder inquiry.'

'Bollocks!' said the young man, his face reddening. 'I'm John Trent, and I haven't murdered anybody.'

'Oh come on, son.' Norman sighed, wearily. 'Do we really look that stupid? We found you through your car. We've seen your photograph on your driver's licence. You might think you know it all, but you really don't, do you?'

'But I haven't done anything wrong!'

'What were you doing in the back garden of number 17 Canal Street ten days ago?' asked Norman.

'Never been there in my life,' the man on the doorstep answered, a bit too quickly. 'I don't even know where it is.'

'So how did your car get there?' asked Jolly.

'It wasn't-'

'It was,' interrupted Jolly. 'I saw it there myself and noted the registration number, just after I saw you running through the back gate.'

'Look. I told you I'm a reporter. I don't have to tell you anything.' He folded his arms and leaned defiantly against the door.

'Like I said before,' said Norman, smiling pleasantly, 'you don't know quite as much as you think you do. Just so you understand, I'll tell you again – this is a murder investigation, not some schoolboy game. Even if you are a reporter, you still have to talk to us. It's true that if you tell us something second-hand you don't have to reveal your source. But that's not quite the same thing, is it?'

'And just so you understand, mate, I'll tell you what you can do–' barked the young man, taking a step forward and jabbing his finger at Norman.

Norman watched with no small amount of pleasure as Jolly grabbed the man's hand, twisted his arm up behind his back, slammed him up against the door and slapped on the handcuffs.

'Now that was a silly thing to do,' said Norman, patiently. 'Now we can add threatening a police officer and resisting arrest to that list of charges. And think yourself lucky. If my colleague hadn't been so quick off the mark, I might have been able to add assaulting a police officer to that list.'

Then, as an afterthought, he added, 'And just so you know, I am not, and never will be, your "mate".'

He looked at Jolly and nodded his head towards the road. Jolly began to drag her prisoner towards the car.

'Ow!' yelled Trent. 'That hurts, you bitch. I'll f–'

'Foul and abusive language, and threatening behaviour towards a second police officer,' interrupted Norman, following along behind. 'At this rate, I'm gonna need a bigger notebook.'

'Do you know how difficult it is to even keep near our budgeted costs?' Bob Murray asked, exasperated.

'I appreciate you're under a lot of pressure,' sympathised Slater. 'But–'

'And now you want me to provide protection to someone who might be in danger, but you don't exactly know for sure, and you don't have a clue why. Come on, David, you need to be a bit more convincing than that.'

These rants about spiralling costs were certainly becoming more and more frequent, so Slater figured the pressure from above must be really getting to Murray. It explained why he seemed to be here seven days a week recently. He thought it couldn't be much fun for an old school copper, who had spent his entire career doing whatever had to be done to get a result, to suddenly have to start worrying about balancing books. Murray sounded like a man who'd just about had enough.

'We believe Mr Winter died because he had some information somebody wanted very badly,' he said, trying to stay calm and reasonable. 'When it couldn't be found at his house, that same somebody decided Winter must have passed it on to his solicitor John Hunter. Now his office has been turned over, but nothing was found. It seems reasonable to assume the next place to be targeted is going to be Hunter's home. We've already had one murder, and we believe the person behind this wouldn't hesitate to murder again.'

'How long's it going to take?' asked Murray.

'How long's a piece of string?' replied Slater, tritely.

The scowl on Murray's face immediately told Slater he'd spoken out of turn, and wished he could take the words straight back.

'Don't get clever, Sergeant,' growled Murray. 'This isn't some bloody game we're playing here.'

'Yes sir. I'm sorry sir,' mumbled Slater.

Murray sighed, heavily.

'There's no need to grovel,' he said. 'I shouldn't be snapping at you like that.'

Slater thought that was as near as Murray was going to get to an apology, but he also knew he had spoken out of turn.

'No. You're right to have a go. I was out of order,' he admitted.

'D'you know,' said Murray, tiredly, sitting back in his seat. 'There was a time when I used to love this job, but now I sometimes feel as if they want us to catch criminals with our hands tied behind our backs. How can we do the job with no bloody funds? It makes me so bloody angry!'

It was unusual for the old man to swear, and when he did it usually signified he was particularly angry about something. Right now Slater was losing count of the 'bloodys', and he had no wish to become the object of Murray's ire, so he decided he should keep his mouth firmly closed.

'Let me think about it,' said Murray. 'I'll let you know later.'

'Ok, Boss. Thank you,' said Slater, climbing to his feet. At least the old man hadn't said no. He figured it would probably be a good idea to get out while he was ahead.

'Have you thought anymore about what we were talking about the other day?' asked Murray, before Slater could escape.

'Boss?' asked Slater, dumbly.

'About becoming a DI.'

'Ah. Right. Yes,' said Slater, awkwardly. 'I have as it happens, but as there's no vacancy for a DI here, it seems to me I'd have to move away. At this particular time, I'm not ready to do that. Maybe in a year or two.'

'Serious this time, is it?' asked Murray.

Slater looked nonplussed.

'The new girlfriend. D'you think she might be the one?'

Slater felt himself going red. He didn't know what to say. He didn't think Murray had the faintest inkling about Cindy.

'Don't look so surprised,' Murray said, smiling. 'It's my job to know if people are happy or not, and I'd have to be blind to miss the fact that you have a spring in your step at the moment.'

He nodded his approval.

'I do understand,' he went on. 'But just remember these career opportunities won't always be there just when you want them. That's all, David, thank you.'

'Err, right. Thanks, Boss,' said Slater, eager to get away before Murray embarrassed him any further.

CHAPTER TEN

'Is that Rita Myers?' asked Norman into the phone. Rita was both editor and owner of Tinton's only local newspaper, *The Tinton Tribune*.

'Speaking,' said a business-like voice on the other end of the line.

'This is DS Norman from Tinton police. We're questioning a young man who claims to work for you.'

'Who is it?' she asked.

'His name's Danny Trent,' said Norman. 'Says he's a reporter.'

'Ha!' she laughed. 'That boy has ambition, but I'm afraid he's rather exaggerating his own importance. He's not exactly reached those lofty heights just yet.'

'So he's definitely not a reporter,' Norman said.

'He's just the office junior at the moment,' she replied. 'Look, I'm sorry if I sound rather flippant, but what's he supposed to have done? It's nothing serious, is it?'

'We're just asking him some questions relating to an inquiry. But he's claiming because he works for the press as a reporter he doesn't have to speak to us. To tell the truth, he could be in a lot of trouble if he's not careful. He's not doing himself any favours and he's likely to get charged with wasting police time at the very least, but it could be a lot more serious than that.'

'Would it help if I come in and talk to him?' asked Rita.

'I was hoping you might say that. Would you really be willing to?' Norman jumped at the opportunity to get through to this stupid kid.

'What's he being questioned about?' she asked.

'Off the record?'

'Yes, of course.'

'It could be that a death that we thought was an accident may actually be a murder,' said Norman.

'I didn't know there had been a murder,' she said in surprise. 'Would that be the old man who was found dead in Canal Street?'

'That's the only one we've got,' said Norman, hoping he wasn't going to regret telling this to the local press.

'Give me five minutes and I'll be on my way,' she said, hanging up the phone.

True to her word, Rita Meyers was there within less than fifteen minutes. She was a smartly dressed, no-nonsense sort of woman, and gave off an air of calm efficiency. Norman figured she wouldn't be someone who tolerated bullshit in any form – and he had been right. When Norman pointed her in the direction of the interview room, she hadn't hesitated to march straight in and deliver her message to the unsuspecting Danny Trent in no uncertain terms. Watching through the two-way mirror, Norman thought he was glad *he* wasn't the one getting the bollocking.

'Right,' she said, to Norman and Slater when she'd finished. 'I've explained to him that he's not a reporter and even if he was, he wouldn't have some sort of magic immunity, so I think he'll talk now. Do you want me to hang on, just in case?'

'How about if you sit in with him?' ventured Slater.

Norman opened his mouth to protest, but Slater didn't give him the chance.

'We wouldn't normally do this, of course,' he continued, 'but I think maybe if we make the whole thing a little less formal Danny might be more inclined to talk, and he trusts you, doesn't he?'

'Are you going to record this "chat"?' she asked.

'I thought maybe we'd try informal first,' said Slater. 'Then we can do the full statement afterwards.'

It was a gamble, but Danny Trent obviously didn't trust the police and was unlikely to talk to them alone, Norman thought, grudgingly.

'And what's in it for me?' she asked.

'We can probably make sure you get to take him back home rather than spend the night in one of our cells,' said Slater. 'And I must ask that you keep this quiet, or Danny could be in danger. And that means not printing anything about this case.'

'That sounds very melodramatic,' she said, teasingly.

'It's for real,' said Norman. 'You'll have to trust us on that, but it's not something we'd joke about, believe me.'

She looked from one to the other, clearly weighing up her options.

'Okay,' she said, finally. 'Let's do it.'

Two hours later, Norman watched her walk out of the station with Danny in tow, the office junior having promised to make sure he went straight home and behaved himself.

'What do you make of that?' Slater asked Norman.

'He's an arrogant little bugger, but he's no killer,' said Norman. 'His alibi for the night of the murder checks out.'

'He's a size ten shoe, though. And that's just the right size for the break-in, even though he says the house was like that when he got there that morning.'

'Well, yeah,' said Norman, doubtfully. 'But he says he doesn't have any expensive trainers like that, and when I called his mum she confirmed that. Even Rita said she's never seen him wearing a pair like that. Even if it was his, that shoe print was down by the gate not up by the house. I would say that tends to back up his story that he was just being nosey and panicked when Jane turned up.'

'That's what I think, too,' agreed Slater. 'He's got an attitude on him, but he's no house-breaker and definitely not a killer.'

'But what do you make of this story about a London journalist he says he's working for?' asked Norman.

'Well, Rita did say he's ambitious. I think perhaps this guy's found a naive kid to do some running around for him. In turn the kid probably thinks it's going to fast track him to the big league.'

'Rita didn't look too impressed when he told us about his freelance gig,' said Norman, grinning. 'I bet he's getting his ears roasted on the way home!'

'Yeah, he's just being used,' said Slater. 'I'm sure about that, and I'm sure Rita's telling him exactly the same thing on the way home. The interesting question is: why? Why would a London journalist be sniffing around the seemingly unimportant murder of a little old man?'

'Maybe he knows there's a much bigger story behind the murder.'

'Yeah,' agreed Slater. 'In which case he knows a lot more than we do. But it's the only reason that makes sense, isn't it? We need to find out who he is and what he knows. Until we do, I think we might have run into a brick wall.'

'Here, look at this,' called Jolly, half an hour later.

Slater and Norman turned from their desks and joined her.

'It's the website for this journalist Danny Trent claims he's working for. He's some sort of freelance investigative journalist by the look of it.'

'Ah. A sleazy muck-raker,' said Norman derisively.

'It looks like he does his fair share of that,' agreed Jolly. 'But he's also a bit of a crusader for good causes.'

'So what's the guy in charge look like?' asked Slater. 'Are there any photos of him?'

'Here,' said Jolly.

She clicked a link and a head shot of Geoff Rippon, journalist at large, appeared.

'Hey, wait a minute,' said Norman. 'I know that face.'

He retrieved his mobile phone from his desk and fumbled with it for a moment.

'I thought so,' he said, smiling. 'Here, look. It's the guy who was creeping about at the back of the funeral.'

He showed the photograph from his mobile phone. Even thought it was blurry, it was obviously the same guy.

'My instincts told me not to delete it,' he explained. 'I also have a photo of his car registration.'

'Let's have it,' said Jolly. 'Maybe I can find out where he lives.'

'Is there no address on his website?' asked Slater.

'Just an office address,' said Jolly. 'And a couple of phone numbers. Here.'

She handed Slater a slip of paper with the two numbers.

'Let me give these a ring,' said Slater, turning back to his desk.

Over the next few minutes, he tried the two numbers but all he got in reply was the same voicemail message. He wasn't really surprised. That would have been way too easy, wouldn't it? But at least they now had a name and a face. It was a start.

'Any luck with that car, Jane?' he asked, turning back to her.

'It's a hire car,' she said.

'Huh! Just when I thought we'd got lucky,' said Norman.

'We have,' she said. 'It belongs to that car hire place down by the railway station. Apparently, he picked it up the day before the funeral and he's got an open booking. He told them he's staying at the Station Hotel but doesn't know exactly how long he's going to be here. I'm just printing it out now.'

Norman went to the printer and snatched up the sheet of paper as it finished printing. He scanned the sheet and grinned.

'PC Jolly, come and stand out here. I feel I should prostrate myself at your feet,' he declared, grandly.

'I'm pleased you appreciate my efficiency, but that actually sounds rather pervy,' she said, doubtfully, looking over her shoulder. 'I think I'll stay here and make do with a simple "thank you", if you don't mind.'

'Rebuffed again.' Norman staggered back, clutching his hands to his heart in faux hurt.

'I hate to interrupt,' said Slater, before Norman could get into his stride. 'But we do have an investigation to get on with.'

'Yes, PC Jolly,' said Norman, looking suitably serious. 'Quit fooling around!'

Jolly poked her tongue out and turned back to her computer.

'Are you okay with carrying on with Mr Winters' background check, Jane?' Slater asked, noticing she looked a bit harassed.

'I'd rather be busy than twiddling my thumbs,' she said. 'I'm actually quite good at this family tree stuff. It'll keep me out of trouble for a while.'

'I'll take Norman for a ride. That way he can't keep distracting you,' said Slater. 'We'll be at the Station Hotel if you need us.'

CHAPTER ELEVEN

They found Geoff Rippon in the bar at the Station Hotel. He was on his own at a corner table, pecking away at a laptop. A cigarette smouldered away in an ashtray next to his half-empty pint of beer. Slater thought there was something sleazy about him, although he couldn't have said exactly why. Perhaps it was just that Geoff Rippon looked rather cold and hard. He seemed to be painfully thin and had extraordinarily white skin. His greasy, black hair was plastered across his head in a vain, but futile, attempt to hide its sparseness.

He appeared to be engrossed in his writing and didn't notice their approach.

'Geoff Rippon?' asked Slater.

Rippon glanced up but continued typing. He had a large hooked nose and sharp, beady eyes, which glared at them from behind huge spectacles. In that moment, Slater thought there was something of the vulture about him, and somehow that seemed appropriate.

'Who's asking?'

'Detective Sergeants Slater and Norman.'

They produced their warrant cards. Rippon didn't appear to be unduly interested in them, but he did stop tapping at his keyboard and gave them his attention.

'Have I broken any laws?' he asked.

'Not that I'm aware of,' replied Slater.

'I didn't think I had,' said Rippon, returning to his keyboard. 'Now, if you don't mind I'm rather busy.'

'We'd like a few words, if that's ok,' said Slater, ignoring the rebuff.

Rippon sighed heavily then sat back in his seat and looked at Slater and then at Norman.

'Alright,' he said. 'I can see you're not going to give me any peace, so what do you want to talk about?'

'Mind if we sit down?' asked Norman, pulling out a chair opposite Rippon. Slater did likewise and they both sat.

'They're nice trainers,' observed Slater, pointing at Rippon's shoes. 'I fancy a pair of them myself, but I can't afford them on my salary.'

'I do a lot of running,' said Rippon. 'And I can afford the best, so I buy the best. Is there a law against that, now?'

'Not at all,' said Slater. 'What size are you?'

'Nine,' said Rippon, 'I'll take one off so you can check if you don't believe me. I'm blessed with small feet, but I make up for it in other areas.'

He gave them a sickly grin and Slater felt disappointment wash over him.

'We're curious,' said Slater. 'We can't help but wonder why someone like you would have come down here to attend a funeral. It's not as if you knew Mr Winter, is it?'

'I just wanted to see what it's like when someone with no friends gets buried,' said Rippon, seeming completely unfazed by the question. 'It's a bit of research for something I'm writing about sad and lonely old people.'

'Yeah, right!' Norman smiled at him. 'Like you don't have many examples up in London.'

Rippon smiled right back at Norman.

'There's no law against attending a funeral.'

'We're also curious to know why you employed a local youngster to nose around and interfere with a crime scene,' continued Slater.

'I didn't ask him to do that,' snapped Rippon. 'He was just supposed to let me know if anything significant happened.'

'He thinks you've employed him as co-writer,' said Norman.

'Well, he thinks wrong. He's just a runner. If he did more than I asked, that's his problem, not mine.'

'Oh, don't worry,' said Slater. 'We didn't think for one minute you'd actually care about what happened to him, and we certainly didn't expect you to accept any responsibility for what he's done.'

'You're not going to be disappointed then, are you?' sneered Rippon.

Slater looked hard at him. He really did seem to be a most unpleasant human being.

'So what is so interesting about Dylan Winter's death?' asked Norman.

'You really have no idea, do you?'

'So why don't you give us a clue?'

'What's in it for me?' Rippon's lips pressed into a tight line.

'Ah!' Norman smiled pleasantly. 'What a surprise. And there I was hoping you would be a public-spirited citizen willing to help us.'

'Why should I?' Rippon sneered again.

'So you don't think you should help us solve a murder?' asked Slater.

'Ha! Cover up a murder, more like! You lot are all the same. You're all bent as nine bob notes. He contacted me in the first place because he didn't know if he could trust you lot!'

'Winter contacted you?' asked Slater in surprise. 'Why would he do that?'

'Because he had a story to tell, of course.'

'And you're telling us he would trust someone like you with this story,' scoffed Norman.

'When did he contact you? What story?' asked Slater.

Rippon said nothing.

'Why didn't he trust us?' Norman furrowed his brow

'I never actually found that out,' said Rippon. 'But I suspect it was because he crossed swords with some bent coppers in his past. Same reason I don't trust you.'

'So that means we're all bent, does it?' asked Norman, sighing heavily.

'If the cap fits.' Rippon smiled unpleasantly, showing yellowing teeth.

'Actually it doesn't bloody fit.' Slater smacked his hand down on the table, making Rippon jump. 'Yes, unfortunately there are some bent coppers, but we're not. In fact, we've both been the victims of bent coppers.'

'Yeah, sure you have,' said Rippon, raising an eyebrow.

'If you've got some information that will lead us to his killer, and there's any police involvement, we'll be happy to bring it out into the open. We've done it before,' explained Norman.

'Well, you would say that, wouldn't you?' muttered Rippon.

'You're the journalist,' said Norman. 'Do your homework and you'll see we're telling the truth.'

Rippon looked doubtfully at Norman and Slater.

'I tell you what,' said Norman. 'How about we give you a couple of days to check us out and think about it?'

'And how am I supposed to do that?'

'Like I said,' answered Norman, as he rose casually to his feet, 'you're the journalist. And somehow I can't believe you don't know how to access that sort of information.'

'We'll be back.' Slater, taking his cue from Norman, stood up too. 'Same time, same place.'

They turned together and walked from the bar, Slater feeling Rippon's eyes burning into his back as he left.

'That guy gives me the creeps,' he said, as they approached their car. 'He reminds me of a vulture.'

'You're exactly right,' Norman said, snorting with laughter. 'I knew he reminded me of something, but I couldn't think what it was.'

'D'you think he actually knows anything?'

'I can't imagine Winter would want to talk to a creep like that.' Norman unlocked the car, and climbed into the driver's seat. 'But even if he did, I don't think he told him much. Let's be honest now, if you were old and on your own, and that guy turned up at your home, would you feel you could trust him?'

'Good point.' Slater nodded as he buckled up his seatbelt. 'He certainly wouldn't put me at ease.'

'He knows something, though,' said Norman. 'And I guess anything would help, right now. Let's see what a couple of days does for us. If he still doesn't want to talk to us, we'll have to think again. He obviously wants this story or he wouldn't have come down here.'

'Did he want it so badly he murdered for it?' suggested Slater, as Norman started the car and pulled out of the space.

'That would have to be one seriously big story to want to murder someone for it,' said Norman. 'To be honest, I can't see it. But even if he did, he wouldn't have taken the risk of involving the kid, would he?' said Norman.

'Having a pair of eyes and ears down here would keep him informed.'

'Hmm, maybe, but I'm not convinced,' said Norman, after a moment. 'If Winter had the story, why would Rippon kill him? Surely that would rather defeat the object.'

'Do you think he'll do a runner?'

'No. I don't think so,' Norman said, chuckling quietly. 'Because if he does, he's going to promote himself from possible suspect to definite suspect, and that would be pretty stupid. Whatever our Mr Rippon might be, he certainly ain't stupid.'

CHAPTER TWELVE

It was 6am on Saturday morning and it was still dark. A mobile phone was ringing incessantly somewhere close by.

For God's sake, thought Slater. *It's so bloody annoying. Why don't people answer their phones?*

He felt a finger jab sharply into his ribs.

'Tell them to answer that bloody phone or I'll arrest them for disturbing the peace,' he mumbled, sleepily.

There was another jab, but much harder this time.

'What the-' he began.

'Issyourphone,' mumbled an even sleepier voice up close behind him.

'What?' he said, only half awake but totally confused.

'It's your phone,' repeated the voice, a little less sleepy this time. 'And if I have to answer it for you I'm going to throw it out of the window.'

He slipped an arm behind his back and felt the cosiness of the soft, warm body pressed up against him. For the briefest moment, he wondered where he was and who was sharing his bed. Then he smiled to himself as he awakened sufficiently to recall exactly where he was and who was snuggled up next to him. He fumbled around until he found her hair, and then the softness of her face.

He had met Cindy Maine during a case and had been attracted to her right from the start. To his surprise, she had seemed to be equally attracted to him. Once the case had been solved, they had started dating, and now, three months later, they seemed to have become something of an item. They didn't see each other every night, and each had their own house, but they seemed to be spending more and more time together. It just seemed right somehow. He smiled to himself as he thought about how lucky he was to have her as a girlfriend. Then he yelped as she bit his hand.

'Ouch!' He grimaced. 'Jeez, that's not very friendly.'

'Nor's poking your fingers in my face and allowing your phone to keep ringing. If you don't answer it right now, I'll show you just how unfriendly I can be!'

He sat up, swung his legs over the side of the bed, switched on the bedside lamp, and grabbed the phone.

'I hope I'm not interrupting anything,' said Norman in his ear. 'Only it's been ringing for ages.'

'You're only interrupting my beauty sleep,' said Slater, yawning.

'And mine,' shouted Cindy, loud enough for Norman to hear.

'Now, in her case I can believe it's beauty sleep.' Norman chuckled. 'But I have to say, it's not working anywhere near as well for you.'

'That's because people keep calling me in the middle of the night and waking me up.' Slater yawned again. 'Anyway, if you've just called to share your beauty tips, I have to tell you not to bother. They don't work. Just look in any mirror and you'll see what I mean.'

'You're only jealous,' said Norman. 'I don't know what that beautiful young woman sees in you. I mean she coulda had me. It was just lucky you got there first-'

'Ha!' Slater laughed loudly. 'In your dreams, mate, in your dreams. She fell for the one with brains, as well as looks, and you know it.'

Cindy was now wide awake, and seemingly none too happy about it.

'I don't believe you two,' she snapped in Slater's ear, loudly enough that Norman could no doubt hear too. 'It's six o'clock on a Saturday morning, and I should be sound asleep, but instead I have to listen to you two sad people twittering on about how good looking you are.'

'Oh dear,' said Norman. 'I appear to have set fire to the blue touchpaper. I guess the safest thing for me to do now is deliver my message and get the hell away.'

'Yeah, right. Thanks for that, Norm. So what is it that's so important, anyway.'

'They had another break-in at Hunter's last night. This time the place has been taken apart.'

'Oh crap!' Slater sighed. 'So much for my lie in. Okay, give me half an hour and I'll be there.'

He shut the phone off, stood up, stretched, and yawned so expansively he nearly turned his head inside out.

'I'm sorry, love, I'm going to have to go in,' he said, turning to face Cindy, but she'd pulled the covers over her head and Slater didn't think she would be coming out anytime soon.

'Cindy?' He tugged gently at the covers. 'I know you're in there.'

'Go away,' she said. 'I'm asleep.'

'Okay,' he said, moving away towards the bathroom. 'I'll leave you to it-'

'No. Wait,' she said, pushing the covers back from her face. 'You can't just go off and leave me like this.'

'But I have to,' he pleaded. 'You know how it works.'

'Yes, I think I've known you long enough to know exactly how it works,' she said. 'Work comes first, and I come a poor second.'

'Now you know it's not like that,' he said. 'There's nothing I'd like more than to spend all my time with you, but I have a job to do, and a duty-'

'I know,' she interrupted with a sigh. 'I know you have to go, but surely you can spare a few minutes, for me, before you go.'

She had that look on her face. The one that he just couldn't resist.

'It's all warm and snuggly in here. Look,' she said saucily, raising the covers just enough to suggest what he was missing.

Oh my, thought Slater. *This just isn't fair. But what can a poor boy do?*

'Five minutes, and that's it,' he said.

'Oooh!' she teased. 'Does this mean I'm going to get the extended version?'

'Ha, ha, very funny,' he said, huffily. 'Of course, I could just say I don't have time, and leave you to it.'

She poked her tongue out at him and raised the covers a bit further so he could now see exactly what he was missing.

'Mmmmm. I don't think so, do you?'

And he had to admit, she was right...

'I won't ask what took you so long,' said Norman, over an hour later, when Slater finally arrived at Tinton police station.

'I got held up,' said Slater. 'I can explain.'

'Please don't,' said Norman.

'But, my car wouldn't start,' began Slater.

'Yeah, right,' said Norman. 'You forget I'm a trained detective, and right now I detect a shedload of bullshit heading my way. I think I can probably guess what happened, and I have to point out that telling me about it is totally inappropriate. It's also going to make me jealous, so please, let's just say the matter's closed, okay?'

That suited Slater just fine because he had no excuse anyway. Well, at least, not one that he was going to tell Norman about.

'So what's this about Hunter's?' he asked instead.

'I got a call at 4.30 this morning,' said Norman. 'The duty sergeant thought we should be told as we were there yesterday. I went down to take a look, and I can tell you there was no subtlety about it this time. They ignored the alarm, smashed the door down, and tore the whole place apart. By the time anyone responded to the alarm they were long gone.'

'Is there anything missing?' asked Slater.

'How can you tell when the place looks like it was hit by a bomb?' Norman shrugged. 'Forensics are on their way down there now, and I've called Hunter. He's going to meet us there at eight o'clock. In the meantime, two uniforms are guarding the place. You wanna go take a look now?'

'Might as well,' agreed Slater. 'Otherwise there was no point in me getting up so early. I'll buy us a coffee on the way.'

W hen Norman had said it looked like a bomb had gone off, Slater had thought his friend was exaggerating. Perhaps he was annoyed about having to get out of bed so early. However, now that he could see the damage for himself, Slater thought it was actually a pretty accurate description.

At first glance, it appeared that nothing had been left untouched. Every cupboard, filing cabinet, and drawer appeared to have been emptied and then flung across the office. But, despite the appearance that this had been some sort of frantic, drug-fuelled robbery, Slater was convinced Ian Becks and his forensic team wouldn't find a single shred of evidence to indicate who was behind it.

Slater had felt a huge amount of sympathy for John Hunter when he had arrived and seen the damage. He had been deeply shocked by the scene, and Slater had been wondering how he was going to cope with sorting the mess out, but then the cavalry had arrived in the form of Hunter's formidable secretary, Sheila Bettsan, and his wife, Belinda. It seemed the two women were made of sterner stuff than Mr Hunter, and by the time Slater and Norman were leaving they had the situation firmly under control.

'I take it you're now prepared to accept this break-in is related to the previous one here and at Canal Street?' asked Norman, as they walked back to their car.

'It would be hard to think otherwise, wouldn't it?' agreed Slater. 'As far as I'm concerned, there's a very strong link. It can't be a coincidence.'

'I think there's no doubt now that someone thinks Winter had some information, and now they think Hunter's got it.'

'But Hunter's adamant he's not been given anything.'

'Well, someone doesn't believe that,' said Norman. 'And that someone doesn't care that we know they're looking for it. In my experience, if someone doesn't care we know, that means they're desperate to get their hands on whatever it is they're looking for, and desperate means dangerous.'

Norman plipped the car locks as they approached and they both climbed in.

'It has to be something that was expected to be found on a computer, right?' ventured Slater.

'For sure,' agreed Norman. 'But that means it could be on a CD or a memory stick. It could even be stored somewhere in the cloud.'

'Talk about looking for a needle in a haystack,' said Slater, sighing and wondering how anything could be stored in a cloud. 'And right now we don't have a bloody clue who, what, where or why.'

'I think this calls for some abstract thinking,' said Norman, starting the car. 'We might not have Mr Winter's computer, but maybe he had some sort of online account that would give us a clue.'

'But we don't have that sort of expertise,' said Slater. 'And the waiting list for that sort of help will be a mile long.'

'Only if we go through the official channels.' Norman smiled, putting the car in gear.

'What?' said Slater, with dismay. 'You're not suggesting we involve your friend Vinnie again, are you?'

Vinnie the Geek, as he called himself, was a young man Norman had helped way back in the past, who just happened to be a genius with computers. Apparently, Norman had helped to turn his life around, so he always seemed ready to help whenever Norman asked. It just so happened he was also someone Slater found particularly difficult to get on with.

'Have you got any better ideas?' asked Norman. 'Cos I think we need to act now before this gets out of hand. We already have one murder on our hands...'

He left the sentence unfinished.

'Do you really think the risk is that high?' asked Slater.

'I think desperate equals dangerous,' said Norman. 'So yes, I do.'

'But what if there's nothing to find?'

'We can't take that chance,' said Norman. 'There must be something for someone to go to all this trouble. Maybe Winter was threatening to expose someone.'

'A geriatric blackmailer?' asked Slater. 'Do you really think that's likely?'

'We have to consider the possibility. Like I said before, we can't afford to take any chances,' persisted Norman. 'You know how good Vinnie is. If he can access Winter's email account, or any online accounts he might have, who knows what we'll find? We've got his bank statements so we should be able to see who he was paying for stuff like that. Vinnie doesn't even need to come down here – I'll send him the information and he can get onto it from home.'

Slater knew Norman had a point. It couldn't hurt to take look, now could it?

'D'you think this will convince the Old Man we have to put some sort of guard on John Hunter's house?' he asked.

'I know he won't like it,' said Norman. 'But yeah, I do.'

'So do I. But he'll be going spare about it. He's trying to keep the overtime bill down, and we're going to be spending it hand over fist.'

'He'll go ballistic for sure.' Norman grinned wickedly. 'I'm glad it's not me that has to ask him. I'd love to be a fly on the wall, when you have that conversation.'

CHAPTER THIRTEEN

'Coffee!' announced Slater, coming backwards through the door into the incident room. In his hands, he balanced a tray with three cups of coffee and a plate of assorted doughnuts. He placed the tray down on his desk, set the coffees and cakes into three places around the desk and dragged up two more chairs.

'Come on, over here' he called to the other two. 'Jane, get away from that screen for ten minutes. Norm, leave that paperwork and get your backside over here!'

'I can't eat all those doughnuts,' cried Jolly in alarm, looking at the two cakes Slater had placed alongside her coffee. 'What about my figure?'

'I think your figure's fine.' Norman smiled as he eased himself into a chair next to her. 'But if you really don't want to eat all of those doughnuts, don't worry. Whatever you don't eat won't go to waste.'

'That's very gallant of you,' said Jolly. 'But I really don't think you need them either.'

'It's a sacrifice I'm prepared to make, for a lady,' said Norman, letting out a theatrical sigh. 'It's a tough job, but someone's gotta do it.'

Slater let the conversation become a discussion about the wisdom of Norman's diet, and then on to what TV they watched last night and then their varied opinions about the latest news. After about fifteen minutes, he felt it was time to get back to the matter in hand.

'So how's your search going, Jane? Anything interesting?' he asked.

'This is what I've got so far,' she began. 'Henry Winter was born in 1946 and lived with his mother in Andover. His sister Julia arrived in 1951. Then in 1958, both parents were killed in a car crash. Neither of the parents appear to have had any relatives, and all the grandparents were dead, so the two children were sent to an orphanage.'

'I thought his name was Dylan,' said Slater, confused.

'Bear with me,' said Jolly. 'I'll come to that in a minute. Henry Winter resurfaces when he joins the Army in 1964. While he was in the Army, he built up quite a substantial property portfolio which he sold for over a million shortly after he left in 1993. He bought the house in Canal Street then, and appears to have been existing quietly there ever since, presumably living on his pension and the interest from the proceeds of his property sale.'

'Now that's a shrewd investor,' said Norman, admiringly. 'I bet he spent near enough all his wages on houses and they just sat there growing in value. And that was the period when house prices were growing like crazy.'

'So where's all that money now?' asked Slater. 'Didn't John Hunter say the only asset mentioned in his will was the house in Canal Street?'

'He certainly didn't spend it on a lavish lifestyle,' said Jolly. 'Not if his house is anything to go by.'

'We didn't look back very far into his financial affairs.' Norman sounded thoughtful. 'I'll go back to the bank and ask for more information on Monday.'

'So how come he's now called Dylan?' asked Slater.

'In 1994 he also changed his name from Henry to Dylan, by deed poll,' said Jolly.

'Do we know why?'

'No idea. But people change their names for all sorts of reasons. Maybe he just fancied a change.'

'What about the sister, Julia?' asked Slater. 'Where's she been?'

'I can trace her going into the orphanage in 1958 with her brother, but then after that she seems to disappear.'

'Was she adopted?' asked Slater. 'Or did she die? It wasn't unheard of for kids to die in those places back then.'

'I've found no record of either so far,' Jolly said.

'Where was this orphanage, and when did it close?' Slater's curiosity was well and truly aroused.

'That's my next job,' she replied.

'See what you can find out about it. Maybe there will be some records stored away somewhere.'

'Okay. I'm on it,' she said, heading back to her desk.

A n hour later, his thoughts were interrupted from across the room.

'This orphanage,' Jolly said. 'It was called Hatton House. It's only about five miles from here. It was closed back in 1964 and fell into disrepair.'

'Good work, Jane,' said Slater.

'That's very interesting,' chipped in Norman, 'but I'm not sure it helps us much.'

'Ah! But that's where you're wrong,' said Jolly, beaming. 'I haven't finished telling you what I've found yet. Here's the really interesting bit. It was bought for £600,000 in 1995, by one Dylan Winter of 17 Canal Street, Tinton.'

'What?' said Slater and Norman in unison.

'Why would he do that?' asked Slater of no one in particular. 'Does it say what he's done with it?'

'Now *that* I can't tell you,' said Jolly. 'I've just checked the local council website, and there are no planning applications associated with Hatton House, Dylan Winter, or Henry Winter.'

'So what does that mean?' asked Slater. 'Is it still derelict? Why would you buy an old wreck of a house and do nothing with it?'

'To stop someone else buying it?' ventured Jolly.

'Maybe there's something in that old orphanage that he wanted to make sure no-one else could get hold of,' Norman said. 'Maybe that's what the big secret's all about.'

'Perhaps it has something to do with his sister's disappearance,' Jolly added, quietly.

'I hope you're wrong.' Norman shook his head. 'I really don't need another kid's death to deal with.'

'Hang on a minute,' said Slater. 'Listen to yourselves! I thought I was supposed to be the negative person here. Right now we have no evidence to suggest any kids have died.'

'I hope you're right,' said Norman, sighing. 'But I'm getting a bad feeling about this case.'

'See if you can find us a map or some directions, Jane, please,' said Slater. 'We'll take a drive out there on Monday, or Tuesday, and have a poke around.'

Before Norman could say anything more, his mobile phone began to rattle out its terrible ringtone. He looked at the incoming number and cursed quietly.

'I have to take this,' he said, standing up and heading for the door.

Slater watched him go through the doors and turned to Jolly.

'Does he have a girlfriend or something?' he asked.

'Not that I know about,' she replied, looking up. 'Why?'

'He just seems to be getting a lot of private calls all of a sudden,' said Slater absently, returning to his work. He knew it was none of his business, but Norman was his friend as well as his colleague.

It was a good five minutes before Norman came back into the room.

'You're popular all of a sudden,' joked Slater. 'Have you got yourself a woman?'

'Sorry?' said Norman. He looked distracted, turning his mobile phone over and over in his hands.

'All these phone calls?'

'Oh, right. Yeah,' said Norman, with a grim look. 'I guess I'm just Mr Popular all of a sudden.'

Norman sat back down at his desk and kept his head down, focused on the screen. Slater got the hint.

CHAPTER FOURTEEN

'So let me get this straight,' said Norman. 'You think we should blackmail this guy by suggesting we think he's the murderer?'

They were on their way to the Station Hotel to see Geoff Rippon again.

'I wouldn't put it quite like that,' Slater said, smiling. 'I think it sounds much better if we say we're going to focus his attention on the matter in hand.'

'By suggesting we think he murdered Winter,' added Norman.

'I'm just going to present our evidence,' explained Slater. 'He was making phone calls to Winter when we believe the threats were made. He paid someone to poke around and find out what's going on this end, and now he's here in person claiming there was a big story. That's a powerful motive for a greedy journalist, don't you think?'

'It's a bit flimsy, is what I think,' said Norman. 'And if he's half the journalist he's supposed to be, he'll know how vague it sounds. If you want to focus his attention, you're probably going to have to make it worth his while.'

'What?' cried Slater, in dismay. 'You think we should make some sort of deal with this guy?'

'Look, I don't like the idea, either,' said Norman. 'But, unpleasant as it seems, it may be the only way we're going to find out what he really knows. Believe me, I've had to deal with these guys before. In their world, if there's nothing in it for them, there's no deal. Like you said yesterday, the guy's a vulture.'

'I'm not sure I like this idea,' said Slater, gloomily.

'I promise you I'm not exactly ecstatic about this myself,' said Norman. 'But here's the thing. If you start suggesting he's a suspect, he's gonna think we're as bent as all the other coppers he knows, and that we're just trying to stitch him up. And if that happens, it'll be end of story before it even starts.'

Slater brooded on this stark reality for a few moments. He knew Norman was rarely wrong in his assessment of these situations, but even so...

'Alright,' he agreed, finally, and reluctantly. 'You're probably right. You lead the interview and I'll try not to put his back up.'

'If I get the slightest inkling I'm wrong, I'll step back.'

'You're going to get it wrong one day, you know,' said Slater, with a grim smile.

'Ha! In your dreams.' Norman grinned back at him. 'You know it makes sense. That's why you like working with me.'

Slater thought of a smart retort, but he chose not to use it. After all, he couldn't argue. Norman was right.

They found Rippon in exactly the same place he had been before. Everything about him seemed to be exactly the same, Norman thought; he even seemed to be wearing the same clothes. The look on his face when he saw them made him look as if a bad smell had just drifted under his nose. Obviously his attitude hadn't changed, either.

'Oh!' he said, sarcastically. 'You two again. What a pleasant surprise.'

'And good day to you too!' Norman smiled broadly at him and pulled out a chair.

Slater did likewise but said nothing.

'So, did you do your homework?' asked Norman, looking Rippon straight in the eye.

'Now, why would I do that? I don't take orders from the likes of you.'

'I don't suppose you do,' said Norman. 'But then I didn't order you to do anything. I just suggested you could confirm what I told you, if you wanted to.'

'But why would I want to?' Rippon sneered unpleasantly.

'Because without our help you've got zero chance of writing this story.' Norman looked more confident than he actually felt about this statement, but he reasoned Rippon would have written the story by now if he knew what it was.

'Oh, and you're going to help me, are you?' Rippon's sneer seemed to be getting worse.

'You know as well as I do that we can't just hand over our files,' said Norman. 'But if you help us, we can probably help you. We can certainly make sure you get it before anyone else does.'

'How do I know I can trust you,' asked Rippon, a little less hostile now.

'You don't,' said Norman. 'But then how do we know you're not going to give us a load of bullshit?'

Rippon stared at Norman but said nothing.

'You have to make a judgement,' continued Norman. 'Doing your homework should have helped you to do that. And you have done your homework, haven't you?'

'I don't need advice from you about who to trust,' said Rippon. 'You'll be telling me how to write next.'

'That would never do. Your stories just wouldn't sell without all the exaggeration and hype.'

'You do your job, and I'll do mine.'

'We are doing our job,' said Slater, irritated. 'But you don't seem to want to help.'

'And why should I?' said Rippon.

Slater looked at Norman, and Norman nodded. He knew what Slater was about to say next.

'Because you're a possible murder suspect,' said Slater.

'What?' said Rippon, his face reddening and his fists clenching.

'You're making this up! I thought you said you guys aren't bent. How can you possibly suggest I'm a suspect?'

'If you'd just answer a few questions instead of trying to prove how clever you are, perhaps you'll understand,' said Slater.

'This is bullshit,' said Rippon angrily.

'Did you get a phone call this morning, Mr Rippon?' asked Slater.

'I get loads of calls every day,' said Rippon, glaring at him.

'Did the caller hang up when you answered?' asked Slater, ignoring Rippon's smart remark.

'How did you know?' Rippon sounded surprised.

'How do you think I knew?' Slater sighed and shook his head. 'It was me. I was going through Mr Winter's phone records and this number kept cropping up, so I dialled it to see who it was.'

'My, my,' said Rippon, his voice heavy with sarcasm. 'Well done, Sherlock Holmes. Aren't you the sharp one? But I already told you he had been in contact with me.'

'That's the funny thing, you see,' said Slater with a wicked grin. 'There's not one call made from him to you. All the calls are from you to him. It's almost like you were stalking him.'

'Bollocks,' growled Rippon. 'The first contact was made by him, in a letter.'

'Oh good.' Norman pounced. 'I take it you've still got the letter so you can prove it.'

'I'm not sure,' mumbled Rippon, looking at the floor. 'I might have thrown it away.'

'How convenient,' said Norman.

'It's the timing, you see,' Slater went on. 'We believe he was threatened into believing his life was in danger, and we also believe that threat was made four or five weeks before he died. That's when you were making all these calls.'

'But he contacted me,' said Rippon. 'I didn't even know the bloke existed until then.'

'What did he tell you?'

'He said he had something really big, and that he needed someone who would tell his story to the world. He thought I would be a good person to do that.'

'It's a sleazy story, then, is it?' asked Norman.

Rippon scowled at him.

'So what's the story?' asked Slater.

'I dunno,' said Rippon, shrugging. 'I never found out. He didn't get around to telling me.'

'So you threatened him, and when he wouldn't tell you, you came down and killed him,' suggested Slater.

'Don't be bloody stupid,' said Rippon, in exasperation. 'What would be the point? You don't kill the goose that lays the golden egg, do you?'

'But what if you came down here to reason with him and it got out of hand?' asked Slater.

A small smile began to form on Rippon's face.

'You're really clutching at straws here, aren't you?' he said, his smile turning into a grin. 'Have you got any real suspects?'

'Apart from you?' asked Norman. 'Sorry, we can't discuss an ongoing inquiry with the press.'

'That means you haven't,' said Rippon. 'But you needn't think you're going to fit me up–'

'No one's trying to fit you up, Geoff,' interrupted Norman. 'Is it okay if I call you Geoff?'

'I suppose so,' said Rippon, grudgingly.

'We need your help. We believe Mr Winter found out something about someone, and that person has silenced him. It makes sense to us that this is the big story he wanted to tell you. So anything you can tell us could lead us to that person.'

'Believe it or not,' said Rippon, much calmer now, 'I would like to help. I only met Mr Winter once, and he was a lovely old guy. But I think the world dealt him a pretty crappy hand, you know? He wanted to right some wrongs while he still could.'

'So what did he tell you?' asked Norman.

'Well, that was it really. He gave me that much, and then he said he wanted to check me out to make sure I was the right person to do what he wanted. All he would tell me was that it concerned someone who was a household name with a very dark side that he kept hidden from the public.'

'And you accepted that?' asked Norman. 'You didn't push him for more?'

'I understood his need to check me out. He was an old man who didn't know who he could trust. Like I said, I liked him and I figured it was going to be worth my while to win that trust.'

'But surely you would have been well pissed off if he'd come back later and said no?' said Slater.

'Sure,' agreed Rippon. 'But people often change their minds about telling a story. It happens all the time – it's not something I'd murder for. I also get offered stories that turn out to be a crock of shite – someone holding a grudge against someone else, and hoping to create a scandal. It happens. That's life. It's all part of my job, but it's not worth killing someone. You must get the same sort of thing in your job. It's bloody annoying, but you don't murder people for it, do you?'

'So where did you think Mr Winter fitted in? Did you think he was for real?' asked Norman.

'Yeah, I did,' said Rippon. 'That's why I was willing to give him time to check me out.'

'Did he tell you he'd been threatened?' asked Slater.

'He didn't say as much,' said Rippon. 'But I spoke to him a couple of days before he died. He asked me if I could come down and get the job done as soon as I could. The problem was I was working up north. I was going to come down as soon as I finished up there.'

'How did he react when you told him that?' asked Norman.

'He was disappointed. He said he hoped that wouldn't be too late, but he wouldn't elaborate on that. I thought maybe he was ill, you know? Maybe he had cancer or something like that. That's why I found the kid. I asked him to keep an eye on the old boy's house and let me know if anything happened. I was thinking if he had cancer or something and he was on his last legs he might get rushed off to hospital. It never occurred to me he was going to get bumped off.'

'But, if he's dead, why are you down here?' asked Norman.

'You're supposed to be the detectives,' said Rippon, patiently. 'It's not rocket science, is it? If he was murdered, it adds weight to the idea there's a big story to be uncovered, and it makes that story even bigger. That's why I was at the funeral. When we were talking, he mentioned his sister. I got the feeling the story concerns her in some way. I was hoping she might be there and I could ask her what it was all about. But there was no sister at the funeral. Anyway, now I'm here I thought I might take a look around. Maybe I'll find something.'

Norman thought it unlikely a successful journalist like Rippon had done no research. He must know about the orphanage and how Winter's sister had disappeared years ago. It was no matter – he could play that game too.

'So what have you got for me?' asked Rippon.

Norman was about to answer, but Slater got there first.

'Like my colleague said earlier, we can't discuss an ongoing investigation. And as for Mr Winter's story – well, you started weeks before us, and it sounds as if you're way ahead of us.'

Rippon didn't look convinced, but Slater looked him hard in the eye.

'So that's it?' said Rippon. 'You're going to give me nothing!'

'Right now, we have nothing we can give you,' answered Slater. 'But even if we had, I don't think it would be a fair exchange at this point, do you?'

'You thought he was holding back, too, huh?' asked Norman as they climbed into their car.

'Definitely,' agreed Slater. 'I don't think he knows enough to write his story yet, or he wouldn't be here now, but he certainly knows more than he's letting on. There's no way he'd waste his time down here unless he thought he was on to something.'

'You think he knows where the orphanage is?'

'Yeah, he must know that much.'

'Then we'd better make a start by visiting that house this afternoon. Maybe that can help us figure it all out before he does,' said Norman. 'Otherwise there's a good chance the whole world's gonna know before us.'

CHAPTER FIFTEEN

Hatton House was just a few minutes from the centre of Tinton, yet Slater had been completely unaware of its existence. As a fairly new resident of Tinton, Norman obviously hadn't a clue, but he was surprised that Slater had never heard of the place. It had turned into something of a mystery trip for both of them. With Norman driving, and Slater navigating, they almost missed the narrow lane that led away from the bypass in the general direction of Hatton House.

Once they were on the lane, though, it soon became clear why they had never seen the house before – it was in the middle of nowhere. The lane was so narrow there wasn't room for two cars to pass, but Norman observed it was unlikely to be a problem, as it looked as if no one ever came along this lane anyway.

They finally found the driveway that led up to the house. In its heyday, the drive would have been lined with privet hedges on either side, but it was obviously years since anyone had tended to them and they were in a sorry state. In some places they had grown so tall, they had collapsed onto the drive, making it necessary to zigzag around them. Eventually they reached a pair of large, rusting iron gates bound together with a huge padlock and chain.

'Looks like we're on foot from here,' said Norman. 'Good job you suggested outdoor gear for this trip.'

'I had a feeling it wasn't going to be in perfect condition,' said Slater. 'I think we would have been overdressed in suits, don't you?'

They were both kitted out in walking boots, jeans and waterproof jackets, and carried small rucksacks with a few bits and pieces they thought might come in useful.

There was a smaller side gate, which appeared to be unlocked. It creaked alarmingly, but then swung reluctantly open as Slater pushed against it. There was no sign of a house up ahead, and Norman began to wonder if perhaps it had fallen down over the years, but then he realised the drive was going uphill. Soon they spotted a roof as it began to level out, and then the house came into view as they came over the top of the hill.

It was a large, sprawling old house and the roof sagged alarmingly, but somehow it seemed to be intact.

'The oldest part's Georgian,' observed Norman. 'And that extension on the west side is probably Victorian.'

'You know this stuff?' asked Slater.

'I used to be a member of the National Trust,' replied Norman. 'I've been to loads of places like this. You see enough of them, you sort of pick it up.'

'You're full of surprises, you know that?' Slater said, grinning and shaking his head as if in wonder.

'Well, I wouldn't want to bore you,' Norman said, smiling back. 'Have you noticed it's not quite so overgrown here as you might have expected?'

'Maybe he paid someone to clear it back some time.'

'Yeah, maybe.' Norman wasn't convinced.

They made their way to the front door which was slightly ajar. Norman gave it a gentle push and stuck his head inside. A large pile of dead leaves had accumulated inside, no doubt blown in by the wind. There was an air of decay about the place and it smelt of damp.

'We need to be a bit careful,' warned Norman. 'This place is not far from falling down, so watch where you put your feet and what you hold on to.'

They poked around downstairs for ten minutes or so, but it was a frustrating exercise as someone had boarded up every window, and their torches didn't help much in the gloom.

'We need to get outside and take down those bloody boards so we can see what we're doing in here,' grumbled Slater.

'Let's take a look upstairs first.' Norman led Slater back across the hall to the staircase.

'Don't trust the middle of the steps,' he told Slater, with a grin. 'Keep to the edges, and let me go first – if they can take my weight you'll be just fine.'

'That's true enough,' agreed Slater, with a grin of his own. 'But you be careful. I'm not sure I could carry you out of here on my own.'

'Yeah, right! Thanks for that,' said Norman. 'Okay, let's get on here and see what happens.'

Gingerly, keeping well over to the left, he started up the stairs. There were a few creaks and groans of protest from the old staircase as he ascended, but it seemed solid enough and he heard Slater begin to follow. Norman reached the floor above and made his way over to the nearest window. Slater was still only halfway up.

'Wow!' said Norman. 'Now that is a big surprise.'

'What?' called Slater. 'What's a surprise?'

'Look at this,' said Norman, pointing out of the window.

Slater joined him at the window

'Well. I didn't expect to see that, and look, smoke!' he said, pointing towards a small clump of trees at the bottom of the garden where a small thread of what looked like smoke spiralled lazily towards the sky.

'Let's check that out,' said Norman, leading the way back to the staircase. 'We can come back here later.'

They made their way carefully back down the stairs, out through the front door, and onto the drive, where a path curled around the back of the house. Negotiating the side path was difficult as it was overgrown with brambles and more collapsed privet hedging, but they made use of a stack of disused boards to create a makeshift path across the vegetation to the side gate. To Norman's relief, the gate opened easily.

Going through the gate was like stepping from a wilderness into another world. Beyond the gate, a weed-free, gravel path led them down the side of the house, past a freshly clipped hedge. Reaching the end of the path at the back of the house, a large, well-kept lawn was revealed, dotted with carefully tended flower beds and shrubs, which ran down to a clump of trees forming a small wood at the far end. A wall ran a good way down one side with a gap halfway down.

They stopped to take it all in. Neither could claim to have much interest in gardening, but they could both see that someone went to a lot of trouble to keep these gardens at the back of the house in pristine condition. But, who? And, why?

'I bet that's a walled garden, behind there,' said Norman, pointing at the wall. 'I'm betting there's gonna be vegetables growing in there, and greenhouses and stuff.'

'You're kidding me,' said Slater. 'Out here in the middle of a wilderness?'

'Like I said before, I've seen these places. Whoever the gardener is, they know what they're doing.'

Slater's mouth had dropped open. He was clearly having a great deal of trouble getting his head around what he was seeing. Norman didn't blame him – it was so unexpected after the unruly mess at the front, and inside the house. But then something caught his eye and he nudged Slater, nodding towards the small wood. Another tenuous wisp of smoke hovered above the trees before dissolving into the slight breeze.

'Maybe our gardener's having a bonfire,' he suggested. 'Let's go take a look.'

A path ran alongside the wall down to the bottom of the garden. Just as Norman had thought, when they looked through the gap in the wall they saw a fully enclosed vegetable garden, complete with green-houses, a potting shed, and two compost heaps. Being February, the garden wasn't in full production, but Norman had seen enough of these things to know it was prepared ready for the coming growing season.

'Someone spends one hell of a lot of time working in this garden,' he said, admiringly.

'I don't know anything about gardening,' admitted Slater. 'But I'm guessing you could feed a family with a vegetable patch this size.'

'Oh, easily. Back in the day it would have supplied the entire household with fruit and veg,' explained Norman.

'Come on,' said Slater. 'I want to know what's going on here.'

He led the way on down the path towards the trees. A neatly manicured beech hedge, about six feet tall, separated the lawn from the trees, making it almost impossible to make out exactly what was beyond. Norman could just about see a patch of mixed woodland that stretched across the garden and beyond. He estimated it probably stretched for about a quarter of a mile from side to side, but how far it stretched back was anyone's guess. In the corner where the wall met the hedge, a small children's play area had been fenced off. The ancient toys were mostly falling to bits apart from a small roundabout, a slide and a swing which were all obviously well-used and well-loved. As they followed the path around the play area, Norman couldn't help but wonder whose kids were using it.

There was a gap in the hedge at the end of the path and they stepped through. If it had been summer and the trees had all been in full leaf, they would have been lucky to have seen much of anything, but at least half the trees were leafless at this time of year. A well-trodden path wound its way through the trees towards a dense clump of conifers. As they approached, there was a clatter from behind the trees and a figure could be made out heading away through the trees. Norman watched as Slater took off in pursuit. *Wasn't that...?*

A s Slater charged beyond the conifers, he could see his quarry about thirty yards ahead. It was definitely a man. A tall, thin man, with black greasy hair. *Rippon*, he thought. *How did he get here?*

The man seemed to be following another path, but Slater had made the decision to cut through the trees to try to head him off. As branches slapped at him and brambles tore at his legs, he knew almost straight away he'd made the wrong choice, but if he turned back now he'd never catch his man.

Rippon, bizarrely, seemed to be pretty fit. Slater was surprised, given how unhealthy he had looked when they had met him previously. He saw Rippon look back at him, a confident smile on his lips. Slater glared at him, and at the very moment he took his eyes from where he was going, his foot caught a thick bramble and he crashed to the ground, the fall knocking all the breath from his lungs with a hearty 'whoof'. He lay, face down, his hands throbbing from the impact. He climbed slowly to his knees just in time to see Rippon disappear from sight beyond the trees.

'Bugger!' He sighed, panting heavily. 'Bugger, bugger, bugger.'

'I take it you didn't catch him,' asked Norman, when Slater eventually returned, his whole body aching.

Slater gave him a dirty look.

'Please don't tell me you did catch him and he gave you a good hiding,' said Norman.

'No I didn't bloody catch him,' snapped Slater. 'And, no, he didn't give me a good hiding. "We" might have caught him if "we" had both been chasing.' Slater knew he sounded sulky but was too annoyed to care at the moment.

'Seriously?' asked Norman. 'The guy was like a damned greyhound. Anyway, you know I don't do running.'

He watched Slater puffing and panting and slowly looked him up and down.

'Did you fall over?' he asked eventually.

'Actually,' said Slater, his patience wearing thin, 'I thought maybe it's time I followed your lead. I've merely adjusted my style to match yours.'

'Oh, really?' said Norman. 'I don't think you've ever seen me in torn jeans, and as for that green slime-'

'Enough,' snapped Slater. 'I fell flat on my face, alright? But I'm okay, thanks for asking.'

Norman looked away, but Slater could tell from the way his shoulders were heaving that he was laughing.

'Arsehole,' he muttered. 'We'll catch up with Rippon later. I found out how he managed to get here without a car anyway. The canal's over the other side of those woods. The old towpath looks as if it leads all the way into town. It's pretty overgrown, but there's a definite, well-used path along it, too.'

'Come and see what I found behind these trees,' said Norman, pointing to the clump of conifers which turned out not to be a clump of trees after all. It was an artfully planted hedge, which hid a small log cabin.

'This is bizarre,' said Slater. 'It's like a gingerbread house in a fairy tale.'

'It's pretty neat, isn't it?' said Norman. 'There's even a little wood-burning stove inside. That's where the smoke was coming from. There's no-one home, but someone definitely lives here.'

'So who's living out here in secret?'

'Well, my guess is it ain't Snow White and the seven dwarves,' Norman said, smiling. 'But whoever it is coulda been here for years, and who would have known?'

CHAPTER SIXTEEN

'I wondered how long it would take you to get here,' said Rippon, with a big smile, when they caught up with him later.

They were back from Hatton House and had tracked him down to the bar at the Station Hotel. It hadn't really taken much tracking – the man seemed to live at his corner table in the bar. He'd obviously been back long enough to shower and get changed and he appeared relaxed and refreshed while Slater and Norman were still in the same clothes they'd been wearing at Hatton House. For once, Slater thought, ruefully, Norman looked the tidier of the two.

'Why were you running away from us?' he demanded.

'I wasn't running away from anyone,' said Rippon. 'I was out jogging along the towpath. I decided to run through the woods and I was just heading back when I saw you. I thought you wanted a race.'

'Come on, Rippon. Cut the bullshit,' said Norman. 'You went out there to check out Hatton House. You were there for the same reason we were. You think there's a link to Mr Winter and his story. But we think this could also lead us to his killer, so wouldn't it be in both our interests to share what we know?'

'It seems I know a whole lot more than you lot,' said Rippon. 'It strikes me I'd be the one doing all the sharing, not you two.'

'You do a lot of running, do you?' asked Slater, doubtfully.

'I told you I did, but you didn't believe me.' Rippon smiled. 'I do marathons mostly, including London every year, and half a dozen others. I'd never win any medals at the Olympics, but I can usually get round in under three hours.'

Slater was both surprised and impressed. That was a pretty good time for a man in his late forties. He knew he certainly couldn't get anywhere near a time like that.

'I thought most London runners do it for charity,' he pointed out.

'What makes you think I don't?' asked Rippon.

'You don't look the charitable type.'

'Never judge a book by its cover. You, of all people, should know that, Sergeant.'

'Charities like who?'

'Great Ormond Street Hospital when I'm doing London,' said Rippon. 'I've got half a dozen smaller children's charities I support, too. If you don't believe me, look on my website. I don't make a big deal about it, but you'll find them listed under my other interests.'

Slater wasn't sure he was convinced, and a glance at Norman told him he wasn't the only one.

'I know.' Rippon laughed, holding up his hands. 'It's hard to believe isn't it? I pride myself in being a true contradiction. Complete hard-case arsehole at work, but with a soft centre, especially where kids are concerned.'

'So, if there is a soft centre, as you say,' said Norman, 'can I appeal to it for help in solving what appears to be the murder of a lonely little old man?'

'I'll help you, if you help me.'

'But you said know more than we do,' said Slater.

'At the moment,' agreed Rippon. 'But there's going to come a point where you know more than me. If this is what I think it is, we're sitting on one very big story, and I want it all to myself.'

'Is this where the hard-case arsehole comes into it?' asked Slater.

Rippon smiled an evil smile.

'This is a cut-throat business, Mr Slater. People will tell you I'm a nasty piece of work and I'm selfish. Those people only know me at work. If you want to succeed at this job, you have to be ruthless, and I am. Very. Do I feel bad about that? Sometimes, yes I do. Perhaps helping kids is how I make up for it.'

Slater had to admit the man seemed to be surprisingly honest, but even so, he had his reservations. He looked at Norman who shrugged his shoulders.

'Look. You don't trust me, right?' asked Rippon. 'I can understand that. It goes with the job. I don't find it easy to trust people myself. So here's the deal. As a gesture of good faith I'll give you some of what I know, and we'll take it from there. What do you say?'

Slater looked at Norman again.

'We could do with the help,' admitted Norman.

'I suppose it couldn't do any harm,' agreed Slater. 'Okay,' he said, turning to Rippon. 'So what have you got?'

'I haven't got much more than you lot really,' he began. 'But maybe I'm just a bit more observant.'

'What's that supposed to mean?' asked Slater.

'Well, we both think there's a big story here, and we've figured out Hatton House is involved. I'm assuming you know it was an orphanage way back, and that Mr Winter bought it back in the nineties, but did you know he then set up a trust fund to own and maintain it?'

'So that must be where all his money's gone,' said Slater, trying to hide his surprise at this news. 'But I'm not sure I'd say it's being maintained very well.'

'That would depend on how you define "maintain",' said Rippon, quietly.

'What's that supposed to mean?' asked Slater, puzzled.

'You're the detective. You think about it,' said Rippon. 'I'm not going to do all your work for you.'

It looked for a moment as though he was going to withdraw his assistance and stop talking, but then he started again.

'You're probably also aware he had a sister when he went into the orphanage, but she never came out again, right? So, what happened to her?'

'According to his solicitor, Mr Winter swore she's still alive, but claimed he didn't know where she is,' said Norman.

'Oh, really?' said Rippon. 'Do you believe that?'

'To be honest, we're not sure what to believe,' said Slater. 'But so far, we've no reason to think otherwise.'

'He never actually told me anything about his sister,' said Rippon. 'I suppose that would have come after he decided to trust me.'

He thought for a few moments before continuing. He was obviously trying to decide if he should share any more with them.

'But maybe that was a good thing. If I'd known she was supposed to be missing, I might not have made the connection at the funeral,' he said. 'I think you'll find the story about his sister being missing is a red herring.'

'What connection at the funeral?' asked Slater. 'And why is it a red herring?'

'Didn't you see the little old lady who was hovering around at the funeral?'

'Well, yeah,' said Slater. 'But she's just a bag lady. I did try to find her after, but she disappeared. I figured she was just being nosey or looking for shelter.'

'She's very good at that disappearing thing,' said Rippon. 'She did it this morning when I found her just before you two arrived.'

'So you're saying you think she's the missing sister?' asked Norman. 'Are you sure?'

'No, I'm not sure. But it's a bit of a coincidence, don't you think? First she turns up at his funeral, then I track her down to a big house that he owns. And she's obviously been living there for a long time.'

'But if he knew she was there, why does he say she's missing?' asked Slater.

'Why do you think?' said Rippon. 'It's obvious. She doesn't want to be found, and he's helping her to stay hidden.'

'So how did you find out where she was hiding?' asked Norman.

'I did what you lot should have done.' Rippon smiled smugly. 'I've been keeping an eye out for her. I watched where she went and I followed her.'

Slater felt somewhat chastened. He'd had the chance to follow the old woman, but she had outwitted him and vanished. Yet somehow Rippon had managed it.

'So what did she say when you spoke to her?' he asked.

'Ah, now that's where we have a problem. She wouldn't say anything to me, and she took off as soon as she got the chance. The thing is, she's probably spent years preparing for the day when someone comes looking for her. She knows those woods like the back of her hands. I bet she's got some great hiding places right where we were and we'd never spot them in a million years.'

'I wonder why she's hiding?' said Slater, to no one in particular.

'I've worked on stuff like this before,' said Rippon. 'That's why Mr Winter came to me in the first place, I think. I've done two or three stories about old orphanages and how they were used as places to abuse kids. My suspicion is that this was one of those places, and it's possible his sister, your bag lady, is one of those abused kids. Maybe she knows something someone would rather she didn't know.'

'You're making a lot of assumptions, don't you think?' asked Norman.

'Maybe,' conceded Rippon, looking pointedly at Slater. 'But perhaps that's better than asking lots of stupid questions, don't you think?

'Whether I'm right or wrong, I'll tell you this much – when that woman saw me she was bloody terrified. Now, I know I'm not blessed with good looks, but I don't usually frighten people just by looking at them. I think she was frightened because I'm a man. I've seen it before, and I'd put money on it. If you're thinking you might like to speak to her, and I can see why you need to, I'd suggest you send a woman.'

'I suppose it wouldn't hurt to get Jane to talk to the old dear, would it?' Slater asked Norman as they headed back. 'Or would it be wrong to let someone like Rippon tell us how to do our jobs?'

'He didn't exactly tell us what to do,' said Norman. 'He just made a suggestion. And frankly, if he's right about her being frightened of men, we'd just be wasting our time.'

'Yeah, I know,' agreed Slater. 'But I think you should go with her.'

'Me? Why me?'

'Because someone has to go with her, and you have a much better bedside manner than me. You can keep out of the way when she tries talking to the old girl, but if you do have to get involved you can do the "gentle approach" without thinking.'

'Well, I do have a lot more patience than you, that's for sure,' agreed Norman. 'And I quite like wearing this gear.' He indicated his clothes. 'It's much more comfortable than a suit.'

'Maybe you should work for the parks department,' suggested Slater. 'Then you could wear jeans all the time.'

Norman was clearly so used to Slater taking a dig at his dress sense that he was oblivious to it. The insult sailed harmlessly over his head, seemingly unnoticed.

'Oh, and go in by the towpath,' added Slater. 'I don't think she ever uses the front way, and I reckon she can probably see anyone coming from the front of the house long before they get anywhere near her hideout.'

They drove on for a couple of minutes in silence before Slater spoke again.

'Do I really ask a lot of stupid questions?'

'I think you sometimes speak your thought process out loud,' said Norman.

'So I do ask a lot of stupid questions, is that what you're saying?'

'No, that's not what I'm saying. The way you think things through is by working your way through a series of questions, and sometimes those questions are obvious. There's nothing wrong with that. The thing is you sometimes say them out loud, in front of people who don't know how you think.'

'And I come across as stupid,' finished Slater.

'You're just vocalising your thoughts,' explained Norman, clearly struggling to get his point across. 'And the thinking you're vocalising isn't stupid thinking, it's thorough thinking. You're not frightened to ask the obvious, and you prove again and again that you're anything but stupid. Trust me, if people think you're stupid they're making a big mistake.

'Look at me. People think I'm stupid because I'm fat, and because I don't seem to care what I look like. That's fine by me, because I know I'm not stupid and I don't give a shit what people think. I use it to my advantage to catch crooks. It doesn't matter if people sometimes think you're stupid, all that matters is that you know you're not stupid.'

'Wow,' said Slater after a few moments thought. 'There you go again with your positive thinking stuff.'

'Dolly Parton once said she doesn't mind if people think she's a dumb blonde,' finished Norman, 'because she knows she ain't dumb, and she knows she ain't blonde. You could do a lot worse than think that way. You know you're good at what you do, and that's all that matters. If it ain't broke, don't fix it. Right?'

He looked across at Slater.

'Right, I've got it.' Slater grinned back at him. 'I ain't dumb, and I ain't blonde.'

'What does this little old woman look like?' asked Jolly, when they told her what she and Norman would be doing next morning.

'Looks like a little old bag lady,' said Slater, picturing her at the church. 'Quite small, long white hair and a dirty off-white coat tied up with string.'

'That sounds like Florence,' said Jolly.

'You know her?' exclaimed Slater.

'Everyone knows Florence, don't they?' asked Jolly, looking expectantly at the two detectives.

Slater's mouth was agape.

'Or perhaps not,' she said. 'But then you two don't pound the beat, do you?'

'No one pounds the beat these days, Jane,' said Slater.

'You know what I mean,' she said. 'Those of us who patrol the streets on early shift probably see Florence once or twice a month. She tends to walk through the town in the early morning, before everyone else is up and about.'

'Where does she come from and where does she go?' asked Norman.

'I don't think anyone knows. She just seems to walk the streets.'

'Hasn't anyone ever asked her?'

'I'm afraid she doesn't like the uniform,' said Jolly. 'So if you do stop she won't talk.'

'Do you know why?' asked Slater.

'Afraid not,' Jolly said, smiling. 'And I can't ask-'

'Because she won't talk to the uniform,' finished Norman.

'Exactly. She doesn't do any harm, so we leave her alone. The only person who seems to be able to communicate with her is the baker's wife. She sometimes gives her a loaf of bread.'

'But she must be eighty if she's a day,' she added after a pause. 'She's too old to be Mr Winter's little sister.'

'I dunno,' said Slater. 'I thought he looked twenty years older than he actually was. Maybe it's in the genes. Talk to that baker's wife and see what she can tell you about her.'

'As luck would have it, I'm going to be escorting you tomorrow, Jane.' Norman grinned at her when Slater had finished talking. 'But I want you to promise you won't take advantage of me.'

'That's a promise I shall find very easy to keep.' She smiled sweetly.

'Oh, and don't bring your best clothes,' said Norman. 'Dress for the great outdoors.'

'Well obviously I'm not going to wear uniform if I want to get her to talk, am I?' said Jolly. Then she rolled her eyes in mock horror. 'You know I never thought I'd be taking fashion advice from you.'

'Just pin your ears back,' Norman said, grinning. 'Watch and learn. Why d'you think they used to call me Joe Cool?'

'Oh come on, Norm,' Slater said chuckling and shaking his head. 'No one could possibly ever have had any reason to call you Joe Cool.'

CHAPTER SEVENTEEN

It was a pleasant enough walk along the old towpath at the Canal Street end, and Norman thought it was easy to see why the spot had become so popular since it had been cleaned up. There were even a few ducks paddling up and down in anticipation of a bread handout. Norman and Jolly were both carrying rucksacks with food and one or two goodies that they were hoping would win Florence over, but they didn't have time to stop and feed the ducks or enjoy the views.

'So what did the baker's wife tell you about the bag lady?' asked Norman, as they walked along.

'Florence,' corrected Jolly. 'She's a real person. Her name's Florence.'

'Okay, sorry. What did the baker's wife tell you about Florence?' said Norman, contritely.

'Not much really. She said Florence comes into town once or twice a week, always in the early hours, which she thinks she does to avoid other people. She started giving her a little food parcel a couple of years ago, but in all that time she's never actually managed to befriend her. And Florence always retreats if her husband appears.'

'That confirms what Geoff Rippon said. He reckons she's terrified of men.'

'Apparently all Florence ever says is "have you seen Dougal?"' added Jolly.

'Who's Dougal?' asked Norman.

'She has no idea. It could be a person, or a lost dog. Who knows?'

'Have you ever heard of The Magic Roundabout?'

'Wasn't that a children's TV series?' asked Jolly. 'A bit before my time I'm afraid. Why do you ask?'

'It was late 60s and early 70s,' said Norman. 'It was intended for kids really, but it became something of a cult. I'm pretty sure Dougal, Dylan, and Florence were characters. It just seems a bit of a weird coincidence, that's all.'

'Were they all people?'

'If I remember right,' said Norman, thinking hard, 'Dylan was a sort of hippie rabbit, Florence was a little girl, and Dougal was a dog. They all finished up on the roundabout at the end of every episode I think.'

'Wow. Sounds amazing,' said Jolly, derisively.

'You had to be there,' Norman said, smiling nostalgically.

'But how does it fit in here?'

'It probably doesn't. It just seems a bit of a coincidence.'

They stopped as they reached the point where the path clearing had stopped. From here on, it was going to be a matter of working their way through weeds and brambles.

'This trail must be the route Florence follows in and out of town,' said Norman, indicating a faint trail that seemed to wind its way through the undergrowth. 'It's going to have to be single file from here on.'

'She must come along here in the dark,' observed Jolly. 'How on earth does she manage?'

'I guess it's what you get used to,' said Norman. 'Maybe she only comes into town when it's a clear night and there's a bit of moonlight to help her out.'

Norman looked Jolly up and down.

'I know it should be ladies first,' he said, 'but I'm gonna pull rank. I'll go first. Just in case.'

'Just in case what?' asked Jolly.

'Just in case there are lions or tigers,' said Norman. 'I don't know. I just think it's right I should go first.'

'It's got nothing to do with rank, has it?' she said. 'If it was, you'd send me in first. You're just being gallant.'

'Don't kid yourself,' said Norman, but his body had betrayed him and he felt his face turn bright red.

'I didn't know you cared,' she teased.

He turned away from her to hide his embarrassment.

'More than you know,' he muttered to himself, then added, much louder, 'Come on then, follow me.'

It was almost an hour before they finally reached the woods at the back of Hatton House. Norman was puffing hard, and his muscles ached from all the unusual activity, but he was pleasantly surprised. He had actually expected to feel much worse.

'Okay, Jane,' he said. 'How do you think we should play this?'

'If she's really terrified of men,' said Jolly, 'you'd better keep well out of the way. I'll go up there on my own and see what happens.'

'Are you sure you'll be alright? I'm supposed to be here to look after you.'

'I honestly don't think I'm in any danger,' said Jolly. 'I think it's a pretty safe bet she's more likely to run away than attack me. I'll be fine.'

'Remember, the log cabin's hidden behind a conifer hedge, through these woods, in that direction,' he said, pointing through the trees. 'I'll follow at a safe distance, but I'll try to keep out of sight.'

'Right,' said Jolly, beaming at him. 'Let's get this show on the road.'

Jane Jolly headed off through the trees in the direction Norman had indicated, following a faint path that she presumed had been made by Florence. Creeping along as quietly as she could, Jolly made slow but steady progress and soon, up ahead, she was able to see what she presumed must be the conifer hedge hiding the log cabin. She could just make out a roof and a chimney through the tops of the conifers. A thin wisp of smoke curling lazily into the air from the chimney gave her some hope – surely Florence must be home, she thought.

But suddenly, without any warning, a small dog was barking furiously and snapping away at her ankles. She was forced to hop on one leg as the dog managed to sink his teeth into her jeans and began tugging furiously.

'Let go, you little bugger,' she hissed, but there was no way he was releasing his prize any time soon, and her curses just seemed to make him even more determined.

With one huge heave, he gave an almighty tug, and, caught by surprise and unbalanced by the unfamiliar rucksack on her back, Jolly fell heavily to the ground. Through it all, she heard the dull sound of footsteps from beyond the hedge, but they were receding, and Jolly knew it must be Florence running away. Completely unprepared for what was happening to her, and convinced this fearsome little terrier was about to start biting her, Jolly had no time to consider what Florence might, or might not be doing. She began to panic and covered her head with her arms.

The little dog clearly had other ideas, though. He promptly set about snuffling around her head and trying to lick her face. There was no way in for him, so he settled for plunging his tongue into her ear and then sticking his nose down the back of her neck. In spite of herself, and the seriousness of the situation, Jolly began to giggle as she realised the dog just wanted to play and be friends. She pulled her arms free of the rucksack, rolled over and sat up, the joyous dog climbing all over her in his excitement.

'So you're all bark and no bite,' said Jolly, scratching the dog's head. 'Why didn't you say so at the beginning?'

She climbed to her feet, lifting the dog, tail still wagging furiously, into her arms.

'You're the alarm system, aren't you?' she asked the dog. 'You create a diversion while your mum does a runner. Why didn't anyone warn me about you?'

She was annoyed to think she had probably blown their chances of getting through to Florence before she'd even started.

'Oh well, I've come this far, there's no point in turning back just yet,' she said, more to herself than to the dog.

She put him back down on the ground.

'Come on then,' she said. 'Let's find the way in.'

The little dog disappeared back under the hedge and she was suddenly on her own again. She brushed herself off, collected the rucksack, and set off, following the hedge off to her right. After a few yards, the hedge made a left turn, and then after a few more yards, she found an arch had been clipped into the hedge, offering her a first glimpse of the log cabin.

She stopped and gazed in surprise. She had been told it was like a gingerbread house from a fairy story, but she hadn't expected it to actually look like that. It really was made from logs, and it was quite small – probably no more than ten feet by twenty, with a door in the centre and windows either side. A small veranda at the front of the little house was home to a wooden rocking chair.

Jolly walked reluctantly towards the house. She felt rather uncomfortable, like an intruder who had no right to be there, and for a moment she was torn between doing her duty, and turning around and leaving this little old lady in peace. Then she remembered that Mr Winter had been murdered and Florence might just be able to help them unravel the story behind his death.

She peered in through one of the windows. The little house looked cosy inside, but it was obvious there was no electricity or any of the modern day luxuries that many people seemed to think they couldn't live without. The room she was looking into had another window opposite, so it was surprisingly light inside. The end wall she could see had no window, but a huge print in an ornate frame hung in the centre. Jolly did a double take, but there was no doubt she had seen the exact same print before in Mr Winter's house.

Having no idea where Florence had headed when she fled, Jolly put the rucksack down and perched on the rocking chair while she considered what to do next. The dog had re-appeared and jumped up onto her lap to renew their friendship.

'Now what do I do, little dog?' She sighed.

She had been sitting on the rocking chair for a couple of minutes, stroking the dog and enjoying the peace, when she became aware someone was watching her. She couldn't see anyone, it was just a feeling, but then the dog pricked his ears and turned his head to confirm her feeling. Someone was behind her, yet she felt no threat. She knew instinctively that whoever was there was a gentle being. Slowly, and deliberately, she turned around in her chair.

The little old lady was standing just a few yards away, watching Jolly with a wistful expression on her face. She was less than five feet tall, her long white hair flowing over her shoulders, almost down to her elbows. Jolly smiled.

'Florence?' she asked.

The dog jumped down and ran to Florence's side.

'He's a nice dog,' said Jolly. 'I think he likes me. What's his name?'

Florence smiled uncertainly and looked down at the dog.

'Dougie,' she said in a quiet, almost childlike voice.

'I'm in your chair,' Jolly apologised. 'I'm sorry.'

She went to stand up, and Florence started to back away.

'I'm not going to hurt you,' said Jolly, but Florence didn't look convinced and fidgeted nervously from foot to foot.

'I'll stay here, then,' said Jolly. 'I just want to talk to you. Will that be alright?'

'Suppose so,' said Florence. 'If Dougie likes you, I suppose so.'

'Where did you get Dougie?'

'Mine,' said Florence, insistently. 'He's mine. Dylan gave him to me.'

'Dylan? You mean Mr Winter?'

'Dylan.'

'You know what happened to him?' asked Jolly. 'You were at his funeral.'

'Gone,' said Florence. 'Dead.'

'How did you know Dylan?'

'Nice man. Kind,' said Florence. 'Only ones. Dylan and Dougal. Only Dougal now. Have you seen Dougal?'

Jolly remembered the baker's wife telling her Florence was always asking after Dougal.

'Who's Dougal?' asked Jolly.

'Dougal kind, too,' said Florence. 'Only Dougal and Dylan, but Dylan gone.'

'Dougal and Dylan are the only kind men? Is that what you mean?'

Florence nodded.

'Well I'm not a man,' said Jolly. 'And I've not come to do you any harm. I'm a friend of the baker's wife. You know the bakery in Tinton, don't you?'

'Nice lady,' said Florence, her smile confident this time. 'Gives me bread.'

'That's her. She gave me a loaf for you, and I've brought you some other things too.'

Jolly reached for the rucksack, opened the neck, reached inside and removed a loaf of bread which she held out to Florence. The old lady looked uncertainly at the loaf and at Jolly, who was just beginning to realise this was going to be a long-term project. Before she could talk to Florence, she was first going to have to win her trust.

'Look,' said Jolly. 'I understand. You're not sure you can trust me, so here's what I'm going to do. I'm going to get up from the chair and I'm going to leave you in peace. I'll leave the bread and the other stuff in the rucksack here. Is that alright?'

'Alright,' answered Florence, but it was obvious she wasn't sure about any of this.

Jolly wasn't sure Slater or Norman would approve of what she was doing, but her instincts were telling her she had to give Florence some space.

'I'll come back tomorrow morning,' continued Jolly. 'If you aren't here, I'll understand you don't trust me and you don't want to talk, but I think you can help me find out what happened to Dylan. You want to know what happened, don't you?'

Florence looked desperately sad, but she nodded her agreement.

Before either of them could say anything else, the dog suddenly pricked his ears and made a rush for the hedge, disappearing underneath it. A look of alarm filled Florence's face and she stared in dismay at Jolly. The sound of barking and cursing came from beyond the conifer hedge, followed by a loud thump as a heavy body hit the ground. Jolly looked towards the sound and then back at Florence, but all she saw was the old lady's back as she showed a remarkable turn of speed in making her getaway.

When Jolly found Norman, he was laying on his back in an untidy heap on the floor, the dog still tugging away at his jeans even though he was on the ground. He reminded Jolly of a stranded tortoise as he struggled ineffectually, his arms waving uselessly.

'You bloody idiot!' she snapped. 'You were supposed to keep out of the way. I was just starting to gain her trust and now you've frightened her away.'

'I was just trying to help. I was getting worried about you,' wheezed Norman from the ground. 'I heard all that barking and then it went quiet.'

'That was ages ago,' said Jolly.

'It's rough going you know,' he said. 'I got here as quick as I could, then this vicious little rat took me by surprise.'

He kicked out ineffectively at the dog but missed and it only served to make it even more determined to chew through his jeans.

'This little rat, as you call him,' said Jolly, 'is Dougie. He's Mr Winter's dog.'

'Great,' said Norman. 'So now you can stop worrying about what happened to him. And do you think you could get him to stop eating my damned jeans.'

'Dougie!' said Jolly. 'Come here.'

The little terrier obediently did as she asked, releasing his death grip on Norman's jeans and coming to stand at her side.

'Good boy,' she said, stooping to pat his head.

'Jeez,' said Norman, puffing his way into a sitting position. 'Rotten little shit, tripped me up.'

'He was protecting Florence,' explained Jolly.

As if to prove he would be equally happy to protect Jolly, Dougie gave Norman a warning growl and showed his teeth.

'It's alright,' Norman addressed the dog. 'I already know your teeth work okay, you don't need to prove you still have them.'

A shrill whistle echoed through the trees and, using his ears to locate the correct direction, Dougie zoomed off like a small rocket. They watched him disappear under the hedge once again.

'So how come he likes you so much?' asked Norman, as he struggled to get to his feet.

'He's like Florence,' said Jolly. 'He seems to think women are more trustworthy than men. They're certainly not as useless.'

'Look, I've said I'm sorry,' pleaded Norman. 'How was I supposed to know you were alright?'

'Because I told you I'd be alright,' she said, still angry with him.

'Yeah,' said Norman. 'And no one's ever said that and been wrong, have they? What if you hadda been in trouble and I'd just sat back there on my backside? What would that say about me as a partner? You would have done the same, and you know it.'

She thought about this for a moment. He had a point.

'I suppose you're right.' She sighed. 'I'm sorry I snapped your head off.'

'And I'm sorry I scared her away,' said Norman, reaching out a hand. 'But it's done now and we can't undo it. Now, could you please give me a hand?'

She grabbed his hand and finally, with her heaving for all she was worth, he managed to get to his feet.

'Thank you,' he puffed, beginning to brush himself down.

'Here,' said Jolly, brushing at his clothes with her hands. 'Turn around.'

She began brushing away at his back.

'There, you'll do,' she said, at last.

'So how did you get on, anyway?'

'You need to understand this isn't going to be a simple case of sitting down and having a chat,' she said. 'This woman is wary, and doesn't trust anyone easily. And she's definitely scared stiff when it comes to men. According to Florence, there are only two kind men on the whole planet. One of those was Dylan Winter, and the other is someone called Dougal, whoever he is.'

'He was the dog in the Magic Roundabout.'

'This is a man, not a dog,' said Jolly. 'But he's another one on the missing list. The baker's wife told me Florence asks if she's seen Dougal every time she sees her, and she asked me the same question.'

'Well, you seem to have done well, considering you don't think she trusts you,' said Norman.

'Another thing,' said Jolly. 'She has the missing print from Mr Winter's house hanging up on the wall in her house.'

'So she has his dog, and the missing picture,' said Norman. 'I could suggest that puts her in the frame for his murder. It could also suggest she broke in the second time.'

'You wouldn't say that if you'd met her, or spoken to her,' said Jolly. 'She's a gentle soul. She's not capable of murder.'

'If her fingerprints are the female prints they found in his house, she's going to need more than a character reference from you, Jane.'

'There's got to be an explanation. He was her brother. He was kind to her. Why would she murder him?'

'We don't know for sure that he is her brother, yet,' said Norman. 'Does she say he was her brother?'

'No,' admitted Jolly. 'She just said he was called Dylan. So maybe he wasn't her brother, or, for some reason, he didn't tell her he was her brother.'

'Why wouldn't he tell her?' Norman sounded incredulous. 'That doesn't make sense, does it?'

'I don't know, do I?' said Jolly, exasperated at having to defend Florence. 'I'll ask her if you haven't frightened her away for good.'

Norman stared at her for a long moment, as if he wanted to say something, but then clearly thought better of it.

'Come on, let's get out of here,' he said.

They began the long walk through the trees to the towpath and back into town.

'Did you agree to see her again?' he asked as they walked.

'Tomorrow morning,' she said. 'I left the food I brought as a good-will gesture and told her she doesn't have to talk to me if she doesn't want to.'

'You can't come out here on your own,' said Norman. 'I'll come with you. If she did kill him she could do the same to you.'

'With respect,' she said, 'I don't think she's going to trust me if you're tagging along.'

'You can't come on your own.'

'Then you keep well out of the way,' said Jolly. 'I'll use a radio and keep it switched on so you can hear me.'

'Yeah, but–'

'No arguing. That's my final offer,' said Jolly, striding off ahead so he couldn't reply.

CHAPTER EIGHTEEN

While Norman and Jolly were ending their eventful morning over at Hatton House, Slater was fielding a telephone call from Rita Meyers at the *Tinton Tribune* offices.

'I think you should get over to my office. I've got something you'll definitely be interested in.'

'Can you tell me what it's about?' asked Slater.

'I've had a package delivered here from Mr Winter.'

'But he's dead.'

'Nothing escapes you, does it?' she said, not unkindly. 'But, dead or not, I have a package from him, and I know you're working on his case, so I think you probably need to see it.'

'Of course,' said Slater. 'Thank you for calling. I'll be there in a few minutes.'

He couldn't quite see how Mr Winter could possibly have sent a package from the other side, but he could worry about that later.

The *Tribune's* office occupied a small shop front just off the High Street. A bell rang as Slater opened the door and walked in. The first face he saw behind the counter was that of Danny Trent. The dirty look Danny gave him suggested his attitude hadn't improved since his visit to the police station.

'Hello, Danny,' he said. 'I'm here to see Rita.'

'Who shall I say is calling?' asked Danny sulkily.

Slater thought about rising to the bait, but then thought better of it. He didn't need this.

'Dave Slater,' was all he said.

Danny picked up a phone from beneath the counter and pressed a button.

'It's the fuzz,' he said into the phone, but from the way his expression changed and his face began to redden, Slater guessed the boss had been none too pleased with his comment. The boy turned away from him as the dressing down was delivered over the phone.

'Okay. Right. I'm sorry,' a chastened Danny said into the phone.

He replaced the phone and then turned back to face Slater.

'She's coming right down,' he mumbled.

'Thank you,' said Slater, with an evil grin.

He could have said a lot more, but it looked as though Rita had said more than enough to put the youngster in his place. There was the sound of a door closing somewhere behind the counter and then Rita appeared.

'Thank you, Danny,' she said, giving him a withering look. 'You can go and have a cup of tea now.'

He was obviously disappointed at being excluded from this conversation but he reluctantly did as she asked and made his way towards the door and the back of the shop.

'Hi,' Rita said, focusing a beaming smile at Slater. 'I called you as soon as I realised what it was.'

She placed a padded delivery envelope on the counter before him. It had been opened.

'It was addressed to me, so I opened it,' she explained. 'Then I read the letter inside and I thought I'd better call you.'

She pushed the letter across to him. As she had said, it was addressed to her, and the message was short and to the point.

'Please hand the enclosed CD to the police', it said. It was signed 'Dylan Winter'.

Slater peered into the padded envelope. The CD was inside.

'Do you know where it's come from?' asked Slater, looking at the front of the envelope.

'Oh yes. It's on the back,' she said.

He turned over the envelope and there was a return address, neatly printed across the back. It was a London address, but it meant nothing to him.

'Have you any idea who these people are?' he asked.

'I googled it while I was waiting for you to arrive,' she said. 'They're some sort of backup service, but I'm not exactly sure how it works. Do you think what's inside is important? It seems Mr Winter went to a lot of trouble to make sure this got to you.'

'I think it's probably a bit more than a greetings card.'

'It's that all you can tell me?' asked Rita, looking him right in the eye. 'That seems rather unfair. First you tell me I can't report a murder in my own town, and now you won't even tell me what's going on. I could have made a copy of that CD, but I did the right thing and called you.'

Slater studied her face for a moment. He thought she looked honest enough, and he had no reason to doubt her word.

'You know I can't discuss an ongoing investigation with you,' he said. 'It's more than my job's worth.'

'But it's a big story, isn't it?' she said. 'If I'm helping you to solve a murder I think it's only right I should get the lowdown on what's going on, not some sleazeball reporter from London. This should be my story, not his.'

'Rippon helped us with stuff that we didn't know.' Slater felt he had to explain.

'I bet I've just helped you a whole lot more.'

'I won't know that until I've had a chance to look at it.'

Slater was feeling rather awkward. He knew she had a point about the local press and the local story, and he actually agreed with her. But it was a delicate and difficult situation. He needed both Rita and Rippon on their side.

'There's nothing to stop me printing the story about the murder,' she argued.

'Please don't do that yet,' he pleaded.

'So when do I get to print it?'

'I promise you'll be the first to know,' he said. 'Now, please can I get on and see what's in this envelope?'

He picked up the envelope and turned to go.

'I'm going to keep on at you, you know. This is a big story in a little town like this, and I want to be the one who prints it first.'

'And you will be,' he said. 'I'll be in touch.'

A s Slater made his way out of the shop, Danny Trent came back from his tea break.

'Look after the counter until lunchtime please, Danny,' she said, as she turned to go back upstairs. 'Then you can come back upstairs with me.'

'Okay,' he said cheerily. 'Whatever you say.'

He waited until he was sure she'd gone, then he picked up the phone and keyed a number from memory.

'P C Jolly,' announced Jolly into the phone on her desk.

'It's John Hunter here,' said the voice in her ear. 'How's Tinton's favourite PC? Have you been anywhere exciting this week?'

'Only if you count a derelict orphanage as exciting,' said Jolly, warming straight away to his charm. 'What can I do for you, Mr Hunter?'

'It appears Mr Winter's missing sister is alive and well and about to pay me a visit.'

'That's interesting,' said Jolly. 'I've not been able to trace the slightest sign of her.'

'Well, she's going to be here in the flesh, around ten-thirty the day after tomorrow,' said Hunter. 'Sergeant Slater said he wanted to be here if she turned up. Is that still the case?'

'Oh, definitely,' Jolly assured the solicitor. 'Either DS Slater or DS Norman will be there. We need to check this woman's credentials very carefully because we believe the real sister is alive and well and not far away from here, and she has been all the time.'

'That's brilliant news,' said Hunter. 'But, are you sure?'

'Not certain yet,' said Jolly. 'But I spoke to her this morning and we have good reason to believe we're right, so we don't want some fake to deny this lady her rightful inheritance.'

'Quite right,' agreed Hunter. 'But where did you find her?'

'I can't really tell you that,' said Jolly. 'But hopefully all will be revealed soon enough.'

'Well I'll be happy to help if I can. I can be very obstructive if I try,' said Hunter, conspiratorially. 'I'm sure I can find plenty of reasons to make life difficult for our fake sister if necessary.'

'We do appreciate your help.'

'No problem at all. By the way, have you made any progress with the break-in at old Mr Winter's house? Sergeant Slater said you thought it was the same person who broke in here.'

'I'm afraid we've drawn a blank so far. But I'm sure we'll arrest someone eventually. Of course, trying to obtain an inheritance by deception is a criminal offence, so that's one arrest we will be making.'

'Sounds fun,' said Hunter. 'We could do with some excitement around here. I'll see you tomorrow, then.'

As she put the phone down, something was nagging away at Jolly, but she couldn't quite put her finger on it. Anyway, this was good news about the "sister". They were making progress. If they could just get some proof from Florence that she was the real sister, they could put some pressure on this other woman. Maybe then they could find out who was behind all this.

M uch as Slater wanted to find out what was on the CD in his pocket, his stomach was reminding him he'd had very little for breakfast, so he decided to head for the canteen as soon as he got back. He hadn't really been surprised to find Norman when he got there, and he listened as his colleague related the story of their meeting with Florence. It was disappointing they hadn't been able to get much from her but perhaps tomorrow would be better. Norman had been as excited as he was at the arrival of the CD, and for once, it wasn't difficult to get him out of the canteen and back up to the office.

'I had an interesting phone call from John Hunter while you were out,' Jolly announced when they trooped back into the office.

'What did he want?' asked Slater.

'Remember he told us he couldn't read the will because he couldn't find the missing sister?'

'Uh, huh.'

'Well, it appears she's alive and well, and got herself a solicitor of her own.'

'So where's she been hiding away?' asked Slater.

'He didn't say, but apparently she knows all about the will. She's coming down the day after tomorrow, in the morning, and she's demanding to have it read as soon as she arrives.'

'This all a bit sudden, isn't it?' asked Norman.

'I'm curious to know how they can be sure it's her if she's been missing for years,' said Jolly. 'I did a quick search and I couldn't find a single trace of her. Doesn't she need to prove who she is first?'

'Presumably she intends to do that when she arrives,' suggested Slater.

'It's all very convenient, isn't it?' asked Norman.

'That's why Hunter called,' said Jolly. 'He thinks he can smell a rat, but he doesn't know what he can do about it.'

'That makes sense to me.' Norman nodded slowly. 'I think I can smell a rat, and I haven't even spoken to the woman.'

'John Hunter wondered if one of you two could insist on being there,' said Jolly.

'Insist?' asked Slater.

'He said maybe you could use the excuse that you need to make sure she understands she can't have access to the house yet. He thinks if you stress this is a murder investigation, she really can't object without looking suspicious.'

'Can we do that?' Slater asked Norman.

'We can try. But I'm not sure where we stand if they insist we have to leave before the will's read.'

'I'm sure I can come up with some bullshit reason why I have to be there,' said Slater. 'In the meantime, let's see what's on this CD.'

He removed the CD from its envelope, and, handling it as if it were the Crown Jewels, he placed it carefully on the desk. He slid open the drawer of his PC and slipped the CD into place. The anticipation was rising inside him. This CD could hold the key to the whole mystery.

'Oh, bollocks!' he cried, staring at the screen in disbelief. 'Can you believe it? He's password protected the bloody thing! What's the point in sending it to us and then making it impossible to read?'

'Let's think about this.' Norman came over to stand behind Slater. 'He went to a lot of trouble to make sure this reached us, right? Now would you go to all that trouble and then set a password that couldn't be cracked?'

'Of course not,' said Jolly, coming over to join them. 'So it has to be something we're going to be able to figure out quite easily.'

'Well, I'm open to suggestions,' said Slater. 'Because, right now, I'm clean out of ideas.'

'Maybe it's something we should have found in his house,' suggested Jolly.

'Was that before, or after it was hit by a tornado?' asked Slater, referring to the second break-in.

'Good point,' said Norman. 'But maybe it's a bit more obvious. What about the dog's name, Dougie? People often use their pets' names as passwords.'

Slater typed in the dog's name, first in upper case, then lower case, and then in a combination of the two, but it was no use.

'I'm concerned there might be a limit on how many goes I can have at this before I get locked out,' said Slater. 'That would be a disaster.'

'Now that's something to think about,' Norman said, nodding.

'There's never a bloody geek around when you want one,' complained Slater. 'If we have to send the damned thing off it could be weeks before we get it back.'

'Maybe I should take it up to Vinnie,' said Norman.

'Who's Vinnie?' asked Jolly.

'Ah!' Norman looked awkward. 'You didn't hear that, Jane.'

Slater had turned round and was glaring at him. He mouthed

a 'sorry'.

'Have I stumbled across something I shouldn't know about?' Jolly looked between Slater and Norman.

'Vinnie's a secret weapon of ours,' explained Slater. 'You know it can take weeks to get anything IT related done the official way, right?'

Jolly nodded.

'Well,' he continued, 'Vinnie is our fast track way of getting geeky stuff done. The thing is, he's unofficial, and if we get caught using him we could get into some deep doo-doos.'

'So he's a sort of high tech version of picking locks,' said Jolly, before adding quickly, 'Which a police officer would never do, of course. Yes, I can relate to that. Good for you. If it saves time and red tape I'm all for it.'

'But it goes no further,' said Norman. 'You can't tell anyone else about it, right?'

'Can't tell anyone about what?' Jolly beamed at him.

'We'll make a detective out of you yet,' said Norman, looking proud.

He looked pointedly at Slater.

'So what do you think?'

'I dunno,' said Slater, who found Vinnie difficult to get on with. 'Do we have time for that?'

'That depends how much time we're going to waste trying to guess the password,' argued Norman. 'That's assuming we don't trigger some failsafe system and end up being locked out forever.'

Slater turned the idea over and over in his mind.

'If I go now, I could be back by morning,' said Norman.

'And if he doesn't crack it?' asked Slater.

'I'll eat humble pie and you can gloat for weeks to come.'

Slater pressed the eject button and the drawer popped out. He slipped the CD back into its sleeve and handed it to Norman.

'I'll give these people who sent it to Rita a ring and see what I can find out from them,' he said.

'I'm gone,' said Norman, slipping the envelope into his pocket. He turned to Jolly. 'I'll see you here in the morning same as today, right? We'll go back out to Hatton House and see what Florence has to say.'

CHAPTER NINETEEN

It had been snowing overnight and next morning everything was covered in a good two inches of the stuff. And it was cold; Norman shivered as his breath filled the air around their heads.

'I take it from your downbeat mood this morning that your friend Vinnie didn't crack the password,' said Jolly, her words creating a visible vapour trail, as they trudged along the old towpath.

'It never occurred to me that he might be away,' Norman said, sighing and forming his own word cloud. 'Good job I phoned him before I drove up there, or I would have wasted the whole night.'

'What did Dave say?'

'Ha!' Norman smiled. 'Him and Vinnie don't get on, so he's torn between being disappointed that we don't have the password and pleased that he doesn't have to thank Vinnie for helping us out.'

'Why doesn't he like him?' asked Jolly.

'Oh you know Dave. He finds it difficult to deal with people who are too sure of themselves, and Vinnie is confident to the point of arrogance. I guess it's because he's out of his depth with all the geeky stuff that Vinnie finds so simple. The guy's a genius and he knows it. I guess he makes Dave feel inadequate or something.'

'It's funny,' said Jolly. 'I never thought of him lacking confidence until we went to the school together. He really struggled with the kids at first.'

'But I bet he was okay once he was the one stood at the front giving the talk,' said Norman.

'Yes, that's right, he was,' agreed Jolly.

'He likes to be in control of the situation. That's why he finds the unexpected difficult to deal with. He doesn't like change. I wonder how he's gonna cope when Bob Murray leaves and they start shaking things up at work.'

'You think they will change things?'

'They have to,' said Norman. 'Tinton's run like it's still the sixties. Once Murray goes they'll send in a new broom, you wait and see.'

'Is the old man definitely leaving then?' asked Jolly.

'I didn't tell you this,' said Norman, 'but they've asked for volunteers to take redundancy and he's applied. I got the same letter, but I'd have nothing to do if I quit. But Murray's different. He sees it as his free ticket from hell. He can't wait to go.'

They'd reached the woods at the back of Hatton House now, and it was time to split up.

'Make sure you keep that switched on.' Norman pointed to the small radio in Jolly's top pocket. 'It's got a range of about 100 yards so I should be able to hear everything you say through my earpiece. If you need me just say so. I'll probably walk about a bit to keep warm, but I won't be far, okay?'

'Okay,' she said.

The path was difficult to make out in the snow, but she was soon gone from view. Norman was happy he could hear her breathing as she walked. They had agreed beforehand that he would avoid speaking so as not to frighten Florence. He would use a simple click switch unless there was some sort of emergency.

'Can you hear me, Norm?' she whispered in his earpiece.

He gave her a click.

'She doesn't seem to be here. There's no sign of the dog either.'

Another click.

'But the door's ajar. I'm going to look inside.'

Over the radio, Norman could hear a door creak open.

'There's no one here. Even the wood-burner doesn't seem to be lit. This isn't right, Norm. I think you'd better get over here.'

'On my way.'

Norman didn't do running as a rule, but the alarm in Jolly's voice left him with no choice. Following her footsteps in the snow, he shuffled along as fast as he could.

Jolly was normally the epitome of cool, calm and collected, but when he found her, Norman thought he'd never seen her in such a state before. She was almost in tears.

'Something's wrong,' she said. 'I think she may have run away. Oh God, you don't think we frightened her away yesterday, do you? I'd never forgive myself.'

Convinced she was verging on panic, he grabbed her by the shoulders and stared intently into her face.

'Jane,' he said. 'Stop this. You can't help her if you start to panic. She could be anywhere. You said yourself she goes into town sometimes. Maybe that's where she's gone now.'

He seemed to have her attention now.

'Right. Yes. Of course,' she said. 'I'm sorry. It's just that–'

'You can't go jumping to conclusions. Let's do this properly. You're sure she's not in the house?'

'Quite sure,' said Jolly. 'But there are no footprints apart from yours and mine. It began snowing at around eleven last night, so she must have been gone all night.'

'Shit,' said Norman. 'So she could be anywhere. Let's have look inside first. Maybe there'll be some indication where she might have gone. Come on, there's not much of it, so it won't take long.'

He led the way into the tiny log cabin. He was right about there not being much of it. Apart from the little wood burning stove, which Florence obviously used to boil a kettle and heat a single pan, there was little in the way of furniture. A rocking chair, just like the one outside, a small table with matching chair, and a narrow dresser were the extent of her furnishings.

'No electric,' said Norman, pointing to a candle in a holder on the table.

The large print in the ornate frame filled the centre of one of the walls with no windows. The wall opposite, also with no windows, was home to a large poster of the old children's TV series The Magic Roundabout.

'Sheesh!' Norman whistled. 'I have never seen one of these before. It must be straight from the seventies.'

'Is that the TV series you were on about before?' asked Jolly.

'Yeah. Florence must have been one big fan,' he said.

'That print.' Jolly pointed to the opposite wall. 'I'm sure it's the one that's missing from Mr Winter's house.'

'But how the hell did it get here?' said Norman. 'Do you think she broke in and stole it?'

Jolly had pulled open a drawer in the dresser that seemed to serve as Florence's kitchen.

'She didn't need to break in,' she said, holding up what appeared to be a back door key. 'It looks like she may have had her own way of getting in and out.'

A large grandfather clock dominated the inside of the cabin. Jolly stepped up for a closer look.

'This clock looks exactly like the one at Mr Winter's,' she said. 'Except this one doesn't seem to be working.'

'Maybe she forgot to wind it,' said Norman.

There were no ceilings as such, just the inside of the roof, but at one end, a narrow mezzanine floor looked as though it might house a bed. A ladder led up to it.

'I'm gonna take a look up here,' said Norman, as he mounted the ladder.

He climbed enough steps to see over the top.

'The bed's on the floor like one of them futon things. She's got some stuff up here but I can't reach it, and I think I may be a bit too heavy for this. I don't want to bring the roof down. Can you come up here, Jane?'

He climbed back down and made way for Jolly to climb up.

'Wow!' she called down to Norman. 'She's one big fan of that TV series. All these cuddly toys look like the characters on that poster down there.'

Norman listened to her rummaging around, and then heard her exclaim 'Oho!'

'What have you found?' asked Norman, as she eased her way back down the ladder. In her hand, she had an MP3 player.

'Now,' she said. 'What on earth would she be doing with one of these?'

'Come on, Jane,' said Norman. 'What's the big deal? So, it's an MP3 player. Nearly everyone has one of those these days.'

'Right, Clever Dick,' she said. 'But most people have the means to charge it when the battery runs down. What does Florence use, candlepower?'

'Okay. Good point,' said Norman. 'Does it work?'

Jolly pressed a couple of buttons and waited but nothing happened.

'Looks dead,' she said.

'Take it back with us,' said Norman. 'Becksy will have a charger for it.'

He turned his attention to the dresser and slid open the remaining drawer.

'There were three ancient black and white photos, and he carefully removed them and went over to the window where there was more light. Jolly went across to join him. There was one photograph of two children – a girl of about five and a boy just a few years older. They were arm-in-arm, both wearing huge grins. Then there was one of the same little girl, smiling her gap-toothed smile and squinting at the camera. But it was the third photograph that caught Norman's attention. It showed what he thought was the same girl, but this time she was holding a man's hand. He was a good deal older than her, and his smile seemed somewhat forced, but it was the girl's face that made Norman take notice. She had a haunted look to her, and any smile that she might have been able to produce was missing and had been replaced by a look of total fear. Whoever this man was, the girl appeared to be terrified of him.

'Oh fuck,' said Norman. 'I don't like the look of this.'

Jolly looked shocked by his outburst. Norman rarely swore, but he couldn't think of another way to express his feelings about what he thought he was seeing.

'Sorry about the language,' he apologised.

'You took the words out of my mouth,' Jolly said, shaking her head. 'Don't worry about it.'

He pulled his mobile phone from his pocket. Slater needed to know about this.

'Balls,' he muttered. 'No damned signal. Come on, Jane. We need to get back.'

CHAPTER TWENTY

When they got back to the station, Norman made a quick trip down to Ian Becks' lair down in the basement.

'Can I charge an MP3 player?' repeated Becks. 'I didn't know you were into such things, Norm. I thought you'd be more of a vinyl record man.'

'It's part of an inquiry,' said Norman, in no mood for joking. 'I need it charged so I can see what's on it.'

'Okay, okay,' said Becks, soothingly. 'I'm sure I've got something that will do the job.'

He looked at the small player Norman had handed to him.

'What are you hoping to find?' he asked.

'I don't know, Ian, that's why I need it charged up.'

'You know this one plays videos as well as music,' said Becks.

'It won't play anything unless it gets charged, right?' said Norman, testily.

Brilliant as Becks was, he could be very trying at times, and right now he was in danger of pushing the normally placid Norman to the point of no return. He went to open his mouth again, but Norman beat him to it.

'Quick as you can, would be really good, Ian.'

'Right. Leave it with me,' said Becks. 'It should be ready in an hour. I'll call you.'

'Thanks. I owe you,' said Norman.

'And so does Slater,' said Becks. 'Make sure you remind him for me.'

Next, Norman made sure everyone on duty was aware they were looking for Florence. He didn't want her stopped, he just needed to know if anyone had seen her overnight, and if anyone should see her today, he wanted to know.

Upstairs in their tiny office, a distraught Jane Jolly was struggling to relate the morning's events to Slater.

'And there was no sign of her anywhere?' Slater asked.

'There were no tracks in the snow,' said Jolly, rushing her words. 'No wood-burner working and no sign of the dog. She must have gone yesterday after we visited her. Oh God. If this is all my fault, I'm so sorry.'

'Jane,' said Slater. 'Calm down. You're not making any sense. Here, sit down.'

He ushered her on to the nearest chair.

'You can't blame yourself for this,' he said, sitting down opposite her. 'We'll learn why she's gone when we find her. She could have been moving on anyway for all you know. If we're going to help her we need to stay focused on doing just that.'

'I know you're right,' she said. 'But I can't help thinking it's all my fault.'

'Let's start again. Tell me what happened, and what you found. Right from when you and Norm got there,' asked Slater, determined to distract her.

'Okay. I'll try,' said Jolly. She closed her eyes and took a deep breath.

'So you found the framed print that's missing from Mr Winter's house, and what you think might be his back door key,' Slater was repeating to Jolly as Norman came into the office.

'Yes,' she said. 'And lots of Magic Roundabout stuff, and some photographs-'

'Which I have here,' interrupted Norman, placing two photos, side by side, on the desk. 'Becksy reckons the MP3 player will be ready in an hour.'

'So what have we got here, Norm?' asked Slater, leaning forward to study the photos.

'I'll hazard a guess,' said Norman, 'that what we have here are a photograph of Mr Winter and his sister together, and then one of the sister on her own. I reckon these must have been taken before they became orphans.'

'Pity they're so old,' observed Slater. 'It would be impossible to say it's them for sure.'

'And then there's this one,' said Norman, placing the third photograph next to the other two.

Although he wasn't averse to the odd curse and swear, Slater usually tended towards what you might call the milder swear words. However, when he saw the latest photograph Norman had placed on the table, he couldn't stop himself.

'Fuck,' he said, pointing at the photo of the man with the girl. 'I don't like the look of that one.'

Then immediately he realised there was a lady present.

'Sorry Jane,' he said, his face reddening.

'It's okay,' she said. 'That's exactly what I thought when I saw that one.'

'Yeah. It's kinda scary,' said Norman. 'Gives me the creeps.'

'So, tell me what you think this is all about, Norm.'

Norman let out a huge, heavy sigh.

'Well,' he said, miserably. 'How many possibilities are there? We have this big secret, which someone is prepared to kill for. The murder victim spent part of his childhood in an orphanage. We have a missing sister, who it seems is not so much missing as hiding from something or someone. And now we have a photograph that seems to show a terrified young girl with an awful creepy looking guy. I really don't wanna think it, but it wouldn't be the first child abuse case to surface from way back then, would it?'

'So what's with all the Magic Roundabout stuff?' asked Slater. 'Where does all that fit in?'

'I might be able to help you out with that,' said Jolly. 'I've read a bit about this stuff. It's not unknown for abused kids to blank out things that happened in their past. Suppose Florence has mentally retreated to a time when she was happy, and she's stayed there. Let's say Florence was abused as a kid, but she associates The Magic Roundabout with a happy period of her childhood. By staying in that happy period, she blots out the unhappy period when she was abused.'

'Yeah, I've heard about that stuff, too,' Norman said. 'And if you think about it, even the names that are cropping up in relation to her fit the same pattern. She's Florence, her brother's Dylan, and she's looking for Dougal. They're all characters from the series. She even lives in a garden with a roundabout.'

'I wondered who had been playing on those things,' remembered Slater. 'Alright. So we agree we think we know what's behind all this, but if we don't know who's behind it, and we can't find any evidence to back it up, we're not really any further forward. We need to figure out the password for this bloody CD.'

Norman's phone was ringing. He could see it was Ian Becks calling.

'Yo. Norman Norman, style guru to the people, speaking. How can I help you?'

He listened hard.

'You have? Wow! That was quick. Did you take a look to see what's on it?'

He listened again.

'Yeah, that's right. It became a bit of a cult among a lot of adults too.'

He made a face at Jolly and Slater.

'And there was nothing else?'

Norman chuckled as he listened.

'Yeah, I'll be sure to tell him. I think we both owe you big time. Thank you.'

'That Becksy gets better and better,' he said as he cut the call. 'He's already managed to get enough juice into the MP3 player to fire it up. All that's on it is a load of episodes of The Magic Roundabout.'

'That supports your theory about her staying in the past,' said Slater. 'But she had no electricity in that cabin. How the hell did she keep the bloody thing charged up?'

'And how did she come to have an MP3 player in the first place?' added Norman. 'And how could she have downloaded those videos without a computer?'

'Right. So someone must have done it for her,' said Slater. 'And she must have had somewhere to charge it up. How about the baker's wife? She seems to have some sort of relationship with her.'

'I spoke to her,' said Jolly. 'She says she never got further than saying hello to Florence, and she never, ever set foot inside the shop. Anyway, I think you're missing a much simpler answer. She appears to have a back door key to Mr Winter's house. The dog she has matched the description of his dog, and that dog is perfectly happy with her. He's known her a long time. I reckon the reason we've only ever seen her early in the morning is because she's been going back home to Hatton House. I think she used to visit her brother under cover of darkness.'

'So you think he knew where she was all the time and he told everyone he didn't know to keep her safe?' asked Slater.

'Yes, I do,' said Jolly, confidently. 'I think he created a home for her to hide in at Hatton House to protect her. He must have thought she was in some serious danger to go to all that trouble, but then if he was prepared to do all that, getting her an MP3 player and setting it up would have been nothing to him. He could have charged it up every time she came to visit.'

'But the dog wasn't there the day you found Mr Winter dead, was it? Do you think Florence was there that night? Maybe she saw who attacked him.'

While Slater and Jolly were talking, Norman was dialling a number on his phone. He turned his back on the other two as he spoke into it. Two minutes later, he turned back.

'I just asked Becks to check the stuff they found at Mr Winter's house. There's a charger for the same model MP3 player, but they didn't find a player. I think that adds a lot of weight to your theory, don't you?'

'I bet those female fingerprints they found at his house were hers,' said Slater.

'So you can forget about her breaking into his house, can't you?' Jolly said, looking purposefully at Norman.

'Okay, okay,' said Norman, holding up his hands in surrender. 'I'm happy to accept that looks very unlikely now, but you have to admit the evidence did make her a possible suspect.'

Slater was thinking.

'So he changed his name to Dylan in 1994, and bought Hatton House in 1995, right?'

'Yes,' said Jolly.

'Here's an idea, then. Suppose he left the Army and came back to Tinton so he could look for his long-lost sister. He's looking for Julia, but finds someone who calls herself Florence living rough at Hatton House. He's clever enough to figure out Florence is really Julia, but she's locked into this Magic Roundabout thing and doesn't want to know about anything else. So he buys Hatton House to make sure she never has to leave, and to keep her safe.'

'But why change his name?' asked Norman.

'I don't know,' said Slater. 'Maybe she was so scared of men he thought using the name of one of the characters would encourage her to accept him.'

'But he was her brother?' Norman argued.

'Perhaps she didn't recognise him as her brother,' said Jolly. 'Don't forget – we think she may have been scarred by years of abuse, and he's been away in the Army. She hasn't seen him for thirty odd years.'

'Good point. Yeah, that works for me,' Norman nodded his head in agreement.

'It's possible, isn't it?' suggested Slater. Then he had another idea.

'When was this Magic Roundabout on TV, Norm?' he asked.

'Mid-sixties to mid-seventies, I think.'

'But Hatton House closed in 1964. If we believe she was abused in that orphanage, she couldn't have seen it before it happened.'

'I'm not with you,' said Norman. 'What are you getting at?'

'This may sound a bit weird, and it could be complete rubbish,' explained Slater. 'But what if Florence didn't see The Magic Roundabout until after she'd been abused, and because of that, she forgot she ever had a brother?'

Norman and Jolly both looked puzzled.

'I'm not explaining this very well, am I?' said Slater, frustrated with his inability to explain his point. 'Look, we're talking about kids focusing on a happy time *before* they were traumatised, right? What if Florence has locked into a happy time *after* she was traumatised? What if she discovered The Magic Roundabout after she escaped the abuse? What if she found it made her forget what had happened, and it helped make her life bearable? Maybe she locked into that so she could blot out everything before it.'

'Which would include the time when she had a brother,' finished Jolly, as she caught up with his thought process.

'And that's why she calls herself Florence, and not Julia,' suggested Slater. 'Maybe being Julia was full of painful memories. Florence was a good character, right?'

'Yeah,' agreed Norman. 'I'm pretty sure Florence was usually in the garden. There were flowers and trees and the sun usually shone. Oh yeah, Florence had a nice, happy life. It sure would have been better than the horror of being an abused kid.'

He thought for a moment before adding one more observation.

'Wow!' said Norman. 'That must have been really tough for the guy to deal with. How would you cope with that?'

'How about by changing your name to become one of the characters in her fantasy?' suggested Slater.

'And selling all your property so you could buy a derelict house,' added Jolly.

They sat in silent contemplation for a few moments. It was Slater who broke the silence.

'Of course, you idiot,' he said, aloud, to himself as moved across the room and sat down at his desk. 'Why didn't you think of that before? It's been staring you in the face all the time.'

He tapped away at his keyboard.

'What?' said Norman. 'What's been staring you in the face?'

'Dah-Dah!' sang Slater, his face beaming. 'Look. I'm in. The password is Magic Roundabout!'

Norman rushed over to Slater's desk and they stared at the open folder on Slater's computer screen.

'This is all very well,' said Jolly, as a gleeful Slater finally gained access to the CD. 'But what about Florence? She could be an important witness and she's gone missing. It could be she's in a lot of danger. We can't just ignore that, can we?'

'Well, no,' agreed Slater. 'But this CD could tell us everything we need to know to sort this out.'

'You've already had to wait this long,' argued Jolly. 'And you think this crime was committed years ago, so do you really think a few more hours is going to make that much difference? There could be a woman's life at stake here.'

'You're right,' agreed a chastened Slater. 'I think we need to find Florence sooner rather than later. If we assume someone else has that hard disk, it's possible they've joined up the dots like we have, and they're looking for her too.'

'Why don't you stay here and check out that CD,' suggested Norman. 'I've already got everyone keeping an eye out for Florence. If she's out on the streets, someone will spot her. Me and Jane can go back to Hatton House and take another look around. We'll check out Mr Winter's house in Canal Street on the way.'

'Okay. I'll call the people who sent the CD out, too. Maybe they can tell us something useful.'

CHAPTER TWENTY-ONE

It was mid-afternoon by the time Jolly and Norman had checked out 17 Canal Street, and had a look around inside the derelict Hatton House, but there was no sign of the missing Florence. The sky was heavy with clouds threatening to bring more snow and the light was already beginning to fade by the time they got back to the log cabin, but still nothing had changed.

'There would have been footprints in the snow if she'd come back,' said Norman.

'I'm tempted to light that wood-burner and stay out here all night,' said Jolly, sadly. She had hoped that they would find Florence, safe and sound, with her little dog.

'I think that would be a waste of time. I doubt it would make you feel any better, and the chances are if she sees you're here she won't come near anyway.'

'But we have to do something,' said Jolly, desperately.

'If she hasn't appeared by the morning, we'll grab some more bodies and escalate this into a full search,' said Norman. 'For now, I think we need to head back.'

Jolly wasn't at all happy about this, but she knew there was a limit to what they could do. Florence was an adult, and if she wanted to move on there was nothing to stop her. Unless they had evidence to suggest there was anything wrong, they had no reason to instigate a full alert just yet.

'Come on, Jane,' said Norman, gently. 'Let's head on back before it gets so dark we can't see where we're going.'

Reluctantly, Jolly followed Norman back through the woods towards the old towpath. Neither seemed to be in the mood to engage in their normal conversation and, with the blanket of snow that covered everything acting as a good sound muffler, a heavy silence settled around them as they walked. They had just turned left onto the old towpath to begin the trek into town when Jolly thought she heard something.

'Did you hear something?' she asked.

Norman stopped and turned to face her. He stood quietly and listened, but there was nothing.

'I could have sworn I heard something,' said Jolly, with a heavy sigh.

'Shh!' said Norman. 'Listen.'

Jolly did as he said.

'There,' she said, turning away from him. 'It's coming from further along the towpath.'

'Here, let me go first,' he said as she began to head off. 'It's getting dark and we don't know what's out there.'

As he finished speaking the noise came again.

'Shit. What is that? A wolf?' asked Norman.

'There aren't any wolves in England, you fool,' said Jolly. 'It's a dog. I'll go first if you're frightened.'

'Of course I'm not frightened,' said Norman, indignantly. 'It's just a weird sort of noise to hear, just as it's getting dark. Now step aside and let me lead the way.'

Jolly stepped aside and allowed Norman to assert his authority. She reasoned that he was the boss, and if he wanted to lead the way that was okay with her. The light was fading fast and Norman took out his torch. In its powerful beam, they could make out a vague path to follow through the undergrowth. There was now no doubt the sound they were heading towards was a dog, but how far away was it? They followed the path for about thirty yards, and then suddenly they were in a small clearing. Someone had cleared the undergrowth right up to the bank of the canal. An old bench, which had obviously been there for many years, stood facing the water.

'Wow,' said Norman. 'I wonder what this is all about?'

'Maybe she liked to sit by the canal,' guessed Jolly. 'It must be a nice, peaceful spot here. Maybe she feeds bread to the ducks.'

There was no sign of the dog, but they could hear it whining on the other side of the clearing.

Jolly got to her knees.

'Here, Dougie,' she called. 'Come here. Good boy.'

The little terrier suddenly ran from the undergrowth and bounded towards her. He jumped into her arms and frantically licked at her face, his tail wagging furiously.

'What's he doing out here on his own?' asked Norman, sweeping his torch from side to side around the little clearing. 'You'd think he'd stick with Florence.'

'It doesn't feel right, does it?' said Jolly. 'Something's wrong for sure. This dog's really stressed, like he's been hiding or something.'

Norman had spotted something caught on a bramble close to where they had entered the clearing. He moved over and crouched down for a closer look, focusing his torch upon it.

'It's a bit of fabric,' he told Jolly. 'Sort of dirty white colour.'

'From her coat?' asked Jolly.

'It could be,' said Norman.

He stood up and headed towards the canal bank, sweeping the water with his torch. This part of the canal was hidden from what sparse sunlight there had been earlier in the day so the thin coating of ice that had formed overnight hadn't thawed at all and was still intact. About three feet from the bank, just beneath the ice, the beam fell upon a dirty white object.

'Oh My God,' said Jolly, following the beam of his torch. 'That's her. Quick, we have to get her out. She might still be alive.'

She rushed to the edge of the canal, still clutching the dog in her arms.

'Jane,' said Norman, moving across and gently taking her shoulders.

'She was in there when the canal froze last night. There's no way she's still alive.'

He guided her towards the bench, sat her down and sat next to her.

'It's all my fault,' said Jolly, rocking backwards and forwards. 'I must have scared her. She didn't run away, she committed suicide, didn't she?'

She held the dog close and buried her face in his neck. Then she began to sob quietly into his fur. Norman placed an arm gently around her shoulders.

'Hello, Jane. Have you found her?' Slater asked into his phone, a few minutes later. 'If she's a witness to what's on this CD we've got a real case.'

'It's Norm. I've got no signal out here, so I'm using Jane's phone.'

'Oh, right. So have you found her?'

'Yeah,' said Norman. 'I think it's her. You'd better get over here with a full forensics team, SOC tent, lights, the lot. She's not going to be a witness to anything. She's in the canal.'

'Oh bloody hell, no!' said Slater.

'And I think we need a paramedic or a doctor. Jane's in shock. She thinks this is all her fault.'

'Okay. Norm I'm on it. I'll be there as soon as I can.'

'It might be best if you lead the guys in through the front gates,' said Norman. 'You know the way, and it'll be quicker than taking hours to walk all their gear along the towpath.'

CHAPTER TWENTY-TWO

By the time Slater had led the forensic team up the front drive and shown them where the site was, Norman had managed to coax Jolly away from the scene of the crime and down to the main house. She was still clutching the dog tightly in her arms when he handed her over to a paramedic and a concerned WPC colleague to get her fixed up and then taken home.

Now they were back at the small clearing which, being the crime scene, was now a hive of activity. The temperature seemed to have dropped several degrees in the hour or so they had been on site, and everyone was puffing huge clouds of vapour. In the glow of the hastily erected emergency lights, and the glow of light from inside the SOCO tent, it created an eerie sight. The rattle of the small generator powering everything seemed to add to the effect.

Florence's body, still wrapped in her dirty white coat, had been removed from the icy water and lay inside the tent awaiting the arrival of the pathologist.

They were all dressed in the new blue paper suits, but for once Slater didn't picture the familiar swarm of smurfs.

'All this bloody snow doesn't help us, does it?' he observed, moodily. 'It's hiding any evidence on the ground.'

'We'll thaw that out and see what we can find,' said Ian Becks. 'The bigger problem is the fact that we've had detectives, divers, and who knows bloody who, wandering all over the site. If there is any evidence under the snow, it's probably ruined by now.'

'It couldn't be helped, Ian,' said Slater. 'We didn't know we were looking for a body when we first came up here.'

'I know, I know,' said Becks. 'I'm not trying to blame anyone, I'm just saying.'

'Can you tell us anything yet?' asked Norman.

'I can tell you we've fished the body of an old lady, in a dirty white coat, out of the canal. And the doctor has justified his existence by assuring us she's dead, but you didn't need a medical degree to work that one out.'

'Yeah, he's not exactly the friendliest of guys,' agreed Slater. 'I thought warmth and compassion were supposed to be part of a doctor's armoury.'

'Not that one,' said Becks. 'Someone should tell him there's no "I" in team. I'm sure it's his fault the temperature's dropped so much since we've been here. It must have gone down a good ten degrees when he arrived.'

'Is he still here?' asked Norman.

'You must be joking. He couldn't wait to get away.'

'I was hoping he might have some idea what happened.'

'Oh he did,' said Becks. 'He said to tell you, she died. I suppose that's in case you were in any doubt. And that's about it so far, I'm afraid. We're not going to be able to work very quickly in these conditions, so I wouldn't expect a major breakthrough anytime soon. The pathologist is on the way. Maybe we'll know a bit more when he gets here.'

'There's not much we can do up here to help,' said Slater, grimly. 'So we'll get out of your way and have a poke around in the cabin.'

'We're going to move down there when we've finished up here,' said Becks. 'But I expect we're going to be up here for a good while yet. Can you try not to destroy any evidence before we get down there?'

'I should warn you me and Jane were in there earlier,' said Norman.

'We were looking for any clues that might tell her where she could have gone.'

'Oh, wonderful.' Becks sighed. 'So you've already contaminated it down there.'

'Sometimes Becksy, you can be an insufferable arse, do you know that?' said Norman, angrily. 'Dave's already told you we didn't know we had a death on our hands until a couple of hours ago.'

Ian Becks looked stunned by Norman's comments.

'It just annoys me that you lot seem to think we can still do our job when you've already trampled all over a crime scene,' he began.

'You know what, Ian?' Slater interrupted. 'Norm's right. You're bloody brilliant at what you do, and we all appreciate it, but we have a job to do as well. I'm sorry if we're not perfect like you seem to think you are, but we don't yet have the ability to see into the future. We have to make decisions based on intuition, experience, and procedure. We don't have the benefit of hindsight.'

He pointed to the tent.

'Right now, there's a little old lady lying dead in that tent and we, as a team, have a duty to find out what happened. Just now you said someone should tell the doctor there's no "I" in team. As the head of this investigation I think I should tell you you'd do well to remember that yourself.'

Ian Becks face had gone scarlet, whether from rage or embarrassment it was hard to say, but before he could take the argument any further, a familiar figure loomed into view carrying a medical bag.

'Evening all,' said Dr Eamon Murphy, the pathologist. 'I hope I'm not interrupting anything.'

He offered a beaming smile to one and all, even though Slater thought the atmosphere could be cut with a knife.

'Hello, Eamon,' said Slater. 'Thanks for coming.'

'What else could I possibly want to be doing on a freezing February night?' said Murphy, cheerily. 'It was an invitation I couldn't refuse.'

'She's in the tent,' said Slater.

'Let's have a look, then.'

'I'll leave you to it,' said Becks, shortly. 'There's one of my guys in there if you need a hand, doc.'

The two detectives led the pathologist across to the makeshift tent where Murphy slipped into one of the blue suits and then they eased their way inside, stepping aside to allow Murphy access to the body. A blue-suited forensic guy nodded to them as they entered.

'Do we know who she is?' asked Murphy as he knelt next to the body.

'Her name's Florence,' said Norman. 'We believe she's the sister of Dylan Winter.'

'Isn't that the guy whose PM you asked me to reconsider?' asked Murphy, looking up at Slater.

'Yeah, that's him. She's been in hiding for years, but we're pretty sure she's his sister.'

'A DNA sample will check that easily enough,' said Murphy. 'I've still got samples of his.'

He turned his attention back to Florence's body. She was lying on her back, her long, wet hair, plastered across her face.

'So you don't think this one's an accident.'

'You'd need to rule that out,' said Slater. 'It could even be suicide, but we don't think so.'

'Can you give me a hand to roll her over?' Murphy asked the forensic technician.

They carefully and gently rolled her over and revealed the ugly mess that was the back of her head. Murphy leaned in closer for a better look.

'As you know, I'm not a forensic pathologist,' he said. 'But I think even I can say, with a fair degree of certainty, that it's unlikely she bashed herself across the back of the head and then threw herself into the canal.'

'Could it be an accident?' asked Slater.

'There's no way you could accidentally do that much damage to your own head,' said Murphy, standing up. 'I think I'd be happy to say we can probably rule out suicide or an accident as the cause of death.'

'I was sort of expecting you to say that,' said Slater, grimly. 'But at least we know what we're dealing with. Thanks for confirming that for us.'

'I'll have her taken down to the hospital now,' said Murphy. 'When I get back, I'm going to flag this one up the line and get a proper forensic pathologist to do the PM. I'll book it for tomorrow at eleven. I'll let you know if that changes.'

After Murphy had left, Slater and Norman were left without much to do. Ian Becks seemed to have split his team so they could make a start on the log cabin so they decided against getting in his way and instead headed back to the main house.

'I've probably pissed Becks off big time,' said Slater to Norman. 'And I really don't need to start another argument right now.'

'I wouldn't worry about it. I think he's had it coming for a long time. It's okay to know you're good at what you do, but a little humility now and then wouldn't go amiss. If he's as professional as he claims he is, he should be able to accept a little constructive criticism and make use of it.'

A generator had been set up outside the front of the main house and someone had set up some lights in the hall. It was probably that same someone who had erected a table and set up a tea urn which was puffing its excess steam up at the ceiling. Slater was impressed with this attempt at providing some sort of refreshment for the workers and he made a mental note to find out who had been responsible so he could thank them.

'So what was on the CD?' asked Norman, as he poured two cups of tea from the urn.

'There are four files,' Slater told him. 'The first one is like a report about what went on at the orphanage. You'll need to read it yourself, but basically what it says is that new kids arriving at Hatton House went through a sort of selection process. The cute looking ones went into a group called the Special Ones. Florence was a Special One.

'They were kept apart from the other kids and got treated much better, but in return they were subjected to regular sexual abuse at the hands of a group of men which included the man who ran the place and assorted dignitaries from Tinton and the surrounding area. Mr Winter is pretty sure these kids never appeared on any register at Hatton House, so officially they didn't exist. '

'Jesus,' said Norman, in disgust. 'So that would explain why he lost track of his sister. But surely there must have been some record of those kids being sent there.'

'Mr Winter reckons the people responsible for those registers were also the abusers, so they were able to cover their tracks quite easily. It makes grim reading, and of course he's had to speculate about some of it. He also claims they were disposed of once they reached their sell-by date.'

'What, you mean murdered?' asked a horrified Norman.

'Well, I guess that would be one way,' said Slater. 'Or they could just have been sold on, I suppose.'

'So how come Florence was still around?' asked Norman.

'He didn't know the answer to that one, but that's why Florence would have been a great witness. She could have told us what really happened and filled in some of the gaps for us.'

'I'm not sure we would have got much out of her, to be honest,' said Norman, sadly. 'She wasn't exactly living in the real world. But it's irrelevant anyway. She can't tell us anything now.'

They sipped their tea in silence for a minute or two.

'Did he name any names in this report?' asked Norman.

'There are two or three names who were supposedly involved in the abuse. None of the names jump off the page at me, but then it's all before my time. A bit of research should help though.'

'So what else is there?'

'There's a list of names, supposedly staff who worked there, but we'll have to check. If it is, maybe we can find someone who can corroborate this story.'

'It's definitely worth a try,' said Norman.

'Then there's a copy of a letter,' added Slater.

'From way back then?' asked Norman.

'Oh, no. This is much more recent. It's dated just a couple of months ago. It's addressed to the man Mr Winter thinks was the ring-leader way back then, so it gives us a suspect for these two murders.'

'Fantastic!' said Norman. 'Who is it?'

'Sir Robert Maunder,' said Slater.

'You're kidding me.' Norman's mouth was hanging open. 'I met him just a few days ago when his house got broken into. The guy's a total arsehole, that's for sure, but I'm not sure he's fit enough to murder anyone. He's over eighty years old.'

'It's amazing what people can do when they feel threatened,' said Slater.

'Well I'll certainly look forward to questioning him. I owe him a hard time.'

'I also spoke to the people who sent us the CD,' said Slater.

'Learn anything?'

'Quite a bit, actually.' Slater grinned, feeling pleased with himself. 'It turns out Mr Winter only opened his account a few weeks ago. He paid for a year upfront, and apparently he was very concerned about security and anonymity. He wanted to make sure there was no way anyone else could find out what he was doing.'

'Just a few weeks ago,' said Norman. 'Are you thinking what I'm thinking?'

'Maybe Sir Robert didn't like the letter he was sent,' said Slater.

'And he threatened Winter,' finished Norman.

'He must have felt he was in a lot of danger,' continued Slater, nodding his agreement. 'So he set up the back-up system to make sure his information stayed safe, even if he didn't.'

'And now we can see why he invited the big story journalist to tell his story,' said Norman. 'No wonder the guy's still sniffing around.'

'He's not off the hook yet. We know he was making phone calls to Mr Winter at the time. We've only got his word for it that he wasn't threatening the old guy.'

'Yeah,' agreed Norman. 'But we haven't found anything to contradict what he told us. I don't fancy him for it, and I don't think you do deep down inside. Don't forget what he said about killing the golden goose. It wouldn't make sense for the scandal-mongering journalist to kill the guy with the juicy story to tell, would it?'

'Yeah, it makes much more sense for the subject of that scandal to kill him, doesn't it?' agreed Slater.

'We'll need to tread carefully if we're gonna catch the old guy,' warned Norman. 'He seems to have a direct line to the chief constable, and I'm sure he's got lots more friends in various high places. He'll run squealing to them as soon as he gets a sniff we're on to him, then they'll all close ranks, and we'll be left, high and dry, right in the middle of a shit storm.'

'We'd better make sure we've got it right before we show our hand then, Norm,' said Slater.

CHAPTER TWENTY-THREE

It was a tired, sad, and depressed team that gathered next morning. Slater and Norman had been up at Hatton House until way past midnight, and had each managed about four hours sleep. Jolly had been administered a rather heavy duty sedative to make sure she slept, and it was obvious to everyone she encountered that she was still half asleep when she arrived at the station that morning.

'What are you doing here?' asked Slater, when she walked in. 'We weren't expecting you to come in today.'

'Like I can sit at home knowing Florence would still be alive if it wasn't for me,' she said glumly. 'I'm here because I feel I have to help you two solve this case.'

'Are you sure?' he asked. 'We understand if–'

'Yes, I'm sure,' she interrupted. 'And I do appreciate your concern, but I really can't sit back and do nothing.'

'Okay, I can understand that. But the deal is you let us know if you're finding it difficult, alright?'

'I'll be fine. Honestly. Where's Norm?'

'He's gone downstairs to see what forensics have got for us. He'll be back in a minute.'

When Norman came back, he was even more concerned for Jolly's welfare. Slater felt he should indulge him for a couple of minutes, but it was Jolly who was quick to point out that she was still alive and that it was Florence they should be focusing upon.

'Right, then,' said Slater, finally. 'Let's see what we've got to work with and where we go from here. If we assume the information on the CD is correct, we now have a prime suspect in the form of Sir Robert Maunder. However, because of who he is, we can more or less guarantee barriers will be erected all around him as soon as his name comes out. So we need to build a much stronger case than we have right now.

'We need to find anything we can that links him to the orphanage. We have a list of names that appears to be staff members. Maybe we can locate someone who can back up Mr Winter's story.'

'What if we find someone who says it's all crap?' asked Jolly. 'I don't want to find these two people have died for nothing.'

'That's a risk we have to take,' said Norman. 'I can assure you Maunder is a complete arse, but at the moment he's an innocent arse unless we can prove otherwise. And anyway, we can't ignore the possibility that Winter just had it in for him and this is all fiction.'

Jolly didn't look at all happy at Norman's suggestion that Mr Winter was making the whole thing up.

'I can't believe that!' she snapped.

'I don't think any of us believe it, Jane,' said Slater. 'But we can't ignore the possibility. That's why we need to find the evidence to prove it. There must have been records of all the kids who were put into the care of that orphanage. It's got to be worth trying to find them. Can you get onto that, Jane? Start with the local council, county council. You know what to do.'

'Why don't I combine that with the search for information about Hatton House?' suggested Jolly. 'It seems they're almost one and the same thing.'

'Good idea,' said Slater.

'Are we ruling Rippon out as a suspect now?' asked Norman.

'I think we can push him back down the queue, but he's still a suspect. What if he's the one with the hard disk? Maybe he was hoping Florence would know the password.'

Slater saw the look on Norman's face.

'If he had a copy,' argued Norman, 'he wouldn't need Florence to help him. The guy's a professional. He must know someone who could access that information.'

'Look. I agree it's probably as unlikely as Winter telling lies, Norm, but he still has a motive. We can't ignore him yet. Anyway, what did forensics come up with?'

'Well,' said Norman with a smile, 'it seems our exchange of words might not have done too much harm. They've pulled out all the stops on this one. It looks like something was dragged from the log cabin to the canal. Their theory is she was killed outside the cabin and then dragged up to the canal and thrown in. It was dragging her body that created the trail.

'They also found a footprint along this trail. It matches the one found at Mr Winter's house, same shoe, same size. So we need to find out where Rippon was yesterday afternoon and evening. I think we also need to ask Danny Trent where he was. We didn't prove he's ever had a pair of those shoes, but after he admitted he was at Mr Winter's house we have to assume he could have been at Florence's too.'

'This is a good start,' said Slater. 'Was there anything else?'

'Oh, there's more,' said Norman. 'In the cabin they found a back door key that they think will fit Mr Winter's back door.'

'If that's the key we saw, I'm sure it's his,' said Jolly.

'They also found a creased sheet of paper that had been roughly smoothed out,' continued Norman. 'Remember the torn piece of paper found in Mr Winter's hand? When they put them together, they found they were a match, and now they can see what the numbers are. It's a phone number.'

He held up a sheet of paper with a mobile phone number printed on it.

'I'm sure I've seen that number before.' Slater scrabbled through the papers on his desk. 'Wait a minute. Yeah. Here it is. It's Rippon's number.'

'There's another question for him to answer, then,' said Norman.

'Is that it?'

'That's it for this case,' said Norman. 'But while I was down there,

Becksy gave me something else that I think you might find interesting. Remember I had to go to Maunder's house when he had this break-in? He assured everyone it was the Night Caller. He even called up the CC to tell him I was an idiot for not immediately agreeing with him.

'Well, Becksy finally got some feedback from Winchester. It's definitely not the real Night Caller who broke in there. Apparently it's not the same calling card, but it's not the usual copycat either. The fakers use the sort of card you can buy anywhere and print from a PC. The real guy uses expensive, fancy card and a very expensive printer you can't buy just anywhere. Whoever broke in at Maunder's used the right card, but then made the mistake of using the wrong ink, wrong font, and wrong size. They also used a PC to do the printing. They might have known about the fancy card but they didn't know the other details.'

'Is it common knowledge about the card?' asked Slater.

'It's been reported in press releases that he leaves a card,' said Norman, with a wicked grin. 'But it's never been revealed that he uses fancy card.'

'So what do you think?' asked Slater.

'Well, I have to say I thought it was all a bit iffy from the start. I mean, they conveniently forgot to set the alarm. The jewellery box was left out in the open, and I'm supposed to believe they both slept while someone came into their bedroom and cleaned the thing out. In my humble opinion it stinks to high heaven, but because he is who he is I was told to back off and leave it.'

'Did he fake it?' asked Slater. 'Insurance fraud?'

'Having seen how they all closed ranks, I think it would be fair to say they think he's squeaky clean. I'm sure he probably knows someone who knows the facts about the Night Caller, and I'm sure if he asked they'd tell him. And, no doubt, once I suggest I need to investigate a bit more thoroughly we'll see them all close ranks again. Isn't that going to be fun?'

'So don't tell anyone,' said Slater.

'But I was ordered to tell the old man if I want to speak to the guy again.'

'But no-one's ordered *me* to stay away,' said Slater. 'We now have a reason for going up there and talking to him. We can use the break-in as an excuse for poking around into his background.'

'And starting a shit storm heading our way.'

'Is that a problem?'

'It's never worried me before,' said Norman, grinning. 'And I'm getting a bit long in the tooth for changing my ways now.'

'That's what I thought.' Slater smiled back. 'But we need to do our research thoroughly before we go up there.'

He leaned back in his chair and fished a coin from his pocket.

'Heads or tails?'

'What am I gonna win if I call it right?'

'If you call it right, you get to stay here and start searching through this list of employees. If you call it wrong, you get to attend the PM.'

'Wow, what a choice. You're just too kind. Okay, I'll go heads.'

Slater spun the coin in the air and slapped his hand over it as it landed on his desk. He tilted his hand just enough to see the coin for himself, but kept it hidden from Norman. His face broke into a broad grin.

'I'm not buying that,' said Norman, suspiciously. 'Lemme see.'

Slater took his hand away to reveal the winning tails.

'Crap,' said Norman. 'I hate watching a PM right on lunchtime. There must be somewhere else we should be. Are you sure you don't want to come?'

'I'd love to accompany you,' said Slater, grinning, 'but we need to get cracking on. Jane can't handle all this research on her own. If you leave now you can have an early lunch before it starts.'

'Watch it on a full stomach? You have to be kidding,' said Norman, looking aghast. 'But I will take you up on the "leave now" bit.'

Slater and Jolly were both engrossed in their computers, the room filled with a deafening silence apart from the clicking of keyboards. Norman had been gone a couple of hours when Slater suddenly cursed loudly.

'Bugger!' he said. 'Norman was right when he said there was somewhere else we should be. One of us was supposed to be at John Hunter's this morning to see the fake sister. I got so involved in Florence's murder I forgot all about it.'

He looked at his watch, then snatched up the phone and dialled Hunter's number.

'Hi, Mr Hunter. It's DS Slater. I'm afraid we've got so involved in another case I forgot I was supposed to be coming in this morning. Has she turned up yet?'

'She's not coming now,' said Hunter.

'But I thought she was rushing down to hear you read the will today. I thought she was insisting,' said Slater, irritated and confused.

'Yes, she was. But now it seems she's decided against coming down.'

'Did she say why? When is she intending to come down?' asked Slater, transitioning from irritation to disbelief.

'It seems she no longer wishes to hear the will and no longer claims to be Mr Winter's long-lost sister.'

'What? Just like that?'

'Perhaps she knew we were onto her,' said Hunter

'So she was a fake, just as we suspected,' said Slater. 'I'd like to know how she came to get involved in this in the first place.'

'Sergeant, there are people out there who do nothing but look for ads just like the one I placed in a large number of newspapers. I suppose you only need to manage to fake it once and you get your hands on a sizable inheritance.'

'If I wasn't so busy right now, I'd be after her,' said Slate, angrily.

'I fear you'd probably be wasting your time,' said Hunter, mildly. 'The chances are she'll have vanished into thin air already.'

Slater sighed heavily. He knew Hunter was probably right. It was so frustrating though.

'Are you any nearer to finding the real sister?' asked Hunter.

'Err, yes,' admitted Slater. 'We think we have found her. We'll know for sure when we get the DNA test results back. The problem is she's dead.'

'Oh my goodness,' said Hunter. 'What happened?'

'I'm afraid I can't tell you that,' said Slater, grimly.

He was finding it difficult to hide his irritation, and so he made his excuses and ended the call, finally throwing the phone back into its cradle in disgust.

'What's happened?' asked Jolly.

'Apparently this missing sister who was so insistent on coming down has decided to drop out of the whole scene. Suddenly she's not his sister,' said Slater bitterly. 'I was hoping we could find out who she was working for.'

'Maybe she was just working on her own. Perhaps she spends all her time on fishing trips like this one.'

'No,' said Slater. 'I'm sure there's more to it than that. There's something not right about this whole thing. I just can't see what it is yet.'

The door burst open and Norman backed in, carefully balancing three mugs of tea on a small tray.

'I come bearing gifts from afar,' he announced, placing the tray carefully on Slater's desk before adding, 'Well, from the canteen, anyway.'

'So how did the PM go?' asked Slater.

'It was grisly, gory, and generally uncomfortable,' said Norman.

'Did you learn anything new?'

'I learnt I don't like watching post-mortems, but I already knew that,' said Norman. 'But that's not what you mean, right?'

Slater nodded patiently. No one enjoyed PMs so he was prepared to accept Norman's need to joke about it.

'There was no water in her lungs, so she didn't drown. It looks like she was killed by a heavy blow to the back of her head and then dragged to the canal and thrown in. Time of death is a bit hazy because of the effects of the cold and being in the canal overnight, but they reckon between 4pm and 7pm the day before we found her, so she'd been in there about 24 hours when we found her.'

'No real surprises there then,' said Slater. 'Did they say what they thought the murder weapon was?'

'That old favourite, the blunt instrument,' said Norman. 'A baseball bat would fit the bill, but they couldn't be sure. I've asked the guys to try searching the canal a bit further afield, but don't hold your breath.'

'Are they doing a DNA comparison to Winter?' asked Slater.

'Yeah,' said Norman. 'I always thought she might be too old, but she was much younger than she looked. I guess that's what being in hiding and living rough does for you. According to the pathologist she was in her late sixties, so that would be about right. She has to be his sister.'

'Talking of sisters,' said Slater, 'we forgot one of us was supposed to be at Hunter's this morning.'

'Crap!' said Norman. 'Did she turn up?'

'Apparently she's decided she's not his sister, after all,' said Slater, sighing. 'She's not coming now.'

'Really? Why's she suddenly got cold feet?'

'Yeah. That's what I'd like to know. It's not right is it?'

'Did she know we were going to be waiting for her?' asked Norman.

'Not unless Hunter told her, but it was his idea, so why would he do that? Anyway he says he didn't.'

'Oh well, if she got cold feet it's one less problem to resolve,' said Norman, optimistically.

'Or it's whole new problem altogether,' replied Slater, ominously.

'Is that what you think?' asked Norman.

'Something's not right,' said Slater. 'I know it, but I just can't put my finger on it.'

'Stop thinking about it and it'll come to you eventually,' said Norman.

He turned to Jolly.

'So how are we doing on these searches?'

'Most of the people on this staff list would be in their eighties or even older,' she said. 'If they were still alive. It seems the mortality rate is pretty high. I haven't found anyone who's still alive yet. I haven't even got started on the search for Hatton House records.'

'What about you?' Norman asked Slater. 'Any luck with your list of possible abusers?'

'I seem to have the same problem as Jane,' he replied. 'Everyone's dead.'

'All except the main man,' said Norman. 'Doesn't that seem a little strange? Or is it just me?'

'I didn't know Jane was having the same issue. But it seems unlikely that everyone would be dead, doesn't it?'

'What about causes of death?' asked Norman.

'Natural. In their sleep mostly,' said Jolly.

'Me too,' said Slater. 'Two of mine had cancer. Neither was terminal, yet they both died.'

'Now that looks like a whole inquiry in itself,' said Norman.

'I don't think we can get side-tracked on that now,' said Slater. 'We don't have the resources.'

'Nah. You're right. But it's something we should maybe flag up at a later date.'

'In the meantime,' said Slater, 'I thought we should check out our favourite journalist, but when I called the Station Hotel they told me he'd gone back to London for a few days. So I called his London office and they confirmed he's been up there for the past three days. But he's due back this afternoon. I thought we could call in on our way home.'

'What about his young accomplice?' asked Norman.

'He's got a good alibi, too. He's out of the country,' said Slater. 'I already checked. It seems he was advised to take a holiday for a week or two until all this has died down.'

'So that's two suspects we can cross off the list then,' said Norman. 'There's only one left really. I do like a short list!'

'Rippon could always have come back down without anyone knowing,' said Slater.

'You really think so?' Norman sounded surprised.

'No, not really,' admitted Slater. 'We should still speak to him, but I agree Maunder looks the favourite right now.'

'So why don't we go over there tomorrow morning and rattle his cage?' suggested Norman.

It was five-thirty when they found Geoff Rippon sat at his usual corner table in the Railway Hotel, furiously tapping away at his laptop. If he saw them come in, he didn't acknowledge the fact.

'Evening, Geoff,' said Slater, as he and Norman carried their pints over and settled into the chairs across the table from Rippon. He looked up, grimaced at each of them, and then returned to his laptop.

Slater and Norman sat and waited as he hammered away furiously, enjoying the first pint they'd had together for a long while. Eventually, Rippon looked up again and glared at them.

'What?' he snapped.

'Cheers,' said Norman, raising his glass to Rippon. 'It's good to see you, too.'

'Don't expect me to be pleased to see you,' said Rippon. 'We had a deal. You were going to share information.'

'I don't think it was quite like that,' said Slater, mildly.

'You didn't tell me you were going to let the star of my story get killed, did you?'

'How d'you know about that?'

'I read the bloody newspaper,' said Rippon, angrily. 'You should try it, perhaps then you might find out what's going on.'

'How d'you know she was a star player in your story?' asked Norman.

'You already know how I know,' he replied. 'It was me that told you she was old Mr Winter's sister, wasn't it?'

'So where were you yesterday?' asked Slater.

'What? Am I a suspect?' asked Rippon, aghast. 'Do I need an alibi?'

'I just asked where you were, that's all,' said Slater.

'If you must know, I was at my office up in London. I've been up there for a couple of days. You can check with my secretary.'

'I will,' said Slater.

'She'll tell you where, what times and who with.'

'To be honest, Geoff,' said Norman, 'you're not exactly our number one suspect, but we wouldn't be doing our jobs if we didn't ask. You do have a motive, and we did find that fancy trainer print of yours again.'

'Only in your eyes do I have a motive,' said Rippon. 'Like I said before, you don't kill the golden goose. And they sell millions of those trainers.'

'I don't think Florence would have been your golden goose,' said Norman. 'She didn't live in the real world. I don't think she would have been any more use to you, as a witness, than she would have been to us. But she didn't deserve to die, and we were hoping you might want to help us find out who killed her.'

'What makes you think I can help?'

'Two reasons,' said Norman. 'One, the journalist in you sees a big story. We know you've been investigating, just like we have. Maybe you know something we don't. Two, we know that inside that tough exterior there's a decent human being. We think that decent human being would want to see her killer caught.'

'Nice speech,' sneered Rippon. 'But we've already done this and I told you what I knew, and then I got nothing out of it. Why should I think it'll be different this time?'

'We have a CD,' said Norman. 'We believe it's a copy of what Mr Winter was going to give you. But we also believe someone else has a copy.'

'Well if it was me I'd have written the story by now.'

'We believe someone has it because they seem to be keeping one step ahead of us,' said Slater. 'So if we thought you had it, we would have arrested you by now.'

He raised his glass to Rippon and took a mouthful of his beer.

'We don't drink on duty,' said Norman. 'This is off the record.'

'Well, I can tell you this,' said Rippon. 'Off the record or on it: if you've got a CD, you've got a bloody sight more than I have.'

'It was sent to us from a back-up service,' said Norman.

'You don't use one of them unless you feel your security's been compromised,' said Rippon.

'That's what we think,' said Slater. 'So do you know anyone who might make him feel that way?'

'The guy who the story's about would have pretty powerful motive, don't you think?' Rippon looked interested and less hostile now.

'Yeah, we figured that one out for ourselves,' said Norman. 'But is there anyone else?'

'You know more than I do,' said Rippon. 'But if you had another copy and you wanted it kept safe, who would you leave it with? The bank, in a safety deposit box, or with your solicitor.'

'But he had the back-up service set up,' argued Norman.

'Maybe he didn't trust his solicitor or his bank,' suggested Rippon.

Slater pondered that as he took another sip of his beer.

CHAPTER TWENTY-FOUR

As the front door swung open, Slater got his first glimpse of Sir Robert Maunder. He was good six inches shorter than Slater but, even though he was in his eighties, he stood tall and erect, his attitude confrontational right from the start.

'Sir Robert Maunder?' said Slater, politely, producing his warrant card. 'I'm DS Slater, from Tinton police station, and this is my colleague DS Norman.'

Norman had been standing behind Slater, but he stepped forward at the sound of his name.

'What do you want?' snapped Sir Robert. Then he pointed a finger at Norman. 'And what's that idiot doing here? I specifically told them not to send him again.'

Norman didn't say anything; Slater knew this was probably a monumental effort on his friend's part.

'Oh. Is there a problem?' asked Slater. 'I'm afraid no-one told me. We're here to discuss the findings of the inquiry into the break-in here recently.'

'Surely there's nothing to discuss,' grumbled Maunder. 'It was this Night Caller chap, end of story.'

'Yes,' said Slater. 'I understand your theory, sir. But there are one or two things I need to clarify if you could spare me a few minutes.'

'Clarify? What do you mean clarify?'

'Perhaps if we could come in?'

They were obviously as welcome as herpes, but after a few moments, Maunder backed into the house and opened the door to allow them in.

'I'll talk to you in the library, Slater,' he said as they stepped inside. 'But your "colleague" will have to wait out here in the hall. I've got nothing to say to him.'

They hadn't been expecting a warm welcome, but even so, Slater found it hard to accept such open hostility towards Norman. He thought about insisting Norman should be in on any discussion, but Norman intervened before he could speak.

'That's okay, Sir Robert,' he said. 'I understand. I'll wait out here. It's better than being outside in the cold.'

Maunder grunted at Norman, then turned his back and led Slater through a door across the hall. Once inside, he closed the door behind them.

'So what do you want to clarify, Sergeant?' said Maunder, settling himself into the chair behind his desk. He left Slater standing, with the desk between them. The battle lines were drawn.

'First off,' said Slater, 'forensic evidence indicates this was not the work of the Night Caller.'

'Of course, it was.' Maunder glared at him. 'He even left his calling card. I hear he leaves it every time. And we're just the class of people with the sort of house he would target.'

'I can't argue about the target,' agreed Slater. 'And I can't argue about the card being left. The thing is, it's not the Night Caller's card. This card was left by someone who wanted us to think it was the Night Caller.'

For a few brief seconds Maunder's eyes narrowed and a trace of panic flitted across his face. It would have been easy to miss, but it was the sort of reaction Slater had been looking for.

'Your people must be wrong,' he blustered.

'I'm afraid not,' said Slater. 'There are very distinct differences between the card left here and the real Night Caller's card.'

Maunder said nothing.

'How often do you forget to turn on your alarm at night?' asked Slater.

'That's a very impertinent question. Don't you know who I am?'

'Yes, sir, I do know who you are,' said Slater. 'I also know how old you are, and, with respect, you wouldn't be the first person your age to have a problem with their memory.'

'I'm not sure I like what you're suggesting, Sergeant.'

'I'm not suggesting anything, Sir.' Slater smiled pleasantly. 'Maybe your wife has a problem with her memory, too.'

Maunder's face had turned an angry red now.

'I think that's enough innuendo and suggestion, Sergeant,' he snapped. 'I think perhaps you should leave.'

As soon as the library door had closed, Norman started to look around. There were two more doors at the end of the hall, one of which was slightly ajar. He walked quietly across to it, stopped, and listened. He could hear nothing, so he gently pushed the door open and stepped inside.

'Who on earth are you?' asked a bright-eyed, sprightly looking old lady.

Norman nearly jumped out of his skin, then quickly realised this must be Maunder's wife.

'Oh, I'm sorry,' said Norman, fumbling for his warrant card. 'I'm DS Norman. I came with my colleague to speak to your husband, but I'm afraid he doesn't want to talk to me. I was just looking for a glass of water.'

'Ah!' She smiled at him. 'Do come in, Sergeant. I can do better than water. I've just made a pot of tea, if you'd like one.'

'Oh, that would be wonderful,' agreed Norman. He already liked this woman, who seemed to be the complete opposite of her grumpy husband.

'Come and sit down.' She indicated two chairs at the kitchen table.

'Thank you.' Norman grinned at her and sat down.

'So you must be the poor soul who came when we had the break-in,' said Lady Maunder, as she fussed around finding a cup and saucer and then pouring tea for him.

'That was me,' conceded Norman.

'I'm afraid my husband's not blessed with a great deal of patience,' she said, setting his tea down on the table, and then settling in the chair next to him. 'In fact just recently he seems to have none at all. But he's not a bad person, he's just never quite managed to retire properly, if you see what I mean. He still thinks he's the one in charge and what he says is all that matters.'

'Maybe something's bothering him,' ventured Norman. 'If someone's worrying about something it can make them seriously short of patience. And I understand what you mean about not retiring properly. My dad was the same. Does Sir Robert have problems with his memory, too? That's what used to make my dad angry.'

'Oh there's nothing wrong with his memory.' She laughed. 'I think it's just that he's so good at everything he doesn't expect anyone to disagree with him.'

'It's a shame you left your jewellery box out that night,' said Norman. 'It must have been sad to lose all that fabulous family stuff.'

'Now that he *did* forget to do,' she said. 'I had already gone to bed. I did ask him to put it away for me when he came up, but it wasn't part of his normal routine, you see, so I expect that's why he forgot it. It was such a pity. Still, at least we don't have any family to pass it on to, so no one's going to miss it, only me.'

'You have no children?' asked Norman.

'No. It obviously wasn't meant to be.' She sighed sadly. 'But then if we'd had children of our own he probably wouldn't have had time for all those orphans and the children's charities he's helped over the years.'

'Oh really?' said Norman. 'I didn't know about that.'

'He never used to make a song and dance about it,' she said, smiling fondly. 'I think it helped him deal with the fact we had none of our own.'

'It's funny you should mention orphans,' said Norman. 'I've only just found out there was an orphanage not far from here. What was it called now...'

'Hatton House,' she answered. 'Oh yes. Robert used to spend lots of time there. It was such a pity when it closed.'

'If you really want me to leave, I will,' Slater said to Maunder. 'But before I go, can you tell me if you know this man?'

He placed a photograph of Mr Winter on the desk.

Maunder looked at the photograph, and then sat back in horror.

'Good God,' he said. 'That's a mortuary photograph. That man's dead.'

'I'm afraid he is, yes,' agreed Slater. 'Do you recognise him?'

'I've never set eyes on him before,' said Maunder. 'What makes you think I would recognise him?'

'I thought you might know him. After all, he sent you a letter a few weeks ago.'

'What makes you think he sent me a letter?'

'We found a copy,' said Slater.

'I think you're mistaken, Sergeant Slater.' Maunder's voice had taken on a menacing tone.

'You're probably right,' agreed Slater, with a condescending smile. 'Us modern-day coppers have got no idea what we're doing. Not like it was back in your day, eh? *Sir*.'

'How dare you speak to me like that?' Maunder leapt to his feet – impressively for a man in his eighties – and rushed to the door, flinging it open with a flourish. 'Get out of my house!' he shouted.

'Good heavens,' said Lady Maunder in the kitchen, as the sound of her husband's shouting reached them. 'Whatever is going on?'

'I think maybe my colleague and your husband have finished talking,' said Norman. 'Thank you for the tea, and I really enjoyed talking to you, but I think I'd better be going, too.'

He stood and made his way back to the hall where Maunder was berating Slater as a disgrace to the police force. Then he spotted Norman coming from the kitchen.

'And what the hell do you think you're doing wandering around my house?'

'Err, your wife offered me a cup of tea-'

'You've been talking to my wife? How dare you?' Maunder roared. 'Get out of my house, the pair of you. You'll pay for this. It's harassment. I'll be talking to the chief constable, and to my lawyer.'

'Right,' said Norman, as he ducked past Maunder to join Slater by the front door. 'We'll let ourselves out then, shall we?'

'That seemed to go well,' observed Norman, tongue firmly in cheek, as they drove off.

'The guy's a real charmer, just like you said,' said Slater. 'He didn't like it at all when I suggested there was something fishy about their break-in. And when I asked him about Winter... Well, he denied knowing Winter, or about any letter. But he went crazy. I thought he was going to go into orbit.'

'Yeah. See, I told you he was an arse,' said Norman. 'But how does a guy like that end up with such a lovely wife? She's his polar opposite, honestly. She's sweet, and gentle. She made me a cup of tea and we had a cosy little chat. She tells me it was her husband who was supposed to put the jewellery box away that night. And she assures me there's absolutely nothing wrong with his memory.'

'That more or less confirms it, then. I bet if we get a search warrant we'll find the stuff's still there somewhere.'

'Yeah. Good luck with getting someone to sanction that. I think we'll have more luck coming at him from the other direction. His wife confirms they have no kids. She says, to make up for it, he's always done lots for children's charities. And get this – he used to spend loads of his spare time down at Hatton House when it was open.'

'Do you think she knows what he was really doing down there?' asked Slater.

'I don't think so,' said Norman. 'She sees him as spikey on the outside but with a heart of gold on the inside. She thinks he's one of the good guys.'

'I've found you a real, live ex-staff member,' announced Jolly, when they got back to the office. 'Gordon Ferguson. He lives in a nursing home down Portsmouth way. I've spoken to the staff there. They say he's a bit of a loner, keeps himself to himself. He's quite frail, but he's also quite lucid, and he never gets any visitors so he'd probably appreciate someone going to see him.'

'Now, we're getting somewhere,' said Slater. 'Well done, Jane.'

'I've also located some records to do with Hatton House,' she said. 'They're archived at the County Council's offices. The only problem is they've got no-one to sort through them, so this afternoon I'm going to go down and start sorting through it all myself.'

'Are you okay with that?' asked Norman.

'It's got to be done,' she said. 'And I'm sure I can do it a lot more efficiently than you two.'

'Ouch,' said Norman. 'I felt that.'

CHAPTER TWENTY-FIVE

When Jolly had finally tracked down the whereabouts of the records she was looking for, she had been warned about the likely condition of both the records themselves and the place where they were kept. Now she had reached that place, she could see they hadn't been joking. She was surprised to find the archive appeared to be run by a young man who looked about thirteen years old. He introduced himself as Ryan.

'Everything you want will be down the far end there,' he said, pointing to the far end of the basement area. He was obviously none too keen on actually going with her to help in any way, although he didn't say as much.

'Right. Thank you,' she said, doubtfully, surveying the rows of dusty shelves packed tightly with boxes and boxes of paperwork. 'Do I get any sort of clue about exactly where it might be? Or what it might look like?'

'Sorry,' he said. 'I've never been down that far, so I couldn't tell you what's down there. I suppose it'll be in archive boxes like the rest of it.'

'Oh, great. That's really helpful,' she said, testily.

'Old Mr Rodgers would know exactly where everything was,' he said.

'Where's he today?' she asked, hopefully. If he was on a day off, maybe she could come back tomorrow.

'In his grave,' Ryan said. 'He died all of a sudden. He had a heart attack. Left me in charge of this bloody lot but I'd only been here a week so he never got round to showing me what's what.'

'That was very inconsiderate of him,' said Jolly, acidly, but her sarcasm was wasted. If the youthful Ryan had detected her tone, it certainly didn't show.

'Yeah,' he agreed. 'He was a bit of a selfish old git.'

'It's been lovely talking to you,' said Jolly. 'But I'm afraid I need to get on. It looks like I've got a lot to do.'

She slung her rucksack over her shoulder and made to walk past him.

'Sorry. You can't take that in there.' He pointed at the rucksack.

'Why not?'

'I don't know what's inside it, do I?'

'But it's just overalls, face masks, and stuff, so I don't get covered in dust and other assorted crap.'

'You might want to smuggle something out,' Ryan said, gravely. 'I can't allow that.'

'I'm the bloody police, you moron,' Jolly snapped. 'I'm looking for evidence, and I can assure you if I find any I don't need to smuggle it out. I'll bloody well walk out with it under my arm! Are you clear on that?'

Ryan looked distinctly embarrassed.

'Alright, alright,' he said. 'I'm just doing my job.'

'No, Ryan,' said Jolly. 'You're not doing your job, you're obstructing a police inquiry, and the police are beginning to lose their patience. Now, are you going to let me past?'

The young man looked like a rabbit caught in the headlights, and quickly stood aside.

'Thank you,' she said. 'It wasn't so difficult, was it?'

She stepped past him and started to make her way through the basement. At the beginning it was all neat and tidy and relatively dust-free. But she couldn't quite get her head around the sheer volume of paperwork that seemed to represent just one month's work. *If this was the paperless society computers were supposed to have heralded*, she thought, *then we're all in serious trouble.*

By the time she had gone back fifteen years, to the turn of the century, the dust was thick enough to write her name. It was time to don the blue smurf suit she'd persuaded Ian Becks to part with. When she told him why she wanted one, he'd also supplied her with goggles, a face mask with several spare filters, and a head torch. She wasn't sure she'd need the goggles, but already she could see the face mask had been a good idea. As she headed deeper into the archive and the lights became less effective, she knew she was also going to be grateful for the head torch.

It took her an hour to locate what she was looking for. The dust was so thick on the top of the boxes it was obvious they hadn't been opened in years. She was undecided if this was a good sign or a bad sign, but at least it meant no one else had been looking here, so perhaps, for once, they were ahead of the game. Then again, she thought, it could mean there was nothing here to find. Finally, she realised all this speculation was getting her nowhere. She wasn't going to know, one way or the other, unless she opened the boxes and looked inside.

Over the next two hours, she looked through six of the archive boxes, but found no reference to Hatton House or any other orphanage. The filing system seemed to be a bit hit and miss. Some boxes seemed to contain everything from a single year and some contained documents relating only to a single subject. The head torch proved to be invaluable in the gloom, but even so, she could feel a headache beginning to develop. She decided to take a break and get away from all this dirt and dust for a while, and made her way back up to the front end of the archive where the air was cleaner and the light was better.

'Jesus,' said Ryan when she emerged, covered in dust and grime. 'Look at the state of you!'

'Yes,' said Jolly. 'Look at the state of your archive, you mean.'

'I honestly had no idea it was that bad,' he said. 'That's disgraceful.'

He jumped up from his desk and pushed at the bars of a fire door.

'Here,' he said. 'Come outside and get some fresh air. I'll get you a cup of tea.'

She was totally unprepared for this change in his attitude, but so grateful to see daylight and fresh air she didn't pass comment. She stepped outside, dragged off her overalls and face mask, and sank onto a chair.

'Here you are,' said Ryan, carrying a mug of tea out to her. 'You shouldn't be working down there in all that shit. It can't be doing you any good.'

'I don't have much choice, do I?' she said. 'It's got to be done.'

'Yeah,' he said. 'But I've got an idea. Why don't we load the boxes onto my sack barrow and bring them up this end where there's some decent light?'

'We?' she said, surprised. 'Are you offering to help?'

'I'll give you a hand if you like. I've got nothing else to do. This job gets so boring I sometimes wonder if anyone actually knows I'm down here. It'll make a change to have something useful to do. If anyone asks what I'm doing, I'll tell them I'm starting to sort out the archive. They won't know the difference anyway.'

'I'd really appreciate that,' said Jolly. 'Thank you, Ryan.'

'To tell the truth,' he said, quietly, 'I think I owe you that much. I don't know why I was so shitty earlier. P'raps it's because I'm so bloody bored, but it's not your fault, is it? There's no excuse for it. I was just being an arsehole because I could I suppose.'

'That's alright,' she said. 'What are you? Eighteen?'

'Yeah.' He nodded, shyly.

'Well that explains it then.' She smiled at him. 'Being an arsehole sometimes goes with the territory. It's part of what being eighteen's all about.'

'You're alright, you are,' said Ryan. 'I tell you what, you drink your tea and then we'll get started.'

Having led Ryan down to the back of the archive and shown him which boxes she wanted to look through, the whole operation began to move more quickly. He proved to be a keen, willing worker, despite the dirty conditions, and was happy to do as directed.

Jolly eventually made her first breakthrough late in the afternoon when Ryan wheeled out a whole box devoted to child welfare. After much sorting, she finally came up with a list of all the children who had been sent to Hatton House from 1956 up to 1965 when it closed. Then, in the very next box, she struck gold in the form of records and documents from Hatton House itself.

She beamed a smile at the now grubby, dusty teenager.

'Ryan,' she said, beaming. 'I could kiss you.'

'Steady on,' he said, doubtfully. 'You must be old enough to be my mum.'

Then, he noticed the look on her face.

'No offence, like,' he added.

CHAPTER TWENTY-SIX

Slater was heading south towards the coast and The Belmont Nursing Home, which sat on a hill, high above Portsmouth, overlooking the town, the old naval dockyards, and out across the sea. He was driving alone as Norman had booked the afternoon off for reasons unknown. Slater was nosey enough to ask, but also understanding enough to accept Norman's stonewalling of his questions. If he didn't want to share his business, that was okay.

The subject of his visit was Gordon Ferguson, the sole surviving member of staff from Hatton House. Ferguson had been the gardener at Hatton House from 1950 when the home had opened, right through until it had closed in 1965, so Slater was optimistic about his chances of learning something useful from his trip.

It was a sunny day, and despite the fact it was late afternoon in February, there were a few hardy souls huddled together on the benches that were dotted about the sun terrace at the back of the building. And then there was one man who sat alone on a bench apart from the rest, staring out to sea. He was wrapped in a huge black coat, with a blue and white scarf coiled around his neck, and a matching woollen hat on his head.

'That's him,' said the carer, pointing. 'On his own as usual. He spends most of his time out here on his own, even when it's freezing cold. He prefers to keep himself to himself, and he can be a bit grumpy, but mostly he's okay.'

She gave him a kindly smile.

'Do you need me to take you over to meet him?'

'I don't think that's necessary,' said Slater, looking at the badge pinned to the front of her uniform blouse. 'Thank you, Maggie. You've been very helpful.'

'That's okay,' she said. 'If you need anything else, you'll find me in or around the reception area. Just ring the bell if you can't see me.'

She hurried back inside. Despite the warm sunshine there was an icy wind blowing in from the sea, and Slater was grateful for his own thick, warm coat, which he kept in his car just in case. He turned the collar up and walked towards the solitary old man. He eased himself onto the bench, close, but not too close, to the old man, who studiously ignored him and continued staring into the distance.

'Mr Ferguson?' he said, after a minute or so. 'My name's DS Slater. I believe they told you I was coming.'

The old man turned to look at him, and Slater's heart gave a little flutter of excitement. His face had the weathered look of a man who had spent his life working outside in all conditions, but he was unmistakably the man in the photograph with the little girl, which was in his pocket.

'Aye. They told me,' the old man said, eventually. 'But they didn't tell me why.'

His voice was a low growl, with just a faint trace of a Scottish accent remaining.

'We're running a murder inquiry,' said Slater. 'Our investigations have led us to an orphanage that was open in the fifties and closed in the mid-sixties. It was called Hatton House. Do you know it?'

'I can't say I do.' Ferguson brushed an enormous, gnarled hand across his face.

'That's funny,' said Slater. 'Because there's a Gordon Ferguson listed as a member of staff. He was the gardener. With hands like that, I reckon you were probably a gardener. Am I right?'

'I'm an old man,' said Ferguson. 'My memory's not what it was.'

'According to the staff here, your memory is just fine,' said Slater.

'You're wasting your time. I can't tell you anything.'

'I haven't asked you anything, yet.'

The old man just grunted in response.

'You must have been good at your job,' said Slater. 'I mean, you were there from the day it opened. And I've seen those gardens. They're beautiful, even now. And that walled vegetable plot. I bet you grew some stuff there.'

'You'll not flatter me, with your fancy talk,' Ferguson said. 'I told you. I can't tell you anything.'

'Maybe you just need something to jog your memory.' Slater slipped his right hand into his pocket. 'How about this?'

He held the photograph out in front of Ferguson so he could see it. The old man's face seemed to almost fold upon itself but then he quickly looked away.

'Remember now?' asked Slater, gently.

The old man continued to stare into the distance but said nothing. The photograph obviously meant something to him, so Slater decided it would be worth his while to be patient and wait a few minutes if he had to.

'Where on earth did you get that?' the old man asked at last, but he wouldn't look at Slater.

'I told you. We've been making enquiries,' said Slater. 'We found this in a log cabin in the gardens at Hatton House.'

'Is the house still standing?' Ferguson sounded surprised as he turned back to Slater, the track of a solitary tear still wet on his face.

'The house is just about falling down,' explained Slater. 'But the gardens are still beautiful. The lady who lives in the log cabin has looked after them really well. She's kept them just as you did. I bet you would be proud if you could see them now.'

'I don't know what you're talking about.' Ferguson looked at the ground. 'I told you I can't tell you anything.'

'Her name's Florence,' said Slater. 'She told us she was looking for someone called Dougal. Do you remember anyone called Dougal?'

The old man's face crumpled again, but this time he didn't hide it and a sob shook his body. Another tear escaped and began its course down his cheek.

'Aye,' he said, sadly. 'I know Dougal. No one ever called me Gordon. I was always Dougal.'

'You're Dougal?' cried Slater in surprise. 'But she's always asking for you!'

'Why is that such a surprise? I was the only one who ever showed her any kindness.'

'But I thought...' Slater's voice trailed off. He studied the photograph again. 'But, in this photograph she looks terrified. We thought that was because you were abusing her.'

'Me? Ferguson looked appalled. 'I didn't abuse any children.'

'But, this photograph–'

'She wasn't terrified of me, you bloody fool.' Ferguson shook his head furiously. 'She was terrified of the man taking the photograph. And so was I!'

'I think you need to tell me about this, don't you Mr Ferguson?'

'It's a bit late now, son. You couldn't do anything about it back then, and it's way too late to do anything about it now.'

'So you knew about the child abuse back then?'

'I already told you I don't know anything,' said Ferguson. 'They told me if I said anything they'd tell the police about what I'd done and then I'd get put away for life.'

'What did you do that you could get put away for life?' asked Slater.

'It was an accident is what it was. But they said they'd tell the police it wasn't an accident. I didn't know what to do, so in the end I did what they told me.'

Slater was thinking hard. They needed a statement from this man, but it had to be done properly. He was old and upset. By the time they got him to Tinton it would be getting late. He had to consider his health.

'I think I need you to come to Tinton and make a full statement, Mr Ferguson. If I send a car, will you agree to come?'

'I don't think so, no,' said Ferguson.

'I think you have to. It's time the record was put straight. Don't you agree?'

'It's much too late for that, now,' said Ferguson. 'I think you should let sleeping dogs lie. I'm not coming Mr Slater. I'm sorry, but I won't do it.'

O n the way back through reception, Slater found Maggie, the kindly carer.

'Was he alright?' she asked. 'Not too grumpy?'

'He's a bit upset,' explained Slater. 'Things from the past, you know. We need to take a full statement from him, but at the moment he doesn't want to help us. I'll give him a couple of days to think about it and then I'll try again.'

'He's not in any trouble is he?' she asked, anxiously. 'Only he's not well you see. He looks okay, but he's got terminal cancer. We're managing it, but he's probably only got about six months left.'

'It's not what he's done, Maggie. It's what he knows about things others have done.'

'Oh, right,' she said. 'Well, if he changes his mind I don't think it will do him any harm. It's funny, he's been here all this time and never had a visitor, then he gets two in two days.'

'He does?' Slater's curiosity was aroused. 'Who was the other one?'

'It was yesterday evening. It's recorded in the book here, but it doesn't say who the visitor was. I was off duty by then.'

'Who was on duty?'

'That'll be Sheila Watts,' said Maggie. 'But she won't be on duty until later.'

'If I leave my number, do you think it would it be possible for her to call me?' he asked.

'Leave it with me. I'll be handing over to her. I'll tell her myself.'

'Thanks, Maggie. You're an angel,' said Slater, smiling at her.

CHAPTER TWENTY-SEVEN

Slater had been so busy with what he had dubbed The Magic Roundabout inquiry, it seemed to have been a long time since he had spent an uninterrupted evening together with Cindy. He had warned her right from the start that the very nature of his job meant he was always on call, but she had been quite convinced she could cope with that. He knew from painful experience, however, that saying you can cope with a situation and actually being able to cope with it, were two very different things. It was one of the reasons he had insisted they should not move in together yet. It would be much better for her, he had explained, if she didn't feel obliged to be there waiting for him to come home.

But tonight, he had promised her on the phone earlier, she would have his undivided attention. In return, she had promised to cook dinner for him. However, she had warned him, if she was going to go to all that trouble he had to be there on time or it would spoil. If he failed to appear by 7.30pm, it would be going into the dustbin.

Taking heed of her warning, he made it back from Portsmouth with just enough time to get home, shower, change, and drive over to her house, arriving at 7.25pm bearing a chilled bottle of champagne.

'Are we celebrating?' she asked, when he handed her the champagne.

'Yes,' he said. 'We're celebrating how lucky I am to have met you. Now put that bottle down and let me show you how much I've missed you.'

He took the bottle from her and placed it on the floor, before enveloping her in a huge hug and giving her a big wet kiss.

'Oh! Goodness,' she breathed into his ear. 'This is going to have to stop right now, or dinner's going to get ruined.'

'I don't care,' he said, breathing in her wonderful smell.

'I'm sure you don't,' she said, pushing him away. 'But I've been slaving away for hours, and if you don't eat now you'll be hungry later.'

'I'm hungry right now,' he said, a wicked grin crossing his face.

'We'll get to that later, Mr Slater. I haven't been cooking all evening so I can throw it away. Food first, afters after.'

'I can't wait,' he whispered, releasing his hold on her. 'I love afters.'

'I'm sure you only want me for my body,' she said, as she returned to her cooker.

'And the cooking,' he teased, coming up behind her and encircling her with his arms again. 'It's almost as good.'

'Go and find two glasses,' she said, flapping a tea towel at him over her shoulder. 'And get that bottle open. Now.'

By nine o'clock, they had finished dinner, and retreated to the lounge where they had settled together on the settee to finish their champagne.

'We need to clear up,' Cindy said, drowsily.

'Later,' said Slater as he pulled Cindy close to him. 'Let's finish the champagne first.'

But they soon forgot all about finishing champagne and clearing up. Laying so close together, something much more urgent was beginning to capture their attention, and it was something that needed satisfying right now.

'Do you think we should go upstairs?' mumbled Slater as he stopped briefly to draw breath.

'Come on then, quickly,' whispered Cindy, huskily.

She almost dragged him from the settee and ran for the stairs. He chased after her and they fell tumbling at the foot of the stairs, exchanging more kisses, their hands all over each other.

'No, not here,' she said finally, breaking free and rushing up the stairs. 'I really need you, but upstairs. Come on.'

By the time he got to her bedroom, she was already naked and slipping under the covers. He felt himself rising to the occasion as he threw off his own clothes.

'Is that a truncheon I see, Sergeant,' she muttered, saucily. 'Or are you just pleased to see me with my clothes off?'

He stood to attention and saluted.

'If you don't behave yourself, madam,' he said, in his best 'Carry On film' voice, 'I just might have to use it.'

'Oh, officer,' she breathed. 'You'd better show me what you mean.'

Slater thought he was going to burst with excitement as he slid into bed and climbed into position above Cindy's gorgeous, waiting body.

And then his mobile phone began to ring.

'Oh for f–' he began to say.

'Shhh! Ignore it,' she pleaded, putting her finger to his lips to stifle his swearing. 'They can leave a message. Focus on me. My need is much greater than theirs, trust me.'

The phone stopped ringing and he tried desperately hard to concentrate his attention on Cindy and give her what she needed, but it was too late; the moment was gone, and so was his 'truncheon'.

And then the bloody phone started ringing again.

'Oh, for fuck's sake,' she snapped, angrily, into his face. 'There. I've said it for you now. What? Am I not supposed to swear? Or perhaps you think it's the sole preserve of men to have the satisfaction of being able to release their frustration with some good, old-fashioned bad language. And believe me, when I say frustration I really mean frustration.'

Her voice had become increasingly aggressive as she delivered her speech, almost screaming and spitting with anger as she delivered the final sentence right into his face.

Slater was still in position above her, knees between hers, propped up with his hands either side of her face, and for a moment, something in his head told him how absurd the situation was. For a split second, he was close to laughing out loud, but fortunately Cindy seemed to mistake it for a grimace of discomfort rather than the grin it almost became.

And this really was no laughing matter. He had been completely unprepared for a situation like this, and he really didn't know what to say next, or what to do next, but he didn't need to worry. Cindy seemed to know exactly what he should do next.

'Will you go and answer that bloody phone?' she yelled.

'Err, yeah. Of course,' he mumbled. 'It's over there somewhere.' He nodded his head towards his jeans, lying in a heap on the floor.

'Well you'd better go and find it, then,' she snapped.

Sadly, helplessly, he climbed out of bed and found his trousers. He took the phone from his pocket and slipped the trousers on.

'Dave Slater,' he said into the phone.

'Sergeant Slater,' said a woman's voice. 'This is Sheila Watts, from the Belmont Nursing home.'

'Ah, right. Yes, of course,' said Slater, remembering now.

He sat down on the edge of the bed and stared absently at the floor as he listened.

'I'm sorry I'm calling so late,' she said. 'We had an emergency that couldn't wait, you know.'

'That's okay,' he said, thinking it really wasn't okay, but he could hardly complain about her interrupting his sex life, could he? After all, he did leave a message asking her to call.

'Maggie said you were interested in old Dougal's visitor yesterday evening.'

'Yes, that's right,' he said. 'Did the person leave a name?'

He was aware of Cindy moving around but he focused on the call.

'Well, he signed in and out,' she said, 'But I think perhaps he was a doctor, or some sort of professional like that. I certainly can't read his signature, and he didn't bother to print his name like people are supposed to.'

Yeah, a clear signature, and printed name. That would have been way too easy, thought Slater.

'Can you describe him, Mrs Watts?' he asked.

'I would say he was sixtyish,' she said. 'Quite nice looking, about six feet tall, with silver-grey hair. He had nice blue eyes. And he had a lovely smile,' she said. 'He was nice. He looked sort of kind, if you know what I mean.'

Slater thought that could be anyone, really, but it could be useful.

'So there was nothing particularly special about him?' he asked.

'Not really,' she said. 'He had nice aftershave on. Unusual smell it was. Not one I recognised.'

'How was he dressed, in a suit?' asked Slater.

'Oh, no. Casual,' she replied. 'Trousers, a shirt, and a sweater. Quite smart and tidy, but definitely casual.'

'Did you see what car he was driving,' asked Slater, hopefully.

'No, sorry,' she said. 'We can't see the car park from the reception desk. I'm sorry if I'm not being very helpful.'

'Not at all,' Slater lied. 'You've been very helpful, and thank you for taking the time to call me.'

He ended the call. Sheila Watts hadn't been a great deal of help really, and certainly not enough to sacrifice his sex life for, but it wasn't her fault. The timing had been unfortunate, to say the least, but it hadn't been deliberate. The problem was going to be explaining that to Cindy.

He got dressed properly and made his way downstairs. Cindy was in the kitchen, slamming things into the dishwasher.

'I'm sorry about that,' he said. 'It was about this murder case. I forgot I asked that woman to call me back. I had to answer it.'

'You didn't have to even have it switched on,' argued Cindy. 'It's supposed to be your night off. You told me I would have your "undivided attention". Those were the words you used weren't they?'

'Yes,' he said, guiltily. 'Those were the words. And I meant it.'

'Well, obviously that's a lie,' she said. 'Or you would have switched your phone off and made sure no-one could disturb us.'

'I didn't lie, Cindy. To say I lied means you think I did it on purpose to deceive you. Do you really think I'd do that?'

'I don't know what to think right now. I hardly ever see you, and when I do I don't know if you're going to stay, or get dragged off at any

moment. I'm sorry, but I'm not sure I want to spend my life competing
with your job. Do you understand?'

'Ah. I see,' he said. 'It's you or the job, is it? I did warn you right
from day one, that it would be like this, didn't I?'

'Yes,' she admitted, sadly. 'But I had no idea it would be this bad.'

She began to cry. He wanted to hold her, but he stayed where
he was.

'Don't ask me to make this choice now, Cindy. We've only been
together a few months. I could throw my job in today, and then in a
few more months find we have no future anyway.'

'I know,' she sobbed. 'I know. It's just that we never get any time
together. Perhaps if we could go away for a couple of weeks.'

She looked into his face, and now he did go to her, but only to give
her a consoling cuddle.

'A couple of weeks away would be great, but the problem would still
be here when we got back,' he said. 'I think it's best if I go home now.
You need some time to think about what it is you want. Call me when
you're ready to talk, okay?'

He left with a heavy heart. Up until now, he'd thought that if it
came to it he would happily walk away from his job for Cindy, but now
he knew that wasn't the case. Perhaps she wasn't the one after all.

CHAPTER TWENTY-EIGHT

Jolly looked at the clock on the wall. It was almost 8.30am, and so far, there had been no sign of Slater or Norman. It wasn't like either of them to arrive more than a few minutes after 7.30am and if they had to be somewhere else they would have called. She was beginning to wonder what could have happened to them.

Across the other side of the station, in DCI Bob Murray's office, Murray's temper was happening to them. They had both been called first thing this morning with a direct order from the Old Man, in person. This was unheard of.

'Be in my office. Eight o'clock, sharp,' had been the curt instruction. Those seven words conveyed the message loud and clear. This wasn't a request. It was an instruction.

They didn't need to be told why they had been summoned. Maunder had promised they would regret calling on him and it seemed he had been true to his word. For almost half an hour, they had been read the riot act, without let-up. It appeared not only Sir Robert but the chief constable and Sir Robert's solicitor had been on to Murray, and they had obviously got their message across. Murray was now passing on that message, with bells on.

'What on earth were you thinking, going to his house?' he asked them, but he didn't wait for a reply. 'I specifically told you, Norman, to stay away from Sir Robert Maunder, didn't I?'

'Yes, sir,' mumbled Norman.

'With respect, sir,' interrupted Slater, 'that was my decisio-'

'Did I ask you to interrupt?' snapped Murray. 'And don't patronise me with that "with respect" rubbish. If you had any respect for anyone, we wouldn't be having this discussion now.'

Discussion? thought Slater. *That's a laugh.* They hadn't been able to get a word in edgeways for the last half hour. And he was getting seriously pissed off with this "let's protect Sir Robert" crap. The guy might have a knighthood but he was still crooked. Why wouldn't any of them see it?

'If the chief constable had his way, you two would be back directing traffic,' warned Murray. 'I take it you shared the decision to go and annoy Sir Robert yesterday, so whatever either of you has to say now, by way of an explanation, had better be bloody good.'

'Oh,' said Slater, ready for war. 'We are actually allowed to speak, then, are we?'

'I think it would be better for all of us if DS Norman made the excuses, and you kept quiet, Slater,' Murray said after a moment. 'Your lack of respect is going to make you say something you'll regret.'

'Yeah, but-' began Slater.

'You will remain silent,' roared Murray, looking well and truly at the end of his tether. 'Do you understand?'

'Yes, sir,' said a seething Slater. 'I understand.'

'Well, that makes a change,' said Murray.

He turned to Norman.

'It was a joint decision, was it?' he asked.

'Yes sir,' said Norman. 'Based on the evidence we've uncovered we have reason to believe Sir Robert Maunder could well have been involved in child abuse back in the sixties.'

'You do realise who this man is? He's a knight of the realm, for goodness sake. One of the reasons he got that honour was because of his charitable work with, and for, children.'

'Yes, we know all that, sir,' agreed Norman. 'But he wouldn't be the first person to receive a knighthood and then turn out to be not quite the wonderful person everyone had thought he was.'

That's an understatement, Slater thought.

'And this is based on what evidence?' Murray asked.

'You remember Mr Winter, the old guy who seemed to have died by accident but we later found had been murdered? It turns out he grew up in an orphanage Maunder used to frequent. Mr Winter's sister was abused on a regular basis there. Mr Winter names Sir Robert Maunder as the ringleader of the abusers. We even have a copy of a letter he sent to Sir Robert naming him as the ringleader. We think that could have been why he was murdered.'

'Where's this sister now?'

'She's our latest murder victim,' said Norman. 'We believe she was killed because she was the only surviving witness to what happened back then. We also have reason to believe the so-called break-in Sir Robert reported was faked.'

'Why would he fake it?'

'That's what we wanted to know.'

'Why didn't you come and tell me all this before you went up there?'

'Can I speak?' asked Slater.

Murray nodded.

'But think first,' he said, a note of warning in his voice.

'The reason we chose not to tell you was because we thought you'd order us not to go,' explained Slater. 'But the way we saw it we had a legitimate excuse for going up there and we figured it made sense, while we were up there, to shake his tree and see if anything fell out.'

'And did anything fall out?'

'He certainly knows a lot more about what went on at that orphanage than he's admitting,' said Slater.

'And his wife tells me there's nothing wrong with his memory,' added Norman. 'Yet he managed to forget to set the alarm, and then forget to put away her jewels, on the same night.'

'So you think he might have been involved in child abuse, but all you have is the written testimony of a dead man, and your only potential witness is now also dead,' said Murray. 'Is that right?'

'So far,' said Norman.

'So really, you've got no proof.' Murray sighed. 'How do you know this Mr Winter is for real? Maybe he just wanted to smear Sir Robert's name.'

'We haven't found anything to suggest that,' argued Norman.

'That doesn't mean I'm wrong, does it? And then there's the break-in? What are you suggesting, insurance fraud? You've seen his house. Does he really look as though he's short of money?'

Slater sighed heavily.

'Why are you all so convinced this guy's a saint?' he asked.

'Because so far, you've given me no compelling evidence to believe he isn't. Why are you so sure he isn't?'

'I just know it,' said Slater.

'Gut instinct isn't a reliable form of evidence. It's certainly not a good enough reason to go charging around accusing someone,' said Murray. 'If you want to change my mind you'll need to bring me something a bit more convincing than your personal hunch. In the meantime, you do not go near Sir Robert, his wife, or his house, without first speaking to me, unless, of course, you'd like to be directing traffic. Is that clear?'

'Yessir,' they choused.

'Now clear off and do something useful, like solving those two murders,' said Murray. 'And I want to be kept informed of all developments. As you don't seem to be able to keep yourselves out of trouble I suppose I'll have to monitor what you're doing. As if I don't already have enough to do.'

'Can I ask one more question?' asked Norman.

'Go on,' growled Murray.

'Who's Maunder's solicitor?'

Murray studied the notepad he'd scrawled the chief constable's dire warnings on.

'Someone called John Hunter,' he said.

Slater exchanged a look with Norman.

'Does it matter?' Murray asked.

'No, probably not. Just curious,' said Norman.

'Well, that just about rounds off a fabulous twelve hours in the wonderfully fulfilling life of DS Dave Slater,' grumbled Slater to Norman, as they walked across to the canteen.

'Problems?'

'I think Cindy's had enough.' Slater sighed, miserably. 'We had a big bust-up last night.'

'Don't tell me,' said Norman. 'It's the old "me or the job" argument, right?'

'You said it.'

'It always happens. I bet there's not a cop alive who hasn't had the same problem.'

They were in the canteen now. Slater was collecting three coffees.

'And doughnuts,' Norman reminded him. 'This is definitely a doughnut morning after that bollocking from the Old Man.'

They gathered up their drinks and cakes and headed back to their office.

'The thing is,' continued Slater, going back to the original conversation, 'I actually thought, if it came to it, I would give up the job for her, you know? But now I'm not sure I would.'

'Torn between two lovers,' said Norman. 'That's bad news. So what are you going to do?'

'I told her we should spend some time apart. See if we can work out what we both really want. I told her to call me when she's ready to talk.'

'Wow. So this is really serious. D'you think you'll work it out?'

'Seriously? No, I don't think we will,' said Slater.

'Oh, shit,' said Norman, and he looked genuinely concerned. 'I'm sorry to hear that. Are you okay?'

'That's the weird thing,' said Slater. 'Now I've slept on it, I'm actually feeling quite relieved.'

'Oh. Right.' Norman hovered for a moment, as if he didn't know what to say. He gave an uncertain smile then pushed their office door open, stepping aside to allow Slater to carry their goodies through.

'I suppose that says quite a lot of negative stuff about me and the depth of my feelings,' suggested Slater as he stepped into the room.

'I think it says a whole lot more about the depth of your relationship with Cindy,' observed Norman, as he followed him in.

Jolly had commandeered the spare desk. She was going through piles of dusty old files and papers she had recovered from the County Council archive.

'Where on earth have you two been?' she asked, looking up from her work. 'I've been worried sick. You never called or left a message.'

'When the Old Man calls, personally, to summon you to his office first thing in the morning, Jane,' replied Slater, placing the refreshments on his desk, 'you're so busy wondering what's going to happen you tend not to think about telling anyone. I'm sorry. We should have let you know.'

'But we have brought coffee and doughnuts as compensation,' Norman piped up.

'He called himself?' said Jolly, looking surprised. 'That must have been important. Am I allowed to ask what he wanted?'

'Two detective sergeants for breakfast,' answered Norman, with a wry smile.

'Why? What have you done?'

'We dared to suggest that the well-known saint, Sir Robert Maunder, might not be quite as holy as the chief constable thinks he is,' explained Slater.

'Apparently if we want to speak to him again, or even mention his name, we have to get special permission,' added Norman.

'That's going to make things rather awkward,' said Jolly. 'If he's out of bounds it's going to be a bit like having your hands tied behind your back.'

'It makes it difficult,' said Slater. 'But not impossible. Even with our hands tied, we can still ask questions. There are plenty of other avenues to explore without going anywhere near Maunder.'

'Speaking of which...' Jolly turned back to her dusty papers. 'I've been looking through this Hatton House stuff I found yesterday. I've got a long way to go yet, but there's a record of kids added to the register as new arrivals. I've compared it with the list of kids sent there through Child Welfare and it seems there were more kids sent than were actually registered as arriving.'

'What?' asked Norman.

'Yes, it's a bit strange, isn't it? I thought I'd made a mistake at first, but I've double checked. There are at least five kids who were sent there but never appeared on the Hatton House register. One of them is Julia Winter or, as we know her, Florence. Her brother is registered, but there's no sign of her name appearing anywhere. According to the records she never arrived there.'

'Because she was a Special One,' said Slater. 'That's exactly what Mr Winter said. The Special Ones were kept apart from the others.'

'And if they weren't on any register they didn't officially exist,' added Norman. 'So anyone visiting the home could check the number of kids against the register but wouldn't realise there were some others hidden away.'

'But what happened to them?' asked Jolly. 'Where did they go? Surely when they grow up they have to move them on somewhere else.'

'Or dispose of them,' said Slater, ominously.

'Oh, don't say that,' Norman said, sighing heavily. 'I hate dealing with dead kids, even if they died fifty years ago.'

'We can't ignore the possibility, can we?' said Slater. 'We're going to have to search the grounds.'

'D'you want me to go and see Becksy?' said Norman. 'We're going to need some fancy equipment, and a lot of search trained people, if we're gonna search those gardens. They're huge.'

'Let me go,' said Slater. 'I think it's time I went down there and made peace, don't you?'

'And what about John Hunter?' asked Norman. 'His name seems to be cropping up a bit too often for my liking. First he's Winter's solicitor. Now he's Maunder's solicitor.'

Jolly had looked up at the sound of Hunter's name.

'So, he's a solicitor,' she said, quickly. 'And Tinton's a small town. I think you'll find there aren't exactly huge numbers of solicitors to choose from.'

'How would you describe him, Jane?' asked Slater.

'What sort of question is that?'

'Just humour me a minute.'

'Well,' she began, her face slightly pink. 'He's in his sixties, six feet plus, nice looking, with silver-grey hair, and blue eyes. He's got a very reassuring manner that creates a sense of trust. Oh, and he smells nice.'

'You fancy him,' teased Norman. 'Do you go around sniffing all the men you meet?'

'No, I do not fancy him,' she protested, but her cheeks blushed a deeper shade of pink. 'I simply mean he wears nice aftershave. He's a very nice man and, I'll have you know, it makes a change to meet a real gentleman once in a while.'

'So what's wrong with us?' asked Norman, looking offended.

'You're different,' said Jolly.

'Thank you, Jane,' said Slater, jumping in before Norman got carried away with his "hurt and offended" act. 'That's almost exactly the description of the man who went to see Gordon Ferguson the night before last.'

'Well, well, well,' said Norman. 'Another coincidence. We'd better put him on our visit list. At least we don't have to ask permission to speak to him, unless, of course, Jane here has a problem with that.'

'Oh, hush,' said Jolly. 'If you want to waste your time, that's your affair. I'm sure he'll have a perfectly good explanation for being there.'

'Wow,' said Norman. 'You really do think he's special, don't you?'

'Of course not,' she said, turning back to her work. But the colour that had risen to her face told a different story.

CHAPTER TWENTY-NINE

After his earlier dressing down, Slater thought it might be prudent to inform Murray what they had unearthed, and of his intention to initiate a search of the gardens. To his amazement, Murray gave him the go-ahead without imposing any conditions. Before the Old Man could have a change of heart, he'd headed straight down to the basement to speak to Ian Becks.

He had been expecting a hard time from Becks after their disagreement, but to his surprise the forensics chief appeared to have forgiven and forgotten. Or at least he said he had. Slater found this hard to believe from a man who had a reputation for sulking and bearing grudges, and he fully expected the situation to come back and bite him on the arse at some point in the future, but right now he was far more concerned with getting a team out to search the grounds at Hatton House.

Half an hour later Becks was on the phone.

'Right,' he said. 'I've got a team ready to start work this afternoon, and I've even managed to rustle up a couple of cadaver dogs to help us out.'

'Will we need them?' asked Slater. 'If there are any bodies out there, they'll have been underground for fifty years. It won't be cadavers we'll find, just skeletons.'

'You don't look a gift horse in the mouth, mate. I think we were offered them because the dogs need the practise, but one of them is a bit of a legend and is supposed to have detected a skeleton before, so it can't do any harm, can it? I've also managed to scrounge one of those GPR – ground-penetrating radar – systems. I did the training ages ago. I was beginning to wonder if I would ever get the chance to put it into practice.'

'Does it find skeletons?'

'Only if we're very lucky. But it can detect the sort of disturbance that would be made in the ground by digging a grave. It works hand in hand with the dogs.'

'So we're all set then,' said Slater. 'What time do you want to get started?'

'Make it two o'clock. The dogs will be here by then, and everyone will have had time to eat before we start.

'I'll go on up there and make sure we can access the site without any hassle,' said Slater.

He hadn't yet mentioned to Becks that they didn't have the faintest idea where to start looking.

As promised, by two o'clock Ian Becks and his team were on site and ready to go. They had all gathered around Slater, looking expectant, but there was a bit of a problem. The sky above them was a dirty grey colour. It wasn't raining yet, but it was on the way.

'What do you mean you have no idea where to search?' Becks asked Slater. 'Surely you must have some idea? You haven't brought us out here on a wild goose chase, have you?'

As the implications of Becks' question sunk in, Slater found himself surrounded by hostile faces and accusing looks. He shifted uncomfortably.

'Alright everyone, I can see how this looks, but let me explain,' he began, awkwardly. 'We know, for sure, that at least five of the kids who were sent here back in the sixties were never registered as arriving, and seem to have disappeared without trace. The reason we're so sure this is fact is because Mr Winter and his sister were sent here at the same time. He appears on the register but she doesn't.

'According to the evidence we have found so far, there was a group of kids called "The Special Ones". We believe these were the pretty kids. Boys and girls, they were kept to one side and don't appear on any register anywhere. So, officially they didn't exist anymore. The Special Ones were being regularly abused.'

He stopped for a moment to let this news sink in.

'Surely someone would have noticed?' asked one of the dog handlers.

'You'd like to think so, wouldn't you? But what if the person who would be in a position to notice was part of the paedophile ring doing the abusing?'

'Oh, no, you're kidding,' said the dog handler, looking horrified.

'Not certain yet, but that's how it looks,' said Slater, grimly.

There were a few angry murmurs, and Slater knew he had them on his side.

'The question is,' he continued, 'what did they do with these kids when they finished with them? Presumably they reach a "sell-by-date" and have to be disposed of.'

'And you think they were murdered and buried here somewhere,' finished Becks.

'We figure it's the most likely scenario, so we can't ignore it,' said Slater. 'But the problem is, I can't tell you where to start looking.'

'Then we'll just have to look everywhere,' said the dog handler, with grim determination. 'It's not right they should just be dumped like so much useless rubbish. They deserve better.'

The earlier murmurs had turned into full voices now, and they were all agreed.

'Right,' said Ian Becks, turning to his search team. 'We will cover the whole place, but we'll do it in sections, and we'll cover each section thoroughly before we move to the next. As it's surrounded by a wall, why don't we start with the vegetable garden? Get those two dogs going and I'll join you with the GPR gear.'

The team headed off towards the vegetable garden, while Becks and Slater headed for the vehicles, parked around the front of the old house; Becks to collect his GPR equipment, and Slater to find his wellies from the boot of his car.

'But some of that ground must have been dug over, again and again,' said Slater. 'Surely that will affect the results.'

'Yes,' agreed Becks. 'But if you had buried a body in there, and you knew exactly where it was, would you keep digging that particular bit of ground over?'

'Ah, right. I see what you're saying.' Slater felt a little foolish.

'I'm afraid we're likely to make a mess of these gardens. Especially if it starts raining.'

'I don't think anyone will complain,' said Slater, sadly. 'The only person who cared is dead now.'

'This has affected you a lot, hasn't it?' asked Becks.

'It's the old man and his sister, Becksy,' said Slater. 'Especially the sister. I mean, can you imagine? She had been in hiding since they were little kids. I'm like Norm, I hate dealing with stuff like this.'

'Where is he anyway?'.

'He'll be here soon. He just had to make a call on the way.'

They had reached the forensic team's Transit van. Becks swung the back doors open.

'Thanks for this, Ian,' said Slater. 'I'm sorry I can't point you in the right direction.'

'No problem,' said Becks. 'If those dogs are as good as they're supposed to be, and there are kids buried here somewhere, we'll find them.'

He looked up at the sky, then reached inside, grabbed the portable GPR machine, and began to sling the straps over his shoulders.

'With two dogs and this magic machine, we can't fail,' he said, smiling confidently. 'It just might take a bit longer, that's all. Just keep your fingers crossed that it doesn't start raining too soon. It'll get a lot more difficult if that happens.'

Slater watched him march off towards the vegetable garden and then ambled across to his own car. He flipped up the boot and began to rummage through the heap of assorted coats, shoes, and general paraphernalia he carried around until he eventually found two wellies and a waterproof coat.

As he stood the wellies on the ground and eased his feet into them, he could hear a car approaching up the drive. The unique assortment of sounds confirmed it must be Norman's. It had to be. No one else he knew would be seen dead in that car. Sure enough, a few seconds later Norman's car appeared coming up the drive. He waved nonchalantly as his car rattled up alongside the others, then he crunched it into reverse gear, and the car whined and squeaked into position alongside Slater's.

Slater stood and watched as the driver's door swung open, dropping a good inch or two on its worn hinges as it did so. As his colleague eased himself out of his seat, Slater was sure he heard the car breathe a sigh of relief, and saw the suspension rise a couple of inches. He then watched as Norman failed to slam the door shut three times before he remembered he had to lift it to make up for the worn hinges.

'You should sell that car to the nearest circus,' said Slater.

'There's nothing wrong with my car,' said Norman, indignantly. 'It works just fine.'

'Yeah, right. But it would look much better in a circus ring. The clowns would love it.'

'You don't know what you're missing. Look and learn. This is a piece of British engineering, history.'

'Yeah. I've looked,' said Slater, laughing. 'And I've learnt this car is from the period when we were making really shite cars.'

'I'm just gonna rise above such ignorant remarks,' Norman muttered.

Slater had just noticed a faint odour that seemed to be surrounding Norman. He stepped closer to Norman and took a cautious sniff.

'Blimey, what's that stink?' he asked.

'I don't know what you mean,' said Norman, haughtily. 'I can't smell anything.'

Slater stepped closer still and sniffed again.

'Have you been and bought some new aftershave?' he asked, suspiciously. 'You weren't wearing any earlier.'

'I might have nipped into a shop on the way over,' admitted Norman, blushing slightly.

'Ha!' Slater let out a roar of laughter. 'You're not trying to impress Jolly Jane, are you? Cos if you are, you've made the wrong choice there, mate. That stuff stinks!'

'Well that's where you're wrong, Mr Philistine. I'll have you know this is the very latest-' Norman began.

'Is this because of what she said about John Hunter?' interrupted Slater.

'Of course not.'

'You're sweet on her aren't you?'

'Crap,' said Norman. 'She's a colleague. I am not-'

'I always thought you had a soft spot for her,' interrupted Slater again. 'You'll be ironing your clothes next.'

'Don't you have any work to do? I didn't come up here so you could take the piss.'

'Well, if you didn't want me to take the piss you shouldn't have come up here smelling like a polecat,' said Slater, beaming.

'Like a polecat!' Norman's face drooped. 'Do you know how much this stuff cost?'

'You paid for it?' said Slater. 'Seriously?'

'Oh, screw you. Your problem is you have no taste. I've told you this before.'

Looking at the offended expression on Norman's face, Slater thought it was probably time to stop teasing him and get back to work. But it had been good to have a laugh for a couple of minutes to lift their mood, even if it was at Norm's expense.

'So what did Mr Hunter have to say for himself?' he asked, returning to the more serious business at hand.

'His story is that he's Gordon Ferguson's solicitor,' replied Norman. 'Apparently he's been doing Gordon's will. He went to see him to finalise the details.'

'Yeah, right,' said Slater, sceptically. 'So it's just coincidental he was there the night before me.'

'Right,' said Norman. 'And did you know, in my spare time I'm the Queen of Sheba?'

'Well, that would explain the smell,' muttered Slater, as Norman creaked open the boot of his car and fished out his own wellies and raincoat.

'What's that?'

'I said that boot creaks real bad when you open it.'

'I need to know a bit more about John Hunter,' said Norman. 'And I intend to do just that when we've finished up here.'

'According to the nurse I spoke to, Gordon doesn't get any visitors,' said Slater. 'So how has he been working on Gordon's will?'

'That'll be one of many questions I'll be asking,' replied Norman, slipping on his wellies. 'In the meantime, let's go see how good these dogs are.'

The walled vegetable garden must have been an impressive sight in its heyday but even now, it was still quite a sight. Whatever difficulties Florence might have had, an ability to grow plants and look after a huge garden was not one of them. When Norman and Slater had been here before, they had only glanced at the vegetable garden in passing. Now they were able to take a closer look it was obvious, even to these two non-gardeners, that she must have put an enormous amount of work into keeping these gardens neat and tidy.

At the far end, almost fifty yards away, Ian Becks was marching around pointing his GPR equipment here and there, while the two spaniels were working busily away at the behest of their handlers, noses to the ground and tails wagging furiously. Three more men were in attendance, armed with a pick, spades, and shovels should they be needed. Slater and Norman took the opportunity to poke around in the two long lean-to greenhouses that ran along the south facing wall. Along one shelf, various seeds had been sown in trays and, on another shelf, small plants were being nurtured and prepared for the coming spring.

'Jeez, look at this,' said Norman, a look of awe on his face. 'Are you sure she was doing all this on her own?'

'Can't be sure about it,' said Slater. 'But who the hell else could have been helping her?'

'I can't believe she did this all on her own. I mean, lots of people can manage to grow a few fruit and veg, but run a garden this size? And look after the rest of the gardens too? It takes training to learn all this stuff.'

'It's hard to believe isn't it?' agreed Slater. 'From what I've seen and heard she wasn't exactly all there, was she?'

'If there isn't anyone else, who's going to grow these on now? What a waste.'

'She was even growing fruit trees against the wall in the other greenhouse.' Slater peered through the window in the wall dividing the two glasshouses.

'If she was a veggie,' said Norman, 'she surely would have been self-sufficient with all this lot.'

'Maybe she found the gardens good therapy,' said Slater. 'I mean, the TV show might have helped, but there's only so many times you can watch the same thing over and over, right? But looking after these gardens would be a full time job, and it changes with the seasons, so it's not the same thing all the time. Perhaps immersing herself in the gardens helped to keep out her demons.'

'And there's the satisfaction of creating. Like growing stuff and eating it. That has to make you feel good, even if it's only at a subconscious level.'

Slater looked to the far end of the garden. Everyone seemed to be gathering in one area.

'Looks like they might be on to something,' he said. 'Let's go and see.'

They stomped across to the search team, which seemed to have become focused around the compost heap.

'Have you found something?' asked Slater.

One of the handlers pointed to his spaniel, which was sitting at one corner of the compost heap.

'There might be something here,' he said. 'But I can't guarantee it. With the compost heap being here it could be there's something inside giving off the same smell.'

The heap was about four feet high. Ian Becks was stood on top, studying the small screen of the GPR, trying to make sense of what he was seeing.'

'What do you think, Ian?' called Slater.

'It's difficult to say,' he answered, stepping from the heap and heading towards them. 'I would imagine a compost heap in a working vegetable garden like this gets disturbed all the time so I'm not surprised I can't get a reading. But if the dog says we should look here, I think we should listen to what it's saying. If you think about it, this would be a bloody good place to hide a body.

'For a start, the heat from the compost would speed up decomposition, and you don't keep moving your compost heap around, do you? I think we should clear the heap down to ground level and then take another look.'

'That makes sense to me,' said Norman.

'It would have been the last place I would have looked,' agreed Slater.

'Right guys,' said Becks, to his two diggers. 'Let's get this lot moved.'

He stood back next to Slater and Norman and watched as his team went into action. After a few seconds, he turned to Slater.

'What's that funny smell?' he asked.

Slater inclined his head towards Norman.

'Someone's got new aftershave,' he said, grinning.

Becks turned his gaze to the unfortunate Norman.

'We're trying to use working dogs, here,' he said, struggling to keep a straight face. 'They've got very sensitive noses. That stuff's going to overpower anything less powerful than a skunk.'

Norman looked at Becks, then Slater, and then back to Becks.

'I have only two words to say to you peasants,' he said huffily. 'And the second one is off.'

Slater and Becks roared with laughter.

Twenty minutes later, the compost heap had been removed and a layer of loose soil removed. The spaniels were set loose again. Almost immediately, the older of the two dogs found what he was sniffing for and sat down to indicate where he thought there was a body. Fine drizzle began to fall as Ian Becks moved in and swept the area with his GPR machine.

'I think we might have something here,' he said, his excitement affecting all of them. But the rain was getting worse now. He looked up at the sky which had turned a dark, slate grey since they'd been on site. 'We need to get a tent over this. If it gets too wet it'll turn into a quagmire in no time.'

The dogs had done their work for now. There was no point keeping them out in the rain just for the sake of it, so they were taken back to their vehicle. It was going to be shovel power from here on in. But by the time the tent was erected, the rain had turned to hail and the sky had become so black it was like night, even though it was still an hour before sunset. Then, as the six figures huddled under the tent, there was a flash of lightning and an ominous rumble from the sky.

'I'm sorry, but I think we're going to have to leave this until the morning,' said Ian Becks. 'We haven't got good enough lights to work out here in this, and I'm not happy having my people out here in this weather. And I can't get the overtime sanctioned anyway.'

Slater wasn't exactly over the moon at this news, but he wasn't really surprised. There didn't seem to be any money available for anything at the moment, and they still had two months to go before the year-end.

'I think you're right,' he agreed reluctantly. 'If there are any bodies under here they've been here for fifty years. Another day won't make a whole lot of difference. Maybe the weather will be a bit brighter in the morning.'

'We'll be back here at eight,' promised Becks. 'There's no point in you coming out here to stand around. I'll call you as soon as we find anything.'

'You sound very confident,' Norman observed.

'I've just got a feeling,' said Becks.

CHAPTER THIRTY

It was nine-thirty the next morning when Slater took the call he had been waiting to hear, but not wanting to hear, from Ian Becks.

'We've found a skull,' said Becks. 'I'm no expert, but I think it's an adult, not a child.'

'An adult?' exclaimed Slater. 'But we don't have a missing adult. All the staff are accounted for.'

'So, maybe they had staff who weren't registered to look after the kids who weren't registered.'

'Yeah, but...' Slater didn't really know what to say. He hadn't been expecting this.

'I've already phoned for the mobile pathology team,' said Becks. 'I had warned them we might need their help. They're on the way here now. They should be here by lunchtime. In the meantime, they've asked us to stop digging until they arrive.'

'Right,' said Slater. 'There's no point in us rushing up there until you've got something for us to see. In the meantime, I think there's someone me and Norm need to speak to about those gardens. And before I do anything I need to speak to a higher authority.'

'I should also let you know the dogs have found another possible site.'

'You're kidding me. I thought you said they couldn't detect skeletons.'

'It might be a false alarm, but it's the same dog that found this one, so I'm not going to argue. This time there's a shed on top, so I figure it's a good bet.'

'What have we got up there, Ian, a bloody graveyard?' asked an appalled Slater.

'It's beginning to look like it, isn't it?'

'Okay. Thanks for calling. We'll call in later this afternoon to see how you're doing.'

Slater put the phone back with a heavy heart.

'Problems?' asked Jolly.

'They've found one body already, and one of the dogs seems to think there's another site close by,' he said.

'Oh. I see. Not so good then,' she said, grimly.

'I'm beginning to wonder what exactly we've uncovered up there.'

'You can see why Mr Winter's death was made to look like an accident now, can't you?' said Jolly. 'And if the house hadn't been ransacked we would never have suspected any different.'

'No. That's not right. You suspected from the start. I was the one who dismissed the idea out of hand. If you hadn't been so convinced it wasn't right, we'd never have got anywhere.'

'Just a lucky hunch,' she said.

'The Old Man told me hunches are unreliable,' said Slater, ruefully. 'That wasn't the case here was it?'

He pushed back his chair.

'Talking of the Old Man,' he said, 'I suppose I'd better go and tell him about our latest development. Maybe now he'll let us start investigating Sir Robert bloody Maunder properly.'

'Come.' Murray's voiced boomed through the door.

Slater opened the door just enough to poke his head through.

'Err, have you got a minute, Boss?' he asked.

'Well, come in, man,' said Murray, mildly. 'There's no need to hide behind the door. I don't bite.'

'I thought you were going to the other day.'

'This isn't about Sir Robert again, is it?' Murray sighed. 'You don't give up do you?'

'You told us to carry on investigating the two murders,' explained Slater. 'And you said it was okay to start a search of the grounds, so we have. Now the search team have uncovered a body. Or at least they've found a skull, but that's what we'd expect if the body's been there for fifty years.'

'Oh bugger,' said Murray, wearily.

'And the cadaver dogs have indicated another grave,' added Slater.

'What do you want from me?'

'I need your permission to investigate Maunder,' said Slater. 'We can't ignore the possibility any longer, boss. We need to interview him properly.'

'Let me make some calls. It might be better if he volunteered to come in and be interviewed. In the meantime, I'll get you a warrant to start checking out his financials etc. But I don't want you making a song and dance about it, right? I want it low key.'

'Of course,' agreed Slater. 'Believe it or not, I'm not enjoying this, Guv.'

'Low key?' said Norman, indignantly. 'If it was anyone else we'd be speeding up there with a search warrant and a dozen uniforms. But because it's Sir Robert Maunder he's going to be invited to come in for a chat. Talk about one rule for us and one for them.'

Slater knew exactly what Norman was getting so uptight about, but there was nothing they could do about it.

'So what do we do in the meantime?' asked Norman. 'Sit on our hands and wait?'

'I've got a much better idea than that,' said Slater. 'Jane knows what to look for so it's best if she stays here and keeps on digging into Maunder's affairs. In the meantime, we are going down to Portsmouth.'

'What's at Portsmouth?'

'Who's the one person who might know what exactly *is* buried in those gardens and where?'

'Of course.' Norman grinned. 'Gordon the gardener.'

CHAPTER THIRTY-ONE

'You'll see why I suggested you bring your coat now,' Slater said to Norman as he parked his car outside the Belmont Nursing Home.

'But these places always have the heating wound up so it's like a sauna,' argued Norman. 'We won't need coats in there.'

'The thing is we won't be in there,' said Slater, with a grin. 'Gordon's a gardener, right? He still prefers the great outdoors. He'll be sitting out on the terrace at the back, all on his lonesome, staring out to sea.'

'What are you, psychic?' asked Norman.

'No. I just thought it would be a good idea to phone ahead and make sure it was okay to come. Apparently it's all he's done since I came last time.'

'No shit. Good job I brought my hat and gloves too.'

They found Ferguson exactly where Slater had left him last time he came. They took a seat either side of him. If he noticed them, he didn't show it, continuing to stare off across the sea at nothing in particular.

'Hello, Dougal,' said Slater. 'It is ok if I call you Dougal, is it?'

'You can call me whatever you like,' said Ferguson without looking at Slater or Norman. 'I've nothing to say to you.'

'This is my colleague, DS Norman,' continued Slater. 'He's working with me on the Hatton House case.'

'We went up there and looked at the gardens,' said Norman. 'Someone's been doing a great job looking after them. We figured it must be someone who knows what they're doing, like a retired gardener, perhaps.'

For the first time, Ferguson moved his gaze away from the sea. He turned and looked at Norman as if he was a gibbering idiot.

'It's all I can do to get from my room out to this bloody terrace, son,' he said. 'I'm dyin' of the cancer. Do you really think I could get up there and look after a garden?'

'I didn't mean you,' said Norman. 'But maybe you had someone helping you back then.'

'The only one I ever let help me in that garden was my wife, and then when she died I was on my own, until young Florence turned up. She loved the gardens. If she's living there she'll be the one taking care of the plants. She won't need any help, she's a natural.'

'Wow,' said Norman. 'She must be even better than I thought.'

'It's time for you to start talking, Dougal,' said Slater. 'You can't keep on saying nothing.'

The old man returned his gaze to the sea once more.

'D'you know what a cadaver dog is, Dougal?' asked Norman.

The old man didn't appear to move, but Norman had spotted the slight, nervous, tic that briefly affected his right eye.

'They're amazing animals,' said Norman. 'Their noses are so sensitive they can detect a dead body underground. They can smell the decay. It's incredible. We've got one that can even detect skeletons long after the body's decomposed.'

The tic worsened.

'The thing is,' confided Norman, 'we've been searching the walled vegetable garden at Hatton House. You remember that walled garden, right? You'll recall there's a big old compost heap. Guess what one of our dogs has found under it?'

The old man said nothing.

'But then, we don't think you need to guess what the dog found, do you, Dougal? You know exactly what that dog found, and you know whose body it is.'

The old man sniffed a couple of times, shifted uncomfortably in his seat, and pulled a huge handkerchief from his pocket. He blotted his eyes, but continued to stare out to sea.

'I should deny it and tell you I know nothing,' he said at last. 'But I've carried that secret for fifty years and now I'm close to meeting my maker maybe it's time to confess and get rid of my burden.'

'Confess to what, Dougal?' asked Slater. 'Is this what you were telling me the other day? About how they had threatened to report you to the police?'

'I didn't kill her,' said Ferguson, vehemently. 'It was an accident. She slipped and fell, hit her head. It was just a terrible accident.'

'Who?' asked Norman. 'Who are you talking about?'

'My wife, of course,' said Ferguson. 'It would have been my word against theirs. I didn't know what else to do, so I did as they said and buried her in the garden. If anyone asked I was to tell them she'd run away with another man.'

'You buried your wife under a compost heap?' asked Norman, aghast.

'So what are you going to do about it?' snapped Ferguson, turning to face Norman, clearly upset by the whole situation. 'You want to throw me in jail? Fine. I'll be dead in six months so what do I care?'

'Just calm down, Dougal,' said Slater. 'No one's going to throw you in jail. But you know it's time you told us everything, don't you?'

The old man turned his gaze back to the sea.

'Even now,' said Slater, 'fifty years on, people are still dying because of what went on back then. Do you think that's right, Dougal? If you tell us what you know we can stop this before anyone else dies.'

'You'll have to arrest me,' said Ferguson. 'And even then you'll be wastin' your time. I'm telling you nothing. Now, what time is it?'

'Coming up for three-thirty,' said Norman.

'They'll be coming to take me in for my doctor's appointment shortly. So you might as well be on your way.'

'Tell me about Florence,' said Slater.

'There's nothing to tell.'

'What about The Magic Roundabout?'

'I don't know what you mean.'

'Oh, come on, Dougal,' said Norman, impatiently. 'She had posters and toys. She was Florence, her brother was Dylan, and you're Dougal. Was it her escape?'

'What do you mean she *had* posters? You said she *was* Florence. What's happened to her?'

'I'm sorry, but she was murdered, Dougal,' said Slater. 'Bashed over the head and then dumped into the freezing canal. It was DS Norman, here, who found her.'

'We think she was killed because someone thought she knew something and was going to talk,' said Norman. 'She had been hiding for the best part of fifty years. So what did she know that make her hide for all that time, and still get her killed?

The old man said nothing, but he seemed to slump even lower in his seat. A tear slipped quietly from his eye and rolled slowly down his cheek.

'Poor wee thing,' he muttered.

'Mr Ferguson,' called an approaching female voice. 'Come on inside now. Dr McKenzie's here to see you.'

'Can you help me to my feet?' said Ferguson, turning to Slater. 'I have to see the cancer doctor just now.'

They helped him inside for his appointment and made their way back to the car.

'So, what do we do now?' asked Norman as they climbed in. 'Poor old guy can hardly walk from A to B. If we arrest him there's a good chance it might kill him.'

'Yeah,' sighed Slater. 'I thought telling him about Florence might have been enough to tip him over the edge, you know?'

'Perhaps it would have if that nurse hadn't whisked him away at the vital moment,' said Norman, gloomily.

'Maybe he'll feel different when he's had time to think about it,' suggested Slater. 'He's obviously scared of something, or someone, but there must be a tipping point. Perhaps we need to find a child's body. Maybe then we would have a big enough lever to overcome his fear.'

'I suppose he's not going anywhere in the meantime, is he?' agreed Norman.

They had only been on the road for ten minutes when Slater's mobile phone began to ring.

'Hi Becksy, what have you got for us?'

'Are you in the car?' asked Becks.

'Yeah,' said Slater. 'But I'm hands free so you're alright. I've got Norm here too.'

'Right,' said Becks. 'You wouldn't believe the progress we've made this afternoon. I was expecting two forensic pathologists to arrive, but they've brought a small army of students with them.'

'Sounds like chaos,' said Norman.

'These are keen students,' said Becks, laughing. 'They've come to learn, and they're not frightened of hard work.'

'So what have you found?' asked Slater.

'They've not finished yet, obviously, so these results are yet to be confirmed, but so far, we've recovered the skeleton of an adult female and two children from beneath the compost heap.'

'Any idea what age these kids were?' asked Slater.

'They're guessing right now, but they reckon about twelve years old.'

'Shit!' said Norman, in dismay. 'So when they finished abusing them they just killed them?'

'Looks that way, doesn't it?' said Becks. 'Do you want to hear the rest?'

'There's more?' asked Norman.

'Well, yeah,' said Becks. 'Remember I said the dog had suggested we check under the shed? Well, with all these workers around it was no trouble to clear the area and start digging there, too. We've found three more children, so far.'

Slater swore, loudly.

'How many more are you going to find?' asked Norman, appalled.

'We've already got more than I ever wanted to have to deal with,' said Becks, grimly. 'We've been working the dogs as well, but they've not found any more sites. They've finished for the day, but they'll be back tomorrow as well.'

'Well, thanks for letting us know, Ian,' said Slater. 'Are you working into the night?'

'We don't plan to. The light's fading already. We think we've maybe got another hour at best, then we're going to call a halt until tomorrow.'

'I'm not sure we can get there before you've finished,' said Slater. 'We'll catch you tomorrow. Thanks for what you're doing, Ian.'

'I'd like to say it's a pleasure,' said Becks, 'but I'll be bloody glad to get out of here.'

'I think we'll all be glad when this is over,' said Norman.

Ten minutes later, the phone was ringing again.

'Hi, Jane,' said Slater.

'I thought I'd better ring,' she said. 'I didn't know what time you would be back, and I didn't want to miss you.'

'What have you got?'

'Maunder's broke,' she began. 'He's already received a payment from the insurance company, yet that money's gone straight out again in cash withdrawals.'

'How the hell did he get paid out already?' asked Norman.

'I guess if you're a knight of the realm, you get special treatment. I've also been looking at his mobile phone records. He doesn't use it very often, but one of the numbers he calls, and gets calls from, is another mobile phone. I've checked but it's not registered to anyone. It's a pay-as-you-go phone.'

'A burner,' said Norman. 'This smells.'

'Oh, it stinks, Norm,' said Jolly. 'All the calls have occurred around the time Dylan and Florence died.'

CHAPTER THIRTY-TWO

'One adult and five children?' Bob Murray looked horrified when Slater and Norman broke the news to him. 'Who's the adult?'

'We believe she was the wife of Gordon Ferguson who was the gardener there at the time. He has suggested he buried her there.'

'What do you mean, "he has suggested he buried her there"?' asked Murray.

'We tracked him down and went to speak to him,' said Slater. 'We're sure he knows what was going on, but something, or someone, has put the wind up him.'

'There's also the problem he's almost ninety years old and he's dying,' added Norman.

'I don't care about that,' said Murray. 'We've got six dead bodies. You bring him in here and find out what he knows.'

'Yes, Guv,' said Slater. 'I'll get him in here tomorrow.'

'What about Maunder?' asked Norman. 'We need to question him. When's he coming in?'

'He's not,' said Murray, shifting uncomfortably. 'We suggested it would be in his interests to come in, but he's refused.'

'Guvnor,' said Norman, impatiently. 'We've got six bodies buried in the gardens of an old children's home. All the staff who used to work there seem to have very conveniently died, except for the old gardener. The only other person who may have some idea what was going on is Maunder. We have no choice. We have to question him, and you know it.'

'On what grounds? Where's the proof?'

'This bogus robbery of his,' cut in Norman. 'He's already had the pay-out and drawn the money out in cash. He gets weird calls from a burner phone around the time Mr Winter and his sister were killed. That looks mighty suspicious to me, and if the chief constable can't see it, it's only because he's got his nose shoved so far up Maunder's arse he can't see anything.'

Slater winced as Norman finished his speech. *Oh shit*, he thought. *Here we go. The Old Man isn't going to like that.* But to his great surprise, the explosion he was expecting didn't arrive.

Murray sagged in his chair, and let out an enormous sigh. He looked thoroughly worn out and fed up.

'Alright,' he said. 'But you need to understand, when the CC finds out he's going to go berserk. I will be his first point of contact, so I need to know exactly what's going on.'

'Right,' said Slater. 'We understand what you're doing for us, Sir. We'll do it by the book, and we will keep you informed.'

'I want that old gardener brought in and questioned as well,' said Murray. 'I don't want it to look as though Maunder's being singled out for special treatment. You'll need a search warrant.'

'Are you going to phone the CC?' asked Norman.

'Of course, I am. I have my orders. I'll call him in the morning, but I'll wait until ten o'clock. You make sure you're at Maunder's by nine and you should have at least an hour. After that I'll probably be ordered to pull you out, so make sure you find what you're looking for.'

'Thank you, Sir,' said Slater. 'We'll get on with it now. And I'll arrange to get Mr Ferguson brought up here tomorrow as well.'

'Right,' said Murray. 'That'll be all.'

When they got back to their office, Jolly was just getting ready to go home.

'I've just left you a note,' she said. 'The sister from The Belmont Nursing Home called. Apparently, your retired gardener has taken a turn for the worse. He's on the way out, but he wants to make a statement while he still can.'

'Time to clear his conscience, I suppose,' mused Slater. 'I'll arrange for a car to pick him up.'

'No can do,' said Jolly. 'I suggested that, but sister says he's too ill to make the journey, and you need to get there sooner, rather than later.'

'He really has taken a turn for the worse, then.'

'Maybe the news about Florence was too much for him,' said Norman.

'Sister says he wants to do it first thing tomorrow morning, and he says he'll only talk to you. And it's not negotiable.'

'But I'm supposed to be up at Maunder's with Norm,' said Slater. 'I can't be in two places at once.'

'The sister says he's adamant. If you're not going to be there, he's not talking.'

'We're a team, right?' said Norman. 'Division of labour. You go down and interview Ferguson, and I'll go and see Maunder. I can handle him. I owe him for causing me all that grief over the so-called break-in, remember?'

'Are you sure?' asked Slater.

'It'll be a pleasure,' said Norman, grinning. 'I'll supervise the search, and then drag his sorry arse back here. I'll wait for you to get back here and we can interview him together.'

CHAPTER THIRTY-THREE

It was exactly nine o'clock the next morning when Norman rang the bell on Sir Robert Maunder's front door.

'Oh. Good morning. It's Sergeant Norman isn't it?' asked Maunder's wife as she swung the door open.

'Err, yes, that's right,' said Norman, awkwardly. 'Good morning, ma'am.'

Her smile slowly disappeared as she took in the small posse of officers and forensic technicians gathering behind him.

'I take it you haven't come looking for a cup of tea, this time,' she said, acidly.

'I'm sorry, ma'am,' said Norman. 'Is your husband in?'

'I'm afraid not, Sergeant. You've just missed him. You'll have to come back later.'

She made to shut the door, but before she could, Norman placed his hand against it.

'It's a pity he's not here,' said Norman. 'But we're going to have to come in anyway.'

'I don't think so,' she snapped.

'I have a search warrant,' said Norman, gently pushing against the door. 'Please, ma'am. You have no choice. Let's not make this any more unpleasant than it already is.'

She looked as though she might burst into tears, but then she seemed to get a grip on herself. Inwardly, Norman breathed a sigh of relief. He really didn't want to see her in tears. He had been hoping it would be Maunder who answered the door. It would have been much easier to play bad cop with him.

She stepped back and let them in. The team had been briefed earlier. They already knew where to go and what to look for.

'I'm disappointed with you, Sergeant,' she said, as they trooped past. 'My husband said you were a sneaky one.'

Norman didn't know quite what to say to that, but in a way he was pleased to see she was ready to fight. He would much rather hear her having a go at him, than see her in tears.

'What's my husband ever done to anyone?' she asked. 'He's a good man. I should know. I've been married to him for over fifty years.'

'I'd rather not discuss this right now,' said Norman, trying to dodge the issue.

'No. Of course you wouldn't,' she said bitterly. 'He's an easy target, isn't he? You should be out catching criminals not wasting your time here. Why aren't you arresting the man who's been calling my husband and upsetting him?'

'I don't know anything about that,' said Norman. 'Has your husband made a complaint?'

'No,' she said. 'He thinks he can deal with it on his own. He thinks I don't know about it, and he won't mention it because he doesn't want to worry me.'

Before either of them could say another word, a PC came out from the kitchen.

'Excuse me, sir,' he said to Norman. 'But there's smoke coming from down the garden.'

Lady Maunder looked guilty.

'I thought you said Sir Robert was out,' said Norman.

'He is,' she said.

'Yeah, right. He's out in the garden. Please wait here ma'am.'

He turned to the PC.

'You come with me.'

He led the way through the kitchen and out to the back of the house. There was a row of old stables and outbuildings across a court-yard. In the centre, an archway gave access to them. A thin trail of smoke could be seen coming from the other side of the buildings.

They hurried through the archway and into yet another courtyard. Norman knew enough about these old houses to know this would have been where the carriage and horses were kept many years ago. There was a larger building off to one side which would have been the coach house and now appeared to serve as the garage. On the opposite side was another large outbuilding. The door was open and from where they were looking it seemed to now serve as some sort of office.

Norman walked across to the office, the PC following closely in his wake. There didn't appear to be anyone around, so he stepped inside and took a look around. It was a rather grand, well-equipped office, with old fashioned wood and leather furniture. Norman thought he would have been very happy to have an office like this.

He stepped behind the desk. A drawer was just slightly open and Norman eased it open a bit further to reveal a collection of rather expensive jewellery. He was sure he recognised a couple of the pieces from the descriptions Lady Maunder had provided after the break-in.

'Get this jewellery bagged up for me, please,' Norman told the PC.

As he made his way back out to the courtyard, he wondered how Slater was getting on interviewing Gordon 'Dougal' Ferguson. Absently he looked at his watch. It was coming up for nine-twenty.

Norman wanted to confront Sir Robert, but he also wanted to know what was on that fire. Maybe Maunder was destroying evidence from the past. It had to be just around this next corner. He crept up stealthily, half expecting to find Maunder stoking a fire, but all he found was an old, wire-cage style garden incinerator. As he approached it, it seemed as though it was just garden rubbish smouldering away.

But then, as he got closer, he could see there was a bit more to it. The garden rubbish was just being used to keep the fire going. To one side of the incinerator, he could see some photographs and what appeared to be letters. They had slid from the top of the fire, and although they were singed and charred around the edges, it looked as though they might be salvaged, if only he could get them out quickly.

Kneeling down, Norman gingerly fished the assortment of charred photographs and letters from the incinerator. As far as he could make out, the photos seemed to show Sir Robert with an assortment of scantily clad women, but there was nothing to suggest Maunder was interested in children. Suddenly, he heard footsteps and started stuffing the documents hastily into an evidence bag.

'What on earth do you think you're doing?' Lady Maunder's voice came in a shrill cry. 'Taking rubbish from a bonfire? Is there no limit to how far you'll go?'

'No there isn't,' he said, looking up at her. 'Not if it means I catch the bad guys.'

'Well, you won't catch any bad guys here. This is an outrage. You will be hearing from our solicitor, I can promise you that.'

'Yeah, yeah. I'm sure we will,' said Norman as he climbed slowly to his feet.

'What have you got there?' she demanded. 'Let me see.'

'I'm not sure what I've got yet,' said Norman, keeping the bag well out of her reach. 'But maybe if you come and see what we found in your husband's office, you'll understand why we're here.'

'You've been in his office?' she shrieked. 'How dare you? Even I'm not allowed in there.'

'Yeah, well,' said Norman, beginning to tire of her ceaseless yelling and complaining. 'The thing is, I have a search warrant. That means nothing's private. If you just stop yelling long enough to read it, you'll see it gives me permission to go anywhere I want. Now just follow me.'

Ignoring her continuing protestations, he led her round to the office.

'Show her the jewellery, Nugent,' he ordered the PC.

The PC held out the clear plastic bag so she could clearly see what was inside.

'Do you recognise any of those pieces?' asked Norman.

'Well, yes,' she said uncertainly, peering at the bag. 'But I don't understand. They were stolen. What are they doing here?'

'Okay, you can take it over to the house, now,' Norman said to PC Nugent.

Lady Maunder was looking genuinely confused, and Norman

realised she wasn't putting on all this indignation. She really *did* think her husband was some sort of saint.

'They were in the drawer of your husband's desk,' he explained. 'I'm afraid it looks as though they never were stolen, ma'am. I'm sorry.'

'What do you mean?' she asked, her face screwed up. 'But that man left his card...'

'I'm afraid your husband staged the whole thing,' explained Norman. 'I'm pretty sure we'll find he printed the card on that printer over there.'

He pointed to the printer. As he did, his sleeve slid back to reveal his watch. It was nine-thirty.

'There must be some mistake,' she said again.

'I don't think so, ma'am,' said Norman. 'Now. Can you tell me where your husband is?'

'He, err, I thought he was out here,' she said, uncertainly. 'Or he'll be out in his Rolls Royce somewhere. He loves that car.'

For a split second they stared at each other in silence, almost as if they were expecting something to happen.

And then it did.

The unmistakable boom of a shotgun being fired rang out from the garage on the opposite side of the courtyard.

This was followed by a stunned silence, and then the sound of running feet as the PCs in the house reacted to the sound. Norman felt his innards turning to water as his mind raced through the possibilities. *But it couldn't have been that*, he thought. *Could it?*

'What was that?' cried Lady Maunder. She was still standing face to face with Norman, looking into his face.

'Err, I'm not sure,' said Norman, carefully. 'Does your husband have a shotgun?'

'Yes,' she said. 'But he's got a licence for it.'

It was almost as if she was trying to ignore the possibility, but Norman's face told her what she already knew.

'Oh my God,' she said, and then she was off and running and

screaming. She was surprisingly sprightly for a woman in her mid-seventies.

'Sir! Over here, Sir,' a voice called to Norman, from the garage.

A female PC intercepted Lady Maunder before she could get to the garage, and after a brief struggle managed to cajole her into moving away from the garage and back towards the house. The PC's face told Norman all he needed to know.

'Are you happy now?' Lady Maunder screamed at Norman, as she was led away. 'This is all your fault, Sergeant Norman. You did this!'

'Ambulance is on its way,' said another PC as he reached the garage.

Norman rushed into the garage. As he had feared, Sir Robert was in the driver's seat of his beloved Rolls Royce. He had even put the seat belt on. When he had pulled the trigger, the blast had spread most of his brains across the interior roof and across the back seats. Released from his grip, the shotgun had slipped down to the floor and rested between his legs.

Norman felt numb, and he clutched onto the door frame. He forced himself to look away from the awful sight. *Holy crap*, he thought. *I have to tell Dave about this.*

CHAPTER THIRTY-FOUR

At nine o'clock, just as Norman was saying hello to Lady Maunder, Slater was composing himself, having spent the previous hour working his way through his full repertoire of swear words. There had been an accident on the A3 on the way down to Portsmouth and, as a result, the busy rush hour traffic had quickly become a ten-mile long queue. It had taken almost an hour of crawling along at a snail's pace to clear the bottleneck.

He knew it was just one of those things, and nothing could be done about it, but he hated being late. Swearing didn't get him there any earlier, of course, but it helped cope with the frustration. As he climbed from his car and made his way across the car park at The Belmont Nursing Home, he consoled himself with the thought that being late didn't really make that much difference in the grand scheme of things. He would still get Gordon Ferguson's statement, so it wouldn't change anything.

Ferguson was propped up in his bed against a pile of pillows. The transformation in his appearance from when Slater had last seen him, less than twenty-four hours previously, was quite remarkable. The feisty, obstinate old devil from yesterday had been replaced by a pale shadow of a man who looked as though he wasn't going to be around much longer.

'I dictated a statement last night,' the old man wheezed as Slater pulled a chair up to his bed. He pointed to a large envelope at the foot of the bed.

'I wasn't sure I'd be here this morning. I've signed it myself and it's been witnessed by two of the nurses.'

'I still need to ask you some questions,' said Slater.

'Read that first, then if you have any questions you ask away.' Ferguson let out a gasping breath. 'I've got a matter of days now, so I've nothing to lose.'

It was ten minutes past nine as Slater opened the envelope, unfolded the statement, and began to read. He read slowly and deliberately, making sure he took it all in. Ten minutes later, he looked up at Ferguson.

'You murdered your own wife?' he asked.

'Aye. I'm not proud of myself. It was a true crime of passion,' he said, his voice hoarse. 'She was the love of my life, and then I caught her in bed with him. I should have killed him, of course, but I wasn't thinking straight. And he was no hero. He ran away with his tail between his legs while I took it out on her. If he was a real man he woulda stayed and protected her.'

'And then you buried her in the garden.'

'That's when they saw me. I was caught in a trap of my own making. After that I had to do what they said.'

'And the dead children you buried? You knew about the abuse, and what was going to happen to the kids when they were finished with, yet you said nothing, and became complicit by burying the bodies.'

Ferguson looked deeply ashamed.

'I'm as bad as him, right?' he said. 'Maybe even a bigger coward when all's said and done.'

'How come you didn't have to bury Florence?' asked Slater.

'I was supposed to. But she wasn't dead when they brought her to me. I couldn't kill a child, so I hid her in my cottage in the grounds and nursed her back to health. I kept her hidden for two years, then the boss saw her in my garden. I told him she was my niece, come to stay for a few days. But he knew. That's why he took the photograph, so he could be sure. But when he came back for her, I'd managed to send her away to my sister. Then, not long after that the place closed and we all had to move out.'

'So why did Florence end up back there, on her own?'

'I went to my sister's to look for her after Hatton House closed, but she'd run away. I had no idea she'd end up back at Hatton House. But she loved that garden, and especially that roundabout.'

They were both quiet for a couple of minutes until Ferguson spoke again.

'Are you gonna charge me?'

'It doesn't look like you're going to be around long enough,' said Slater. 'So there doesn't seem much point. Anyway, I'm much more interested in catching the person who murdered Florence and her brother. It's the same person who organised all the child abuse, isn't it?'

'Without a doubt,' agreed Ferguson. 'But I'm not telling you who that is.'

'Sir Robert Maunder,' said Slater. 'We already know that, we just need a bit of solid proof.'

Ferguson looked at Slater in amazement.

'Is that what you think?'

'What?' said Slater, doubtfully. 'He knew all about–'

'Oh, he knew about it,' interrupted Ferguson. 'But by the time he found out he'd become a regular visitor to Hatton House. Only he wasn't coming for the kids, he was coming to have sex with my wife. He couldn't resist a pretty lady, you see, and they knew it. But once he'd been photographed in bed with her, then got dragged into her murder what could he do? One word out of place and his dirty little secret would have been all over the place. And being a regular visitor it would be easy to implicate him in her murder, abusing kids, and anything that was going on there. He was well and truly buggered.'

Somewhere, not far from where they sat, a clock chimed the half hour. It was nine-thirty.

'So he wasn't involved in the child abuse at all?' asked Slater.

'Och, no way,' said Ferguson. 'He's a philanderer alright, but he's no pervert.

Holy crap, thought Slater. *I need to let Norm know about this.*

'Err, will you excuse me a minute, Mr Ferguson,' he said, pushing the statement into his pocket and rushing for the door. 'I need to make a call...'

S later rushed outside to make his call, but before he could get the phone from his pocket, it began to ring. He fumbled the phone from his pocket and looked at the caller display. Whoever it was would have to wait. Then he saw the number. *That's weird. Why's he calling me?* He took the call.

'Norm? That's weird I was just going to call you.'

'Are you psychic, or something?'

'What? What's going on?'

'You go first. You said you were just gonna call me.'

'I've just been talking to Ferguson. He tells me Maunder wasn't one of the child abusers. He knew about it, but that's all,' said Slater excitedly.

'That's not going to be much consolation to his widow,' said Norman, grimly.

Slater carried on, not really paying attention.

'Apparently, he knew about it but didn't blow the whistle because... What? What did you just say? His widow?'

'Err, yeah. I think it would be fair to say we have a major problem,' said Norman quietly. 'Maunder just blew his brains out with his shotgun.'

Slater felt as if he'd just been punched hard in the guts. He couldn't think of anything to say.

'I shoulda rounded him up,' said Norman. 'But his wife said he was out and I believed her. By the time I realised he was around he must have already been ready to kill himself.'

'I would have called earlier,' said Slater. 'If you'd known earlier you could have stopped him, but I got held up by an accident on the way down here.'

'Are you gonna be long down there? Only I could do with a bit of help up here.'

Slater patted his pocket to make sure he had the statement.

'I'm on my way, Norm,' he said. 'We'll sort this out, don't worry.'

CHAPTER THIRTY-FIVE

It was after five o'clock by the time Slater and Norman got back to the station. Now, once again, they were stood in front of DCI Bob Murray's desk. Slater thought this was becoming a bit too much of a habit – and it was a habit he could happily live without.

The bollocking had been raging for a good ten minutes so far.

'You got it wrong?' raged Murray, his voice rising an octave. 'I'll say you got it bloody wrong! You've hounded a man to death. He's blown his own brains out because two of my officers wouldn't listen to their superiors and let it lie. Well? What have you got to say for yourselves?'

'All the evidence-' began Slater.

'All the circumstantial evidence, Sergeant Slater,' Murray said, pounding on his desk with each syllable. 'Because, that's all you had, wasn't it? Hearsay is not proof. Surely you don't need me to tell you that.'

He sat back in his chair, his chest heaving.

'The CC's going to go ballistic when I tell him, you know that don't you? He was a good friend of Maunder's. He'll be looking for someone to blame, and as you two went and accused him of child abuse, we'll all be in the frame. It's possible we'll all be suspended and those bloody vultures from Internal Affairs will begin an investigation into our investigation.'

'But we found the jewellery in his office,' said Norman. 'There's nothing circumstantial about that.'

'No, there isn't. But that just proves he was trying to get away with an insurance fraud. It doesn't give you the right to accuse him of child abuse.'

'Err, with respect, Guv. We never accused him of child abuse,' said Slater.

'You didn't?' asked Murray in surprise. 'But I thought you said he was your number one suspect-'

'He was,' agreed Norman. 'We had him down as prime suspect for Mr Winter's murder because we know Winter sent him a letter accusing him of child abuse. And if we're right about all that, it would also put him in the frame for murdering Florence. And, if the letter was the catalyst, it gives us good reason to believe he was involved in child abuse back in the sixties.

'But we've never told him as much, and we've certainly never accused him, because we know we don't have any proof. As a matter of fact, until this morning, I've only ever spoken to him about the fake jewellery theft.'

'I asked him if Winter had sent him a letter,' volunteered Slater. 'But I swear I have never accused him of child abuse.'

'So what are you saying? That there's another reason, and it's not our fault?' asked Murray.

He was still red, but Slater sensed he was calming down slightly.

'For a guy in his position, being guilty of fraud could be enough to tip him over the edge,' said Slater.

'When I was talking to Maunder's wife,' added Norman, 'she said he's been getting phone calls from someone. She said he was worried about the calls, but he was keeping it from her. Maybe someone's been blackmailing him. That would explain why he's broke, and why he needed the insurance money, and if he knew we were onto him, and it was all going to come out, maybe that's why he shot himself.'

'And you're quite sure you haven't accused him of child abuse?'

'Definitely not,' said Slater. 'We suspected him, but we never said as much to him.'

'And now you've got a witness who confirms he wasn't,' said Murray. 'Are you sure he's telling the truth?'

'Yes,' said Slater. 'He caught Maunder with his wife back then, so he's definitely not going to be doing Maunder any favours. He could crucify the guy if he wanted to.'

'Well, look, I'm going to have to tell the CC, before someone else does. I'll try to persuade him you had good reason to be there and keep him off our backs for as long as I can. At least we've got the jewels to back that up. In the meantime, you need to find out who's been blackmailing him, and why he topped himself.'

T hey had agreed it was going to be a long night. If necessary, they would go right through every little thing again. But first, Norman had insisted, they needed coffee.

'I think that went quite well, all things considered,' ventured Norman, as they walked away from Murray's office and headed for the canteen.

'You do?' asked Slater. 'I thought he was going to burst a blood vessel.'

'For sure,' said Norman. 'But I think we got off quite lightly. I was expecting to be suspended.'

'That's probably coming later, when the CC gets his way,' said Slater, gloomily.

'Oh well,' said Norman, chirpily. 'Look on the bright side. It won't be the first time, and I could do with a rest.'

They pushed their way through the canteen doors and headed for the coffee machine.

'I'm thinking I spend far too much time stood in front of the Old Man's desk, getting my arse kicked,' complained Slater.

'You and me both,' agreed Norman. 'But, would you rather be a "yes" man?'

He poured two huge coffees into styrofoam cups, pushed the lids into place and paid his dues, before handing one over to Slater and then leading the way back through the doors.

'You know, I've never had a suspect do that to me before,' he said. 'And I hope it never happens again.'

'It might not have happened at all, if I hadn't been delayed,' said Slater, guiltily. 'If I'd let you know what Ferguson had said half an hour earlier, you could have stopped him.'

'You can't think like that,' said Norman, firmly. 'That's like me saying it might not have happened if I hadn't gone up there with a search warrant. For what it's worth, I don't think he even knew we were there, and he wasn't warned we were coming, so my guess is he had planned to do it anyway. Whatever we did this morning woulda made no difference.'

'I suppose you're right.' Slater sighed. 'It's just that it all seems a bit of a mess right now.'

'The whole thing seems a mess right now, for sure,' agreed Norman. 'But I don't think that's our fault. We can only follow the clues where they appear to lead. The thing is I think we're missing the one clue that really matters.'

'We're missing something, that's for sure.'

'It's gotta be there somewhere,' said Norman. 'I just think we haven't seen it yet, or we've seen it and not recognised it for what it is.'

'Maybe we should come at it from a different direction. Ferguson told me that Maunder had been set up in a honey trap, and that if he ever said anything, he would have been implicated in the child abuse, even though he wasn't involved. What if he was being blackmailed ever since? That would explain why he's broke.'

'But what about the big cash withdrawals when Winter and Florence were killed?' asked Norman. 'How does that work?'

'I don't know,' said Slater. 'I haven't worked that one out yet. Unless they were bonus payments for the blackmailer to bump off Winter and Florence. But then why blow his brains out?'

Maybe the blackmailer was going to up the ante if he'd been paid to commit murder. But it would also make sense for the blackmailer to want them dead, wouldn't it? He had a nice little earner going on there, and they could have spoilt it for him.'

'The blackmailer's the key to this,' said Slater. 'If only we can work out who it is.'

They were back in their office now. There was no sign of Jolly, but that was no surprise; she would have gone home ages ago. She had, however, left a note.

'Wow. Jane's been busy,' Slater told Norman as he read it. 'She's been through nearly all those old records from Hatton House. There's just a small pile left on her desk.'

'If that's all there is,' said Norman, looking at the slim pile of papers on her desk, 'why don't I start there? At least then we know we've covered all the evidence we have at least once.'

He sat down at Jolly's desk and began to work his way through the pile of old papers. Slater went to his desk and sorted everything into order. Then he started the long, boring process of reading his way through all the evidence they had collected. It really was going to be a long night.

It was just before seven when his mobile phone began to ring.

'It's Jane. Are you still at work? Or have you been sacked?'

'No, we're still here, Jane,' he said. 'I think we came fairly close to being suspended, but we seem to have been spared for now. Anyway, shouldn't you be bathing kids, or whatever it is you working mums do of an evening?'

'That's what husbands are for,' she said. 'In return I get the dubious pleasure of going to the supermarket on my way home from work. I've just got back, actually. But I bumped into someone while I was there, and we got talking. I think you need to hear what I found out.'

'I'm all ears.'

Norman turned over to the next document just as Slater's phone began to ring. He was getting a headache already and they had a long way to go yet. As soon as he heard Slater mention the name 'Jane', his attention began to waver as he tried to listen in to Slater's end of the conversation. As a result, he almost missed what was on the document in front of him. What he saw didn't make sense at first, and he had to read it through again.

'Holy shit!' he said, aloud. 'This can't be right.'

He studied the document for a minute or two before it dawned on him. *Of course!* There was a way it *could* be right.

He rushed over to his own desk, clutching the document he'd just read, and started tapping an address into his web browser. A website flashed up on the monitor. He clicked on the 'About' page link. As soon as the page came up, he started reading.

'Ha!' he said. 'Now it makes sense. Now a whole lot of things might start to make sense.'

Slater was still listening on the phone. Norman hoped he wasn't going to be long, because he was pretty sure he'd just found what they were looking for. It wasn't that they'd missed it before. They just hadn't got to it until now.

CHAPTER THIRTY-SIX

'Ah. Mr Hunter,' said Bob Murray. 'Thank you for coming in and giving us the chance to explain our side.'

He led Hunter from the reception area and out into a corridor.

'I've saved us a room so we can talk undisturbed,' he said.

'I'm glad to see you're taking this seriously enough to have a senior officer taking charge and not those two clowns who've caused this unfortunate incident,' said Hunter, his usual good humoured smile missing this morning. 'You realise I'm here on behalf of Lady Maunder, don't you?'

'Of course,' said Murray. 'I'm very sorry she couldn't be here. I think she may have found this rather illuminating.'

'I can't imagine you can come up with a good enough excuse for your behaviour,' said Hunter. 'I'll listen anyway, but I must warn you I intend to make an official complaint. And Lady Maunder will be taking legal action.'

'Yes,' said Murray. 'Of course, she will.'

He opened a door and ushered Hunter inside. Slater and Norman were standing behind a table waiting for them.

'What are these two idiots doing here?' snapped Hunter. 'What's going on?'

'These two "idiots" would like to ask you a couple of questions,' explained Murray with a beaming smile. 'I'm sure a legal man, like yourself, would be interested in seeing justice served. Right and wrong. All that sort of stuff, you know?'

'I'm not wasting my time talking to these people,' raged Hunter. 'They shouldn't even be here. They're a disgrace to the police force. I'm leaving.'

'No, that won't be possible. If you walk through that door, I'll have you arrested and dragged back in here. I'm afraid these two "idiots" aren't quite as stupid as you think. Oh, you've been clever, there's no doubt about that, but these two have been even more clever. So, if they're idiots, what does that make you, I wonder?'

'This is outrageous. You can't do this!'

'I think you'll find I can,' said Murray. 'Now, why don't you sit down and let's get this over with.'

Hunter didn't look quite so smug now, and his tongue seemed to have deserted him. Reluctantly he sat down. Murray nodded to Slater and Norman and walked across to the door.

'Oh, one more thing, before I leave,' he said, turning back to Hunter. 'I should advise you that, as we speak, there are teams of officers at your home, and your offices. They have search warrants, of course.'

Murray let himself out. He was going to enjoy watching this from the observation room.

'Good morning Mr Hunter,' said Slater, smiling pleasantly at him. 'It's very good of you to offer to help us with our enquiries. We just have a few things we think you might be able to help us with.'

Hunter looked like he was about to spout forth, but Norman cut him off.

'When we spoke to you before about Mr Winter, you said you'd only met him a few weeks ago,' he began. 'Is that still the case?'

'Yes, of course,' said Hunter, indignantly.

'Then perhaps you could explain why your secretary, Mrs Bettsan, told PC Jolly that he had been a client for many years.'

'She must be mistaken,' said Hunter.

'What about Mr Winter's missing sister, who you said had contacted you out of the blue and was coming in to hear the will being read?'

'I told you what happened about that,' said Hunter, impatiently. 'She was a fraud, an opportunist who chickened out at the last minute.'

'Or maybe she never existed in the first place,' suggested Norman. 'Mrs Bettsan certainly can't recall her.'

'I didn't tell Mrs Bettsan about her,' argued Hunter. 'There was no need.'

'But didn't you tell us it was Mrs Bettsan who had taken the original call?'

Norman was bluffing, but Hunter didn't seem to realise.

'Mrs Bettsan also finds it hard to understand how your alarm system could have failed,' said Norman. 'According to her it has a battery backup system and is supposed to be foolproof. It can only be disabled by someone who knows the code, and you change it every week. That seems to narrow it down quite a bit, don't you think?'

Hunter remained tight-lipped.

'The problem we had,' said Slater, 'is that we assumed all along that the person who murdered Mr Winter had let himself in with the spare back door key from under the mat. But then just yesterday it occurred to us there was another possibility. What if Mr Winter had known the killer? What if the killer had simply knocked on the door and Mr Winter had let him in?

'He would have done that if he'd known that person for a long time and trusted him, wouldn't he? But we didn't have anyone who fit the bill. And then Mrs Bettsan got talking to PC Jolly, and suddenly we had a candidate.'

Slater stopped talking and there was a pause. Hunter sat silently.

'How are we doing so far, Mr Hunter?' asked Norman. 'It's funny. You seemed to have it all to say when you arrived, but now the cat seems to have got your tongue.'

'I have the right to remain silent,' said Hunter.

'That's right,' said Slater. 'And it's okay, really. I don't think you need to say much. We're pretty sure we've got it more or less worked out without your help.'

'You still might have got away with it all,' continued Norman, watching Hunter closely for a reaction to his next statement. 'But we found some old records from Hatton House.'

'Well, well, well. You didn't know they existed did you?' Slater smiled as Hunter's head jerked. 'I guess it takes a special sort of idiot to keep digging until you find these things.'

'It was mostly old records and stuff that wasn't in the least bit relevant to our inquiry, but then right near the bottom of the pile, we struck gold,' said Norman, who was enjoying himself hugely. 'Here. Take a look at this.'

He slid a copy of the legal document he had found the previous evening in front of Hunter. Hunter looked down at the document.

'Recognise that solicitor's name and signature?' asked Norman.

'That's nothing to do with me,' said Hunter. 'Look at the date. It says 1962. I was barely ten years old then.'

'That's right. It's not you,' said Norman. 'But it has everything to do with you. It's your father, isn't it? Hunter and son, right? Only it's not you and your son, is it? It's your father and you. Your father was the solicitor for Hatton House.'

'And what does this prove?' asked Hunter.

'It proves nothing,' said Slater. 'But it gave us a new line of enquiry. You see, up until this came to light, we were sure Sir Robert Maunder was the person we were after. We even had written evidence that accused him of being involved in child abuse at Hatton House back in the sixties.'

'Yes, and because you accused him of that, he blew his own brains out,' said Hunter, grimly. 'And I'm going to make sure you pay for that.'

'We didn't accuse him of that, actually,' said Norman. 'But we can talk about that later. Right now we're-'

There was a loud knock on the door. Slater got up, went over to the door and opened it just wide enough to stick his head through. There was a short, mumbled conversation and then he closed the door and came back to the table. He was smiling with satisfaction. As he sat down, he slid a note across the table to Norman, who read it carefully. Then he looked up at Hunter with a big, beaming smile.

'It looks like the idiots are on a roll,' he said, grinning. 'Guess what we found, already?'

'Is this going to take much longer?' Hunter sighed, tapping his fingertips on the table.

'I'm sorry,' said Norman. 'Are we delaying you? Do you have somewhere else you'd like to be?'

'I would imagine anywhere would be preferable to sitting here listening to you spout this rubbish.'

'I agree DS Norman can be a little tiresome.' Slater smiled, seemingly overflowing with bonhomie. 'Especially when he knows he's cracked a case. But then, he's an idiot, right? So what can you expect? So why don't I take over for a little while? A change is as good as a rest, isn't that what they say?'

Hunter glared at Slater.

'You're going to pay for this,' he hissed. 'You won't even be back directing traffic. You'll be issuing parking tickets!'

'Yes. You're probably right,' said Slater, looking down at the notes in front of him. 'Now what was I just going to say?'

Norman leaned over and pointed to a line halfway down the page.

'Oh yes,' he said, smiling up at Norman. 'That's right. Thank you.'

He turned back to Hunter.

'You never told us what you thought we might have found,' he said. 'D'you wanna hazard a guess?'

Hunter heaved a heavy sigh.

'Go on,' he said. 'Play your infantile game if you must.'

'We found a mobile phone,' said Slater.

'Congratulations,' sneered Hunter, sarcastically. 'No, really, well done. I must have half a dozen mobile phones, so it really wasn't that difficult, was it?'

'Ah. But the one we found is special, isn't it?'

Hunter's sneer slowly disappeared.

'Do you know what a burner phone is, Mr Hunter?' asked Norman.

Hunter said nothing.

'No? Then let me explain. 'It's an unregistered pay-as-you-go phone. It's used by criminals to make a call, say for example to threaten someone, and then it gets thrown away. That way it's untraceable.'

Hunter was beginning to look a little sick.

'I don't have any pay-as-you-go phones,' he said, uncertainly. 'It must belong to my secretary.'

'Yeah, right,' said Slater. 'Sure it does. Do you think it'll have her fingerprints on it, or yours?'

Hunter's face said it all.

'You see, the thing is, this particular pay-as-you-go phone has been used to call Sir Robert Maunder. Maybe you didn't realise his mobile phone was on a contract, or maybe you forgot we could request his mobile phone bills. Whatever. The thing is we have his mobile phone bills, so we know exactly how often you called him using that very burner phone we found. We know how long the calls lasted and what times they were made.'

Hunter stared down at the table in front of him.

'We've also got his bank statements,' said Slater. 'And they've revealed an amazing coincidence. You see, every time you call him, he goes to the bank the very next day and draws out some money. It must have been like using the hole in the wall for you. Need some cash? Just lean on the old guy and out comes the money, right?'

'This is rubbish,' said Hunter. 'You can't prove any of this. I was his solicitor. Why would I start blackmailing him?'

'Oh, you didn't start it. We believe we can prove your father did that. You just carried it on as part of the family business.'

'This is preposterous,' snapped Hunter. 'My father was a respected solicitor. Why would he blackmail one of his own clients? Don't forget we're talking about a man who was chief constable and was given a knighthood.'

'Ah, but he wasn't a chief constable, back then, was he?' said Norman, keen to get involved again. 'Back then he was a DS, just like me. But he had a weakness. He couldn't keep away from the ladies. He had an affair with Gordon Ferguson's wife. Gordon caught them at it and murdered her. DS Maunder was implicated, but he didn't want anyone to find out.'

'I don't know any Gordon Ferguson,' said Hunter.

'That's odd,' said Slater. 'You drove all the way down to Portsmouth to see him a few nights ago. The Belmont Nursing Home. Ring any bells, does it? And before you deny it, you have been identified by a member of staff, and you're on CCTV.'

'Anyway,' continued Norman, 'Maunder had begun to suspect what was going on with some of the kids up there. Once he got dragged into this murder and its subsequent cover up, your father saw the opportunity to trap him and shut him up for good. Maunder's been paying for that mistake ever since. It also gave your father the opportunity to keep Ferguson under control too. He didn't have any money, but he could be useful in other ways, right?'

'You'll never prove any of this,' said Hunter, desperately. 'You've no proof and no witnesses.'

'I have to admit you've been pretty thorough there,' said Norman. 'We looked everywhere for surviving members of staff, but they all seem to be dead somehow. Except for Gordon Ferguson, but all the time he knew you were out there he wasn't going to say a thing.'

Hunter looked briefly relieved, as Norman had hoped he would.

'There's a problem for you, though,' said Norman. 'Gordon didn't die yet. We know you poisoned him when you were down there the other night, but he's a tough old boy, and he ain't dead yet. He's going to die very soon, and if he lasts until the weekend it'll be a miracle, but we told him we were going to bring you in here and you wouldn't be coming back out, so guess what? He told us who the ringleader was up at Hatton House. He also told us how, when that evil man died, his son had carried on terrorising him.'

There was another knock on the door. This time Norman went. When he came back his grin was even wider.

'It's not looking good for you, is it?' he said. 'They've just unearthed a CD given to you by Mr Winter. I bet it's identical to the one we have.'

Hunter's face fell.

'Oh boy.' Norman laughed coldly. 'You didn't know we had our own copy? See, Mr Winter might have trusted you enough to let you into his house the night you murdered him, but he obviously didn't totally trust you, so he made a copy for us too, in the event anything should happen to him. As you know, he thought it was Maunder who was the ringleader, but I figure he guessed your father might have been involved too.'

There was another knock on the door. This time it swung open and Bob Murray stuck his head into the room.

'Sorry to interrupt,' he said, ominously. 'Could I have a word, with both of you?'

They trooped out to join him. Norman wondered what could have gone wrong this time.

'I've just had the chief constable on the line,' said Murray, looking deadly serious.

'Don't tell me we're suspended,' said Slater.

Murray looked at Slater hard, and then he broke into a broad smile.

'Not this time,' he said. 'Apparently Sir Robert Maunder had planned to take his own life. This morning the CC received a letter through the post from Sir Robert. It's a suicide note in effect, but in it he confesses to being involved in covering up the murder of Ferguson's wife. He confesses to having known about the child abuse but not having the guts to do anything about it. He chose his career and reputation over those kids' lives.

'He also names John Hunter's father as the leader of the child abuse ring, and as his blackmailer. He claims the present John Hunter carried this on. He also confesses to having been blackmailed into paying to have Mr Winter and his sister silenced. He couldn't live with himself any longer.'

'I'm not surprised he couldn't live with himself any longer,' said Norman. 'I don't think I could have lived with myself for five minutes.'

'Yes,' said Murray. 'But not everyone has your moral compass, Norman.'

They stood in silent thought for a moment before Murray spoke again.

'Right,' he said. 'I don't think we're ever going to be able to charge anyone over the historical child abuse, but we've got enough evidence to charge Hunter with two counts of murder and blackmail for a start.

You can add another murder charge when Ferguson dies, and we ought to look back at the deaths of all those staff members who've died.'

Slater and Norman stood there.

'Well go on, then,' said Murray. 'Get on with it.'

'Right, boss,' said Slater.

He turned to Norman.

'Who's going to do the honours, you or me?'

'Aw, heck. I don't know. Whose turn is it?'

'I can't remember,' said Slater, fishing in his pocket for a coin.

'Here you go,' he said. 'Heads or tails?'

'Last time we did this I ended up watching a PM,' said Norman. 'I'm sure that coin's double-headed...'

ABOUT THE AUTHOR

P.F. Ford is the author of the Alfie Bowman Novella series, and the Dave Slater Mystery Series.

A late starter to writing after a life of failures, P.F. (Peter) Ford spent most of his life being told he should forget his dreams, and that he would never make anything of himself without a "proper" job.

But then a few years ago, having been unhappy for over 50 years of his life, Peter decided he had no intention of carrying on that way. Fast forward a few years and you find a man transformed by a partner (now wife) who believed dreamers should be encouraged and not denied.

Now, happily settled in Wales, Peter is blissfully happy sharing his life with wife Mary and their four rescue dogs, and living his dream writing fiction (and still without a "proper" job).

Learn more here:
www.pfford.co.uk

Printed in Great Britain
by Amazon

37724639R00145